Praise for *An Hono*

D0684068

"*An Honorable Man* is an unputdownable mole hunt written in terse, noirish prose, driving us inexorably forward. In George Mueller, Paul Vidich has created a perfectly stoic companion to guide us through the intrigues of the red-baiting fifties. And the story itself has the comforting feel of a classic of the genre, redis-covered in some dusty attic, a wonderful gift from the past."

—Olen Steinhauer, *New York Times* bestselling author of *All the Old Knives*

"Cold War spy fiction in the grand tradition—neatly plotted be-trayals in that shadow world where no one can be trusted and agents are haunted by their own moral compromises."

—Joseph Kanon, *New York Times* bestselling author of *Istanbul Passage* and *The Good German*

"A richly atmospheric and emotionally complex . . . tale of spies versus spies in the Cold War. . . . Vidich writes with an economy of style that acclaimed espionage novelists might do well to emu-late. This looks like the launch of a great career in spy fiction."

—*Booklist*

"Paul Vidich's tense, muscular thriller delivers suspense and in-telligence circa 1953: Korea, Stalin, the Cold War rage brilliantly, and the hall of mirrors confronting reluctant agent George Muel-ler reflects myriad questions: Just how personal is the political? Is the past ever past? *An Honorable Man* asks universal questions whose shadows linger even now. Paul Vidich's immensely assured debut, a requiem to a time, is intensely alive, dark, silken with facts, replete with promise."

—Jayne Anne Phillips, *New York Times* bestselling author of *Quiet Dell* and *Machine Dreams*

AN HONORABLE MAN

A NOVEL

PAUL VIDICH

EMILY BESTLER BOOKS
—
WASHINGTON SQUARE PRESS

New York   London   Toronto   Sydney   New Delhi

WASHINGTON SQUARE PRESS
An Imprint of Simon & Schuster, Inc.
1230 Avenue of the Americas
New York, NY 10020

First Emily Bestler Books/Washington Square Press trade paperback edition February 2017

EMILY BESTLER BOOKS / WASHINGTON SQUARE PRESS and colophons are trademarks of Simon & Schuster, Inc.

For information about special discounts for bulk purchases, please contact Simon & Schuster Special Sales at 1-866-506-1949 or business@simonandschuster.com.

The Simon & Schuster Speakers Bureau can bring authors to your live event. For more information or to book an event, contact the Simon & Schuster Speakers Bureau at 1-866-248-3049 or visit our website at www.simonspeakers.com.

Interior design by Dana Sloan

Manufactured in the United States of America

10 9 8 7 6 5 4 3 2 1

Library of Congress Cataloging-in-Publication Data
Vidich, Paul.
    An honorable man: a novel/by Paul Vidich.—First Emily Bestler Books/Atria Books hardcover edition pages cm
    "Atria/Emily Bestler Books fiction original hardcover".—Verso title page.
    Summary: "This gripping first novel in a spy thriller series, set in Washington D.C. at the height of the Red Scare, investigates a double agent in the CIA whose betrayals threaten to compromise the two lead investigators, the Agency, and the entire nation"— Provided by publisher.
    1. Spies—United States—Fiction. 2. United States. Central Intelligence Agency— Fiction. 3. Cold War—Fiction. 4. Internal security—United States—Fiction. 5. Washington (D.C.)—Fiction. I. Title.
    PS3622.I3656H66 2016
    813'.6—dc23
    2015007547

ISBN 978-1-5011-1038-2
ISBN 978-1-5011-1041-2 (pbk)
ISBN 978-1-5011-1040-5 (ebook)

For Linda, with love

MARC ANTONY:

> The noble Brutus
> Hath told you Caesar was ambitious.
> If it were so, it was a grievous fault,
> And grievously hath Caesar answered it.
> Here, under leave of Brutus and the rest—
> For Brutus is an honorable man;
> So are they all, all honorable men;
> Come I to speak in Caesar's funeral.

—Shakespeare, *Julius Caesar,* Act III Scene ii

AN
HONORABLE
MAN

1

WASHINGTON, D.C., 1953

MUELLER STOOD at the apartment's third-floor window and said to the FBI agent, "It's been too long. He won't show." He ground his cigarette into the overflowing ash tray. "We're wasting our time."

"He'll come. He can't resist the bait."

Mueller looked across the icy street at the dilapidated apartment building separated from the sidewalk by a wrought iron fence. Bars protected first-floor windows. There was no activity and there hadn't been since he'd arrived. A streetlamp at the corner cast its amber glow up the block, but it didn't reach the stoop. An unmarked car stood at Twelfth Street NE and Lincoln Park, and a black Buick was around the corner, in the alley, out of sight, but Mueller had seen it on his way over. Further up the block, an agent waited in the dimly lit phone booth, self-conscious with his newspaper.

"He's been scared off."

"He has no reason to believe we're here."

"He doesn't need a reason. It's instinct. Even an amateur would wonder why that man's been in the phone booth an hour. For you it's a job." Mueller dropped the curtain. "It's his life. He knows."

Mueller glanced at his watch. "When do you call it quits?"

"There's time. We spotted her making the drop at five. She's Chernov's wife. She went in the lobby with the package. She came out without it. He'll come."

"You're sure it was her?" Mueller asked.

He waited for FBI agent Walker to respond. Mueller thought Walker flamboyant, enjoying his status as agent-in-charge, eager to hunt. He dressed the part: dark hair combed straight back, polished shoes, double-breasted suit, and thin moustache like a Hollywood leading man. Through the window, street sounds spilled into the darkened apartment—a car's honk, a woman's anger. The agent raised opera glasses and scanned the street and then shifted his attention to the edge of Lincoln Park. Automobiles cruised single men sitting alone on wood benches. A giant mound of dirty snow from the weekend storm buried parked cars.

"We *know* it was her," Walker said in his drawl. "We have surveillance. Two cars. She left the Soviet embassy, took a taxi to the residence, and walked here with the package. It's still inside."

Mueller waited. He looked at his watch again, and then without thinking, he did it again. Waiting was the hardest part. He moved to the center of the room. There was the rank smell of cigarettes in the small apartment, half-drunk coffee cups, and the wilted remains of a take-out dinner. All waiting did was give him time to be irritated. He took a tennis ball from the table and squeezed it, working out his tension, squeezing and resqueezing. At another window he lifted the curtain. The street was dark, quiet, empty. Walker didn't understand that double agents lived in fear, chose their time, and that a cautious man wasn't going to take an unnecessary risk.

Lights in the building across the street were dark except for a top-floor apartment. A big woman at the window pulled her sweater over her head and then reached behind to undo her bra. Mueller looked, then glanced away. A light on the second floor. Had someone entered the building lobby? Through the window an older man stood in boxer shorts before an open refrigerator. He drank milk straight from a quart bottle and then he shuffled off to the kitchen table and sat by a console radio. Mueller looked back at the top floor, but the curtain was drawn.

How long should he stay? Walker and his men wouldn't abandon the stakeout until long after it was an obvious bust. No one wanted to admit failure, or have to invent excuses. Mueller was officially just an observer.

He saw a young man with a notepad approach from across the room. Crew-cut, freckled face, no tie, boyish smile. Too young for this type of assignment.

"You the CIA guy?" the young man asked.

Mueller narrowed his brow. "Who are you?"

"The *Star*." He lifted the press badge hanging around his neck.

Mueller confronted Walker by the fire escape window. Two men standing inches apart in the darkened apartment. Mueller snapped, "What's he doing here?"

"He's okay."

"We said no press. No surprises. No embarrassments." He didn't hide his anger.

"I had no choice," Walker said laconically.

Mueller gave the agent-in-charge a cold, hard glare and considered who in his chain of command had authorized a reporter. He held back what he wanted to say, that under the circumstances the best outcome for the CIA was that their man didn't take the bait, didn't show. "We had an understanding," Mueller said. "This wasn't it."

"He's a kid. He'll write what he's told to write."

"What does he think is happening?"

"Vice squad got a lead on a State Department guy who cruises Lincoln Park. Security risk. We arrest him and book him. Metro Police give the kid the story. He'll write what he's given."

Mueller headed to the apartment door.

"Where are you going?"

"A little fresh air."

Walker raised his voice so that it carried to Mueller in the hall stairway. "He's okay."

Outside, Mueller stood hidden from view on the top step of the building's stoop. He lit a cigarette. Habit. Then thought better of it and flicked it in the snow. His eyes settled on the empty street, where he saw nothing to change his mind that the night was a bust. The Capitol Building fretted the tree line of the park, a gleaming dome in the night, a navigation point above the neighborhood's sprawling poverty. In the distance Mueller heard the anxious wail of a police siren and then behind him, the soft click of the door closing. He saw Walker. They stood side by side without talking.

"I hear you're leaving the Agency," Walker said.

"Who told you that?"

"One of the guys."

Which guy? Mueller nodded. "If we get him tonight I'll be gone by the end of the month."

"What's next?"

"Fly-fishing." A lie.

"That will last a while."

Mueller didn't indulge Walker's sarcasm. He didn't like Walker, but he tolerated him, and he kept him close to keep himself safe. Walker was too ambitious for Mueller's taste, quick to take credit for success, quick to blame others for his own mistakes. Mueller didn't like Walker's having that detail of his personal life. He kept private matters away from his job, but the daily grind made that hard. Each morning he got up to face the endless urgency of ambitious colleagues inventing useful crises. Politics had taken over everything. He was tired of the double life, the daily mask, and he'd lost his ability to appear interested in a conversation when he was bored out of his mind. Walker bored him. But he knew Walker well enough not to trust him. Walker was a good weatherman of Washington's changing political winds and he was a good spy hunter.

Mueller's exhale came at last. "Where'd you get the tip?"

"The mailbox on East Capitol we've been watching. Someone left a chalk mark. This is the dead drop."

"You know, or you think?"

"She left the lobby without the package. What else would it be?" Then, confidently, "He'll come."

The two men stood in the dark. "I don't get it," Walker said. "Great reputation, but your results stink. Vienna was a failure. So was Hungary. Last week you lost Leisz." Walker paused. His breath fogged in the chilly night air. "Word is you guys got the news Stalin died by listening to Radio Moscow." Walker flicked his butt to the snow. "Great reputation, but your results stink."

"Piss off," Mueller said. He thought about the damn fool Leisz. Ignored the rules after he'd been warned, thinking he wasn't at risk, then got sloppy and paid for it.

"Someone's coming." A voice from the window above.

Mueller and Walker saw the young black woman at the same time. Blond wig, leopard-skin coat, stiletto heels, and a tiny rhinestone purse clutched in one hand. She had emerged from the tree line at Lincoln Park and glanced both ways before making a two-step hustle across the street. Mueller and Walker stepped back deeper into shadow.

When she achieved the opposite sidewalk she glanced over her shoulder. Mueller followed her line of sight to the streetlamp cleaving the darkness at the park's edge. From the trees stepped an army enlisted man. Mueller saw the drab sameness of style of someone who sought to fit in, go unnoticed. Long khaki coat, a visor cap pulled down on his forehead, and a steady stride that didn't bring attention to itself. She baited him with exaggerated hip movements and a calculated head nod. The start of another war had kept Washington filled with single men, and with single men came dreary bars with women who sold themselves.

"He won't come with this sideshow," Mueller said.

"They'll leave. Hail a taxi. Go to a hotel."

Mueller lit another cigarette and then regretted his choice again. He ground it under his heel. Drinking and smoking, two occupational hazards that had begun to wear on him.

The woman walked up the block, but slowed her stride to allow the man to catch up. The air was cold and crisp, sharp like flint. Suddenly she stopped. The two talked on the sidewalk. A bargain was struck.

"There's something odd about him," Mueller said.

"Odd?"

"The uniform. His shoes. He's wearing loafers."

The enlisted man opened the iron gate for the woman and then followed her up the steps to the apartment house lobby. He shot a glance over his shoulder before disappearing inside.

"What are you saying?" Walker asked. "It's him?" Then a demand. "You think it's him?"

"Not my call."

Mueller saw Walker's discomfort and he felt the torment of the decision he faced. Both men knew it would be impossible to recover from a bad call.

"So be it," Walker muttered. He pulled on his glove, stretching his fingers deep into the leather, and clenched a fist.

Mueller watched the FBI assemble. Walker signaled his agent in the phone booth, who in turn placed a call. It took a minute, or less, for the Buick and two unmarked cars to converge on the apartment building. Two agents, handguns drawn, stepped from the first car and hustled up the steps to the lobby. Four other men took up positions at their cars, and one crouched agent scrambled toward the rear of the building.

Walker stood in the street barking orders to his team, and the sudden noise brought neighborhood residents to their windows. They saw black cars stopped at oblique angles on the street, doors flung open.

Mueller stayed out of sight, alone. He saw an FBI agent escort the army enlisted man down the stoop, tightly gripping his arm. The enlisted man had lost his hat, his wrists were handcuffed behind his back, and his unbuckled pants rode down his hips. He looked dazed and embarrassed.

A second agent had cuffed the prostitute and guided her, protesting, toward a car. Her wig was gone and she was hobbling on one broken heel, shouting fierce baritone obscenities at the agent who hustled her down the steps.

"Don't rush me," the transvestite yelled, "I'll sprain an ankle."

Mueller waited until Walker emerged from the apartment lobby and then he stepped out from his hiding spot. They met halfway across the street, Walker agitated, his face twisted in a scowl. He waved a stack of bills at Mueller as he walked past. "Keep this farce to yourself," he snapped. "Don't say a thing. Not a word. Hear me?"

Walker slipped in the Buick's front seat and slammed his door shut. In a minute the cars were all gone and Mueller stood alone. There was one orphaned stiletto heel on the sidewalk that he dropped in a garbage can.

He walked rapidly away. He didn't bother to look behind to see if anyone noticed him, or to check on the curious neighbors. But at the end of the street he happened to turn. An instinct he'd acquired in Vienna after the war, the feeling of knowing when he was being observed. There at the corner in the shadow of a mature tree, a tall man in a gray homburg, hands shoved in the pockets of a long trench coat. There was something suspicious about the figure. Mueller read into every stranger the possibility the person was tailing him, and this man got his attention. Mueller stood there thirty feet away on the other side of the street, staring at the motionless figure, who stared back. Mueller couldn't make out the man's face, or the shape of his jawline in the hat's deep shadow.

"Hey, you," Mueller yelled.

He went to cross the street, but a garbage truck fitted with a snowplow lumbered by in a riot of noise. When the truck passed, Mueller looked for the man, but he was gone.

2

THE DIRECTOR

G EORGE MUELLER understood that he was at a turning point in his career in the CIA, but it still haunted him that he hadn't seen, or chose to ignore, the obvious markers of disengagement along the way. His wishful thinking had blinded him to the Agency's troubles, and it was only when he realized it was too late to recover his enthusiasm for the job that he woke up one morning and thought to himself: *It's over. This is the end.*

Things had always come easy to him, so he didn't have the lessons of failure to help him navigate the crisis. Public school in the Midwest and then Yale on scholarship, where he'd met Roger Altman, a year older, who introduced him to crew, dry martinis, and the gentle fun of a cappella singing. Mueller studied political history, read Hemingway like everyone else, and discovered a love for Ezra Pound and T. S. Eliot. He took up with a smart crowd of young men who affected a calculated weariness toward the world.

Mueller left Yale early to fight against Hitler's Germany, caught up in the great patriotism that drove America's young men into the armed forces. Through friends of friends of earlier graduates, he found himself in Texas training for the OSS. He parachuted behind enemy lines to help French Resistance sabotage rail lines and then played a small but dangerous role in occupied Norway that earned him a Purple Heart. He completed his undergraduate degree after the war and through a series of happenstances—choices presented to him—he worked on Wall Street, became bored, drank, and was recruited by his friend Altman to join the urgent battle in Europe against the Soviet Union. Mueller wanted to believe that he could make a difference in the world.

When things started going wrong they went very wrong. He was caught unprepared. It didn't happen all at once, though. Disappointment came in the slow accretion of small setbacks, and his sense of powerlessness grew along the way. In '48 he was newly married, a father, stationed in the occupied city of Vienna, running paramilitary operations from a cramped, unheated office across the Second Bezirk, the Russian zone, where the old Vienna with its prancing statues lay crumbling and desolate with burned-out tanks pushed to the side of the Danube. The girl he'd married worked in the office and their long hours together led to a romance. She was on the team that recruited disenchanted citizens of Soviet satellites for the Allies and organized them to be air dropped into the Carpathian Mountains, or inserted by fast boat on the Albanian coast under cover of darkness. Johana was just twenty-two when she joined the team working as a translator. She was beautiful, in a most Austrian way, with alabaster skin, wavy chestnut hair, and large brown eyes. She had all the English she needed with her wartime education in London, and on returning to her hometown she'd been deemed suitable for a job with the Americans, where she was in the thick of things. Their child wasn't planned.

They watched in dismay as missions failed. A few radio transmitters were turned on by teams inserted behind the Iron Curtain, but in most cases there was only radio silence. Ambushed. Coordinates were known to the Soviets in advance. No one wanted to admit the obvious. The Soviets had penetrated the Agency. Someone inside had provided the Soviets with drop points, and then later, the names of CIA assets. Mueller saw the pattern in Vienna and continued to see it when he was brought back to agency headquarters in Quarter's Eye. Men disappeared, networks rolled up. One by one CIA assets were compromised in Vienna, Berlin, and now there was Alfred Leisz. He hadn't been somewhere in Europe. Leisz had been right there in Washington managing the listening post in the basement of the public library near the Soviet embassy.

Traitor was a word that never appeared in memos; it was unsaid in meetings. But it was whispered at Friday-afternoon vespers when Scotch whiskey released the week's tension among case officers who worked in Quarter's Eye. Mueller too had been reluctant to use the word because it implied a betrayal of unthinkable proportions. Someone in the close group of colleagues was working for the other side. One of them had turned to the Soviet Union. Mueller knew trust was the basis of their work and he had become guarded in his conversations, cautious in what he said, and matters he once openly discussed he avoided, or simply shut down. Mueller found himself among his colleagues with their Scotch whiskeys knowing they were thinking: *Is he? Was he? Could he?*

Everyone privately worried about a Soviet agent in their midst. They worried about other things too, but those anxieties were openly discussed. A great emphasis, by way of defense, was placed upon loud opinions against communism, against homosexuality, against atheism. And this was matched by great enthusiasm for the activities in their lives, the quail hunting, fly-fishing, tennis, drinking. But not discussed, not among themselves or with their wives, who often were in the dark about what their husbands did, or even who their employer was, were their private suspicions about colleagues. Caution depleted camaraderie.

· · ·

The call to meet the director came early in the morning. Dense fog rolled in from the cold Potomac and low visibility in the back of the taxi deepened Mueller's gloomy mood. It reminded him of winter in Vienna. Dampness that penetrated the soul.

Mueller was just shy of six feet, and on the thin side, which made him appear lanky, and he slumped in the backseat. His face was slightly oval, hair parted on the left, and combed straight back, and he wore clear plastic eyeglasses that made him look inconspicuous, a man who could sit in a restaurant and not catch a waiter's eye.

He dressed practically, in gabardine suits that held their form one day to the next and let him keep his trips to the cleaners to a minimum. He used a simple knot for his necktie because it was fast, easy to tie, and quick to remove, and it matched the narrow-spread collar he preferred. His leather shoes needed a shine and their soles were wearing thin, but since his divorce he hadn't found a comfortable rhythm to his personal life.

He had long, delicate fingers with nails that almost looked manicured. His were not hands that could strangle a man. They lacked the strength for that. The grip of a tennis racket had helped, but tennis was the sport he took up only when he wasn't near a boathouse with sculls to put in the river. They were the hands of a man with a desk job, hands of a thinker. A callus on his finger came from after-action reports he wrote in a cramped style with a fountain pen. No one would look at Mueller and think he was the type to pick a fight in a bar.

"On the right," Mueller said. He leaned forward to the driver and cocked his head at an angle that was always the same degree off center when he took an interest in the person he was addressing. "Drop me there at the guardhouse."

Mueller flashed his badge to the military policeman at the locked gate, near the sign that identified the redbrick building as the United States Government Printing Office. It was a silly holdover from the Agency's early days, and taxi drivers weren't fooled; even tour bus guides took pleasure in pointing out what really went on inside the three-story Federal-style building. Who were they kidding? To Mueller the printing office sign fit into the larger pattern of being out of touch, the Agency believing the myths about itself.

Mueller was shown into the corner office by Rose, the director's longtime secretary, who put Mueller on a leather sofa that
anchored a sitting arrangement at one end of the room, across
from a ponderous wood desk. There was no clutter of paper, only
stacked file folders, and the director was absorbed in reading a
letter. A cold draft filled the room, carrying with it the musty
odor of a stodgy Ivy League club. Mounted antelope and moun-
tain lion heads hung on one wall above a shelf of stuffed game
birds, and an antique double-barrel shotgun was cocked open on
the coffee table by the sofa. Everywhere were framed photos of
the director with smiling dignitaries and elegant women. Mueller knew it was unusual to be in the director's office. An invitation meant a rare commendation or a private dressing down.
One never knew which.

"You hunt?" the director said, crossing the room letter in
hand.

"Quail."

"Good man. We should go one day. I know a spot on the bay.
Before the season opens."

The director sat opposite Mueller in a high-backed wing
chair covered in chintz and tatted antimacassars on the arms.
He wore a crimson house robe open at the neck to show necktie, and tan slippers adorned at the toes with floppy dog ears.
His hair was thinning, gray, eyes a keen blue, cheeks flush with
drinker's weight, and his snaggletooth bit on a pipe, which he
removed and tapped on an ash tray, and said, almost to himself
as much as to Mueller, "You have to have a few martyrs. Some
people have to get killed. It's part of this business. I wouldn't

worry about Leisz. He knew what he was getting into when he signed up with us."

He waved his hand in the air at nothing, like the pope. "He's not on my conscience. None of them are. We are not in the conscience business. The Soviets don't play the game that way."

The director added fresh tobacco to his pipe and applied a match, drawing air to brighten the coals. He looked over his rimless spectacles perched on the end of his thick nose. "I need you to see this through to the end." He drew on the pipe, releasing quick puffs. Hints of licorice reached Mueller.

"Take some time off if you need to see your son. If you think it's important. I believe in letting the mind rest so it doesn't fight against the will. . . . This is a grubby business we're in. Someday we'll both get back to the classroom, you and I. It's that fondness for thinking that makes us good at what we do here. The professor finds satisfaction in sorting through details and he feels superior when he passes along knowledge. The spy is the same. The daily grind, the mounds of information, the hours of boredom poking around the mounds of information, punctuated by ecstatic moments of discovery. Good researchers hold no beliefs, make no judgments. Evidence declares itself. Am I lecturing too much?"

Mueller shook his head.

"Kind of you, George, but I know when I'm going on. People sit on that sofa and say nothing because I'm the man in charge, but sometimes I see they're bored. I saw it with my students. Well, to finish the thought. We use intelligence to solve problems and when we look at evidence against our colleagues, our friends, we need to be rigorous and neutral, so our feelings about the men don't corrupt our judgment. Yes?"

The director rose. He stretched with a grimace. "Gout is a terrible thing. Awful. I don't know what I did in my past life to deserve this disease." He bent over his thick girth and sent his outstretched fingers toward his slippers' toes. His face flushed purple and he let out a great heave of effort. "I'm not embarrassing you, am I? Sitting cuts the circulation. I need to move around to get the blood flowing."

The director walked to his desk and lifted a bronze statuette replica of the Nathan Hale statue at Yale. "He was the first American spy. His last quoted words are often misquoted. He didn't say 'I regret that I have but one life to *give* for my country.' He said 'I regret that I have but one life to *lose* for my country.' It's an important distinction. *Lose* or *give*. The distinction between the passive and active verbs is the difference between a patriotic spy, the role history has given Nathan Hale, and a man arrested in the course of a poorly planned mission who was hanged when he got caught. We want to believe in honor and sacrifice, and when it doesn't exist we invent it."

The director returned to his chair. "Look," he said, sitting, "do you wonder why I asked you here?"

"Yes."

"I saw your report on the incident at Lincoln Park the other night. You didn't mention the reporter's name. I assume he was from the *Star*. That's who the FBI is close to, and the Republicans in the Senate. They would like nothing more than to publicly embarrass us. You read the papers. I don't have to spell it out. They've made the State Department into a goddamn haven for effeminate intellectuals. *Sonofabitch*. There is a madness in this country. I can't bear the name calling, the outbursts of hatred and vilification, the repulsive spectacle of red baiting, and the way good men's reputations are tarnished with innuendo." The director looked hard at Mueller. "They are jealous of our mission here and they don't like that I can call up the White House and get the president on the phone."

The director struck a match that he held over the pipe's bowl and drew air to brighten the coals. His fingers were stubby and thick. "Were you disappointed the other night?" the director said, looking up.

"At what?" Mueller asked. "That he wasn't caught?"

"Yes."

"And read about it in the press? No, I was not disappointed."

"A cure worse than the disease. Very messy. Is Protocol alerted?"

Mueller paused. "I suspect he is. We can't know. The money was there. He might have seen the whole thing from a doorway."

"Unfortunate. He'll be coy now."

"He'll go dormant. A week. A month. We got close this time. Very close."

"What about you?" the director asked.

"I'm not ready to stick around for another six months. That wasn't my deal. I've applied for a teaching position in the fall. I need time with my son."

"Yes, yes, yes," the director huffed. "The deal we had. I know. I know. But I can't afford to lose you right now." He slapped a letter on the coffee table. "It's from the senator. He wants me to answer questions in front of his committee. He wraps himself in his sanctimonious anticommunist rhetoric so the rest of us look weak. He is a drunk, but a dangerous drunk."

The director slumped in his high-backed chair. "That reporter bothers me. They are raising the stakes for us."

It didn't have to be said. They both knew. The head of the FBI resented the newly chartered CIA for taking over foreign intelligence gathering and the FBI had no qualms about using the same tactics against the Agency that it used against corrupt politicians and the mob. Gather dirt and spread it.

"They'd like nothing more than to have a headline that provoked the senator to conduct a witch hunt here." The director leaned forward. "We can't wait for Protocol's next move. We need to accelerate this. Take the initiative while we can."

Mueller looked at the director, but said nothing.

"Walker's team can't know. The FBI can't know," the director said. "Do you understand?"

"There's a risk. It's our job to work together."

"They haven't been good partners on this. Frankly, I don't trust them. We will bend the rules a bit, quietly of course. Are you up for it?"

"It?"

"Altman will fill you in. It's his idea. Let me know what you think. I have my doubts. About the idea. About him." He looked at Mueller. "Same class?"

"He was a year ahead. Same college. Davenport."

"So you're friends?"

"Acquaintances."

"Good man?"

"We were in Vienna together after the war. Before that he was in Berlin." Mueller stopped himself from elaborating. There was no need to recite his personal history with Roger Altman. The director had their files if he wanted to know the background. He suspected the director had already done that, reviewed their dossiers, for that was his job, the men who worked for him, knowing who had which skill, which weakness, and which man was right for the job. "I can vouch for him," Mueller said.

"One more thing," the director said. "Leisz. Any more ideas on that?"

"He knew the man. There was no forced entry. His machine uses one-hour tapes and the reel was still running when I found him."

"Strangled?"

"Piano wire."

"Poor bastard." The director dismissed Mueller with a hand wave. "Look after the wife. Make the usual financial arrangements. We don't want her asking questions."

The meeting ended.

There was no such thing as a typical meeting with the director, but this meeting, unlike others he'd been in, which began with a long-winded preamble that was part anecdote, part lore, part lecture, part pep talk, was different in the director's concerned tone, and different too because he had put the director on notice that he had acted on his desire to leave the Agency.

• • •

That afternoon, Mueller was surprised to find three men seated in the cramped conference room on the second floor of Quarter's Eye. Mueller expected to find Roger Altman, because that was who the director had asked him to see, but he also saw David Downes, Operations, a short man, insecure and indiscreet, with a stutter that he overcame with deliberate speech, and James Coffin, Counterintelligence. Coffin had been in London during the war assigned to X2, which he coordinated with his British MI6 counterparts, and in his three years there he'd become a bit of an Anglophile. It came out when he spoke, for he used the British "we" in place of the American "I," and his penchant for secrecy was mistaken by his British friends as polite reserve. His conservative dark suits were bespoke from a shop on Oxford Street and he drove a drafty English sports car wholly unsuited to Washington's weather extremes. Together the four men formed what they called among themselves the Council.

Mueller took the seat he usually occupied in their weekly meeting on Protocol. There was no rhyme or reason to code names. They were picked in sequence from a sterile list and care was taken to select words that had no meaning.

Mueller nodded at one man, then the others. They were side by side, same drawn expression, same reticence while Mueller settled into his seat. Something had been decided.

"Bad outcome the other night," Coffin said. His shoulders still had the broad lines of someone who'd crewed in college, but the rest of him had gone thin from years of cigarettes and bad scotch.

"It could have been worse," Mueller said. He had confused them. "Walker had a reporter there."

"*Jesus.*" This came from Altman, who snuffed his cigarette in an ash tray. The unventilated room was rank with mildew and tobacco.

So they'd been there a while, Mueller thought. There followed spirited debate about the FBI. Coffin called them insular and untrustworthy. Coffin had a beaked nose, black hair swept back from his pale forehead, horn-rimmed glasses that dominated his angular face and concentrated the expression in his eyes.

"They really don't like us, do they?" Coffin said calmly, almost sarcastically.

"They resent us," Mueller said. "They resent that we're not working for them."

"How close was it?" Altman asked.

"They found the dead drop. The money was there."

"Just money?" Altman asked.

"Used currency. Nothing to trace. Twenties. What else do you need?"

Coffin tapped ash from his cigarette. "How did they know it was there?"

"A tail. Chernov's wife. The Russians made a mistake. They didn't expect the FBI to follow her." Mueller's eyes turned from the winter view outside the window and looked at the three men across the table. "Walker blew it. Protocol was on his way."

"Scared off?"

"He was there. Saw the whole carnival. There were witnesses." Mueller looked directly at Altman. Mueller had been recruited by Altman. There was that obligation. Friendly but not friends. Altman had a handsome face, the same slender figure of their undergraduate days, and he dressed impeccably in double-breasted blue blazer with the flourish of a crimson pocket square.

"What's next?" Mueller asked Altman. "The director said you had an idea."

"What did he say?"

"That you'd fill me in."

"Good. Fill you in I will. Walker is playing a game." Altman talked quickly. That was his style. His speech came in staccato bursts. "A game that we don't want to play. His game. His rules. We'll play our game. Use our rules."

Altman moved to the bookcase and a combination safe camouflaged by a painting. Liquor inside. Altman poured himself a generous glass and offered a round to the others. Mueller didn't touch his.

"We need a new approach that doesn't involve the FBI. They are too eager to have us look bad. Nothing would please them more than to prove we've got a traitor among us."

He repeated the word *traitor* as if shocked by it. Mueller preferred *double agent*. It was easier on the ear, more ambiguous.

Altman threw back his drink, finishing it. Leaned against the wall. "A new approach is what we need. You agree, don't you, David? You haven't said a word. Silence is consent here. A new approach. In six months not one name has come off the list. That's a failing grade."

The list. Five people knew of this list. Four were in the room. Twenty case officers who could be Protocol. Protocol had become the catchall that came to mind whenever something went wrong. It was human nature to blame losses on a calculating intelligence rather than on the sloppy work of demoralized staff. And the Council knew they had to take care not to conflate what might be several bad apples into the work of a single man. Doubt, Coffin liked to remind them, was more precious than certainty.

The names on the list had been painstakingly assembled by matching known compromised operations against officers with foreknowledge of the plans; broadened further to include men who could have gotten access if they'd sought it; broadened further to obvious security risks—heavy drinkers, men spending beyond their means, officers with a grudge, men at risk because of some moral weakness. It was a long list. Too long.

Mueller's name could have been on the list, as could the director's for his well-known womanizing, but the list wasn't meant to be a witch hunt. The Council selected men who they believed had access to the Agency's secrets and a motive. Twenty names. Each suspect. The list itself was secret. Mueller knew of it, as did the other men in the room, and the director had seen it. Secrecy protected the investigation from compromise, but it also protected the reputations of the innocent. The end of a good case officer's career was to have guilt unproven and suspicions remain.

Mueller had volunteered his name for the list in the long, spirited debate that accompanied its compilation. He fit the profile, he'd said, without an ounce of irony. No, no, no, he was told. The director pointed out how ridiculous it would look to have a lead investigator be among the prime suspects. "You are in one category or the other, George. Not both. We've chosen you to investigate this, so your name can't be included."

Mueller had been grateful for the vote of confidence, but he was disappointed he hadn't succeeded in his ploy to be taken off the Council. Mueller knew the list had a problem. Friendships had protected some of the men in the Agency whose names had been part of the culling process, but were removed because an officer had vouched for his friend. Mueller joked to the Council that there should be another investigation with outsiders to investigate the investigators. They had all laughed. He'd been just a little provocative, but serious too.

"What's the approach?" Mueller asked. He looked at Coffin, who'd been silent since his comment about the bad outcome. Coffin was a brooder, a quiet man, a hard man to know. His style was flinty and precise, and his handwriting was a cramped expression of this tendency toward precision, as was his speech. "Roger will fill us in, George."

Altman stood at the window looking at the Potomac fading in the early dusk. He turned suddenly, enthusiastically. "We need to take the initiative, George. We need our own source. We need to recruit someone high up in the Soviet embassy."

"Break the law?"

"It's not breaking the law, George, if it's getting intelligence, which is what we do, what our charter requires. The FBI won't know that the intelligence we're seeking is counterintelligence until we're ready to tell them. We need to control this. Have you got a better idea?"

"What makes you think we can recruit a principal?"

"They think we can. They follow their own people. They're worried about defectors. We need to find one who will come to us."

"What's next?" Mueller knew what was next, but he wanted them to lay it out and build their case so he could hear the conviction in their voices. Coffin and Altman looked at Mueller, as did Downes. Ganged up. Mueller gazed back. He didn't have to do this, he thought.

"Let him come to you," Altman said. "Make yourself an attractive target. Give him a reason to approach you. Draw him in and when he thinks you're a prospect we'll close in. They make mistakes too."

"I'm the bait?"

No one answered.

"I'm the bait?"

Altman paused. "You're tired, George. Everyone knows you want out. The reason you want to leave is the same reason we need you to stay and see this through. You're a credible risk."

Mueller choked back an impulse to laugh. The twisted logic of this blandishment appalled his sense of reason. "How long?"

"Two months," Coffin said.

"That's optimistic." Two months would become five, then ten. Mueller knew this was a job he couldn't resign once he was tapped. *He didn't have to do this.*

"We are confident it can be done in two months," Coffin repeated. "We can't lose another man like Leisz."

It gave Mueller satisfaction to know that he had the power to disappoint them. He had made the mistake of sharing his unhappiness in the Agency with his colleagues and they were using it against him. "Who is he?"

"Vasilenko. Maybe Chernov."

Mueller received the two dossiers that Coffin sent sliding across the conference table. He glanced at Vasilenko's blurred photo, taken, it was obvious, surreptitiously at a distance through a crowd of pedestrians, and Mueller thought it made the Russian look thuggish. Chernov's was a formal head shot.

"They're both in a position to know about Protocol," Altman said.

"Assuming Protocol exists," Mueller added.

"I thought we were over that," Coffin said. "Roger and I are past that point."

"Yes, yes," Altman snapped. "We've stipulated he exists. But we need proof. Vasilenko and Chernov are in a position to know. They might not have his name, but they'll have something—a clue, a lead, a crack to let sunshine in. We'll get something that points to the real name."

There was a debate among the four men. Mueller listened skeptically.

"Chernov is the best choice," Coffin said. "Head of GRU in the embassy. Intelligence arm of the Soviet Army. He might be Protocol's handler. His wife made the drop. Old-line Soviet thug."

Mueller read the dossier. Born 1920 or 1921. Private first class, then corporal in the Red Army and one of the lucky few drafted in the summer of 1941 still alive on Victory Day. Served as a machine gunner on the Volkhov front in the Battle of Leningrad. Developed chronic chills in the swamps. Strong, cheerful personality. Model worker, party protégé of Malenkov on the Central Committee. GRU—the main intelligence directorate of the Soviet Army.

"You think he can be turned?" Mueller said this with doubt.

"No," Altman replied. "And he isn't suitable for another reason. The FBI keeps track of him. Two cars have him under surveillance at all times. He knows that. He thought his wife was safe."

Mueller opened the second dossier.

"Vasilenko is new," Coffin said. "He's come here from the consulate in New York as head of the trade mission. Metallurgy. But we think he is NKVD, State Security, tied to the Beria faction, Directorate K, counterintelligence. Rival of Chernov. It's fluid now with Stalin dead. We still don't know if he died of a stroke, as Russian papers report, or was murdered, as rumors suggest. . . . Before New York we tracked him in Berlin and before that we had him in Vienna—'forty-eight." Coffin looked at Mueller. "It says you knew him."

Mueller nodded. The file had their history. Case officers met their Soviet counterparts and made notes to the file of the meetings, and this was the way both sides kept track of authorized contact.

"We worked together with the Brits in MI6 on the food riots. People were starving. It got very tense. He was practical about it."

"Practical?"

"He didn't pound on the table and blame the bloody capitalists. People were dying. We worked together to get aid brought in."

"Chernov?"

"I don't know him. I never dealt with Soviet military intelligence."

"Vasilenko is the best bet. He'll need to come to you."

"How?"

Coffin flicked his wrist with a fly-fisherman's practiced hand and reeled in an imaginary catch. "Still water. Patience. A good lure."

Mueller saw both men opposite patiently waiting for his response, and he saw in each face a terrible compulsion for patriotism. *He didn't have to do this.*

3

LEISZ'S WIFE

MUELLER LOOKED up to see Mrs. Leisz with her head out the third-floor window and staring down at him with a puzzled expression. He'd said his name on the intercom, but he had no reason to believe that she'd remember who he was. He'd said he'd come about her husband. She yelled down that the door buzzer was broken and then she dropped a sock weighted with a key. He let himself in the lobby. Mueller prepared for the questions she would ask that he would have to avoid, politely of course, and still provide sympathy. He couldn't let on any of what he knew beyond what the police had already told her.

The stairs were grim: fluorescent lights, yellowing paint, and hand-me-down baby strollers on each landing that he had to maneuver past on his climb. Fried onion smells filled the air and faint voices drifted up the stairwell. So this was where Alfred Leisz lived. Agency salaries permitted better housing, but European recruits hoarded their earnings. Mueller was uncomfortable entering the private world of the Hungarian émigré whom he'd known only from his work tapping into Soviet telephone conversations from the listening station a block from the embassy. Mueller had found Leisz in a displaced persons camp and brought him to America for his skills as a linguist, translator, and cryptographer. Leisz had discovered that the Soviet voice encryption machines had a serious problem. They sent a faint echo of the uncoded message with the coded one. He was able to figure out how to extract the echo and reveal the clear text, which he transcribed and translated in the basement room that connected to embassy lines via a tunnel dug under Sixteenth Street. Mueller had found Leisz in his basement cubicle. The damn fool Leisz had broken the rules and let someone in.

"I know you," Mrs. Leisz said when Mueller stood at the third-floor landing. She wore an ankle-length smock and held a restless infant in one arm, while a young boy tugged at her free hand. "You were at the funeral."

Mueller nodded. A frown creased his forehead. "Yes."

She blocked the door, but then remembering, pulled her son aside and made room for Mueller to pass. "You were the one who called?" She spoke English confidently with a slight accent.

"Yes."

Mueller found himself in a small living room with a jumble of toys scattered across the floor, which he stepped over, avoiding the littered field of play as best he could. He sat where she directed, a dark sofa that hid its stains. Steam hissing from the cast iron radiators wastefully heated the apartment. Floor-to-ceiling shelves were filled with technical books and literature in several languages.

Mrs. Leisz sat in a bergère chair opposite Mueller. She had thin pale arms, chafed hands, no makeup, prematurely graying hair wound into a bun on top of her head, and tired eyes that she opened wide. "What documents?" she asked. She rocked her infant child and shifted to make herself more comfortable.

Mueller pulled a file from his attaché case and kindly patted the boy's head. "Can I speak openly?"

"Yes, of course. Speak."

"We've arranged for you to receive his civil service benefits. We want to make sure you're doing okay. I'm here to answer any questions." Mueller opened the file. "Has anyone contacted you?"

She looked confused.

Mueller leaned forward, consciously sympathetic. "If anyone comes here and asks questions about his death, I'm happy to have you direct them to me. It's best that we do that so you don't have to be troubled."

"What questions? Who?"

"The insurance company, for example. We want to make sure that you're taken care of."

She nodded, said nothing.

"This must be very hard for you. We want to help. We have expedited your benefits. Payments will come monthly to your account. It starts in two weeks." He pulled out an envelope with cash which he proffered, but she didn't reach for it so he placed it on the coffee table. "This will help in the meantime."

"Anton, stop," she scolded when her son took the envelope.

The baby had fallen asleep in her arms. Mrs. Leisz turned to Mueller. She tried to look grateful, but her face went blank and words tumbled out.

"I don't know what's happened." She stared. "He was a sunny, open man. He came home at night and read to our son, and he was kind to me. Our apartment was a lively place where friends came to eat and drink and talk. Then something happened. Alfred returned from the library on Friday and he wasn't his usual self. He didn't read to the boy. He sat there and drank. He didn't talk. He was a different person. I just knew something was terribly wrong. The whole weekend was very melancholy and then he said he'd made a mistake. He said he was going to lose his job. He wouldn't tell me anything else.

"It was the weekend of the big storm and everything was closed down Friday night. Trolleys weren't running. Cars were buried. He wanted to fix the mistake, he said, but the city was shut down. No trolleys, no way to get to the library. Weather that weekend was cold and gray and deepened his worry. The children picked up his mood. I told him, go outside, take a walk, so we could have some peace here, but the snow wasn't shoveled and had drifted chest high. He came back up and sat there where you're sitting and drank. I wanted to strangle him."

Mrs. Leisz suddenly put her hand out, touching Mueller, who flinched. "I don't mean that. I loved him, but he was in a dark mood."

Mrs. Leisz rocked her sleeping child and brought her eyes back to Mueller. "That night he was quiet at the dinner table. I said it's a shame the adults in this family have stopped talking.

On Sunday night he just had to get out of the house so we left the children with a neighbor. The new film about Martin Luther had just opened and he picked to see it. I thought it an odd choice. It was a serious movie," Mrs. Leisz said. "Not one to see if you're depressed."

She paused. "Alfred went to work early the next morning to change his report, or fix it. I couldn't understand what was so important. It's just a report, I told him. But he wouldn't listen. I confronted him. He said he couldn't talk about it. I said *You work in a library bookshop. You translate Russian newspapers. What is so important?*"

Her agitated voice stirred the baby and she rocked back and forth cooing and shhhing. Mueller watched her carefully. *She knows nothing.* Alfred Leisz had kept his wife in the dark about what he did and who his employer was.

"Read me this book," the boy said, hopping on the sofa. Mueller smiled at the boy.

"On the phone," Mrs. Liesz asked, "you said 'freak accident,' that he was found in a puddle of electrified water? Face burned? How did that happen in a library?"

Mueller nodded. "Yes. It's from the police report." Lies to assure a closed casket.

Mueller could do nothing more for her, and he didn't want to stick around to take her awkward questions. Time to leave. Mueller laid the package of materials, including the police report, on the coffee table. He'd brought Alfred Leisz's personal items from his cubicle: a framed photograph of his son, a fountain pen, a second pair of eyeglasses. Useless to her, but a keepsake perhaps.

He put the release form for expedited death benefits in front of her to sign.

"I need my glasses," she said.

When she disappeared in the bedroom, Mueller turned to the boy. "How old are you?" He took the boy on his lap. The same age as his son, Mueller thought.

The boy held up one hand and counted each finger. "Five. I'm a big boy."

"I have a boy like you. I don't see him enough. How do you like being a big boy?"

"Oh, it's okay. I don't cry anymore. My sister cries. She's still a baby."

"Do you take care of your sister?"

"Oh, yes."

Mueller smiled at the boy's eagerness. He felt an enormous sadness for the moment his mother had told him his father was dead—and explained what death was. No young child should suffer that darkness. The boy reminded Mueller of his own son—same pink cheeks, same curious eyes, same sweet innocence. For no reason, Mueller flashed on his last supervised visit, when it tore his heart to leave his crying boy pleading for Mueller to stay.

"How old is your boy?" the child asked.

"Six," Mueller said.

"I will be six." He held up two hands. "When I'm six I will be smart. What does he look like?"

Mueller smiled kindly. "He looks like you. I love him like your mother loves you."

"Can I play with him?" the boy asked.

"He doesn't live here." Mueller opened the illustrated story-book and they read together. Mueller watched the boy without letting the boy know he was being watched.

The visit ended. Mueller stood at the apartment door and faced Mrs. Leisz, sleeping infant in her arm, son tugging at her hand. "Will you come again and read to him?"

"Of course." Mueller nodded at the child. "He's a sweet boy." *What could he say?* This was the hard part of the job. *Poor woman*, Mueller thought. On his way down the stairwell he felt a stirring of remorse. He felt the burden of what it took to explain a corrupt world to an innocent mind. Mueller stopped suddenly on the landing, his lanky frame bent over, dry heaving an empty stomach. He felt as bad as he'd ever felt. The lies he had to tell.

4

RUSSIAN EMBASSY

FRIDAY NIGHT, Mueller was back in his office on the second floor of Quarter's Eye. The hall was deserted; the whole place had emptied out. The weekend was ahead, but Mueller felt none of his usual relief that he had two days to himself.

He had finished his report on meeting with Mrs. Leisz and he'd included his speculation, for what it was worth, and he knew it wasn't worth much. But it was all he had. Mrs. Leisz was in the dark about everything. She could be of no help, but also no harm. Leisz's mistake? Mueller suspected he'd come across a clue to Protocol's identity in the embassy's cable traffic. A compromising clue in a coding error, a mistake. Leisz probably didn't know what he was looking at. Or perhaps he did? Somehow they got to him first. Mueller had read all of Leisz's intercepts from that afternoon, but nothing stood out. Just stuff Mueller expected to see, about power struggles in Moscow among rival Politburo factions looking to succeed Stalin, and ordinary cable traffic. Ordinary to anyone except the man who knew what he was looking at.

The problems of the Agency were big problems, but he no longer felt they were his to solve. He didn't care. He just didn't care anymore. He had once enjoyed his work, but the pleasure was gone and his interest had dissipated like sun burning off a morning fog. Where once there was a struggle between good and evil, the clarity was gone, and he was in a new gray-toned world where right and wrong blurred. The many innocent people who were collateral damage haunted him. He knew himself well enough to recognize the signs that he was becoming a burnt-out case.

He sat at his desk stodgily for several minutes looking at nothing in particular. The office's one window looked onto the ventilation shaft, so he kept the blind closed. It was musty. A cell, really. And depressing. He removed a page of stationery from his desk drawer and picked up a pen. He composed a brief letter of resignation addressed to the director. "What in God's name are we accomplishing here? Where does respect for human dignity come into play?" He finished the note, put it in an envelope, moistened the flap with his tongue, and sealed it. He placed the envelope in his outbox where his secretary would find it Monday morning. His mind played out the events that would follow. Colleagues he would disappoint, who wouldn't say they were disappointed, but Mueller would see it in the way they avoided him. Everyone knew it was poor form to resign. *We're fighting evil.* Mueller thought about Alfred Leisz struggling against the piano wire around his neck, gasping for air, leaving his face red and wildly contorted. Mueller forced the image from his mind.

Mueller looked at the envelope for a long time without any expression whatsoever, and without any responsibility. *Thank you for helping*, she'd said. What help? Mueller removed the letter of resignation from his outbox and put it inside his desk under his fountain pen.

"Ride home?"

It was Altman. He stood in the open door in his overcoat, his cheeks warm with scotch.

"With you?"

"I'm perfectly fine behind the wheel, old boy, so long as the driver in the oncoming car is sober."

Mueller's ulcer was good cover to pass on the booze. He wasn't sure how his drinking colleagues got their work done. He knew which reports were written in the morning and which after lunch. Good reports were those whose language was efficient, clear, concise. Afternoon writers sealed their thoughts with the cold kiss of gin.

"You should drink less," Mueller said.

"You, George, should be less abstemious. Each of us walks with his devil."

Mueller rode with Altman in his roadster coupé through the city's lightly trafficked streets, wind lifting snow pushed onto the sidewalk.

"So," Altman said. "Did you learn anything from her?"

"Nothing. She's in the dark. She won't ask questions."

"That's a start."

"Leave her alone."

Mueller was surprised when Altman pulled to the curb at Sixteenth Street just across from the Soviet embassy.

"Why are you stopping?"

"There," Altman said.

A brightly lit guardhouse bordered the tall gate and a guard in a cap leaned toward the glass and peered into the night. Behind, the dark Beaux Arts mansion whose shuttered windows gave it a forlorn look. A high fence with sharp iron tips ringed the old building and reinforced its forbidding appearance. Harsh fluorescent light in the kiosk showed the inquiring face of the lone guard. Three cars were parked inside the gate.

"The one in the middle," Altman said. "Vasilenko takes it to the Soviet compound on Chesapeake Bay on weekends. It's your best shot. FBI don't tail them that far. Remarkable, isn't it? Good for us."

Mueller saw nothing unusual about the green four-door sedan except that it was a Buick, not a Moskvitch. "He gets the privilege of his own car?"

"And a driver."

"Anything else?"

"He's a colonel."

"What does that mean?" Mueller snapped his question with more irritation than he intended, and now his mood was out there.

"George, what's bothering you?"

Mueller didn't have an answer. At least not an answer he was willing to share.

"I'm curious, George. You're being goddamned touchy. Head in the clouds about this."

"I know what I need to do."

"I have reservations too. We all do. The ends don't justify the means, George, but they're all we have."

Mueller was dropped off in front of his apartment building. Altman leaned across the seat and spoke to Mueller through the open passenger window. "Come out to our place next weekend. We're across the water from the Soviet compound. Two birds with one stone."

Altman withdrew, but then leaned toward the open window, and yelled after Mueller, climbing the building's steps. "My sister is there, old boy. In her is the end of breeding. She would like someone to speak with and you may be just the one to commit that act of bravery."

. . .

A cover story had already been arranged for George Mueller. It didn't surprise many people in Quarter's Eye that he was placed on medical leave. These people were reassured that the ulcer he'd developed in Vienna would not interfere with his work, but he needed to seek treatment at a sanitarium, and during that time he'd be in the office less, reducing his workload. During those next few days he complained to whoever cared to listen that the Agency was losing its way, and there was rapidly deteriorating morale. Bright, patriotic professionals had been recruited with promises of exciting overseas service. Then they were put in dead-end posts as glorified messengers and typists. He shared these opinions openly, perhaps recklessly.

On the day he cleaned up his office there were colleagues who came to see him off who didn't expect him to return. He'd been removed from the routing list of daily intelligence summaries in the standard procedure for men on medical leave, but some saw it as a sign he was out. After that colleagues stopped speaking to him about work, or spoke to him not at all, or diverted the talk to safe and inconsequential topics. Everything was made easier by his ulcer because it was real, as were his opinions about the state of affairs in the Agency. He could plausibly explain himself to colleagues and the explanation had the benefit of being true.

Rumors circulated that the losses in Europe were his fault in some way, and he'd been asked to leave, but no one had specific details, so office gossip invented ludicrous scenarios. There was his divorce in Vienna; there was the incident, repeated several times by vigilant janitors, that he had left his office safe unlocked and that was how Leisz's cover had been blown. The accumulation of little oversights and lax behavior fueled speculation that Mueller was a security risk.

5

CHESAPEAKE BAY

THE BAY was a boisterous gray under a low ceiling of angry clouds.

Mueller straddled his bicycle on the windswept road that snaked along the bluff. He was stopped there at the viewpoint within sight of the cove's far shore and the weekend beach homes that dotted the coastline. Cold rain had begun to fall and the intermittent drops hit fiercely. Too warm for snow, but not so warm that he could ignore their biting cold. In the distance, sheeting rain fell from dark clouds moving across the bay.

He spotted the Soviet compound on the spit of land beyond the other homes. It was where they said it would be, and it looked as he'd been told it would look, but there was a sense of moment, being there and seeing what had been described. The pink Belgravia-style mansion was approached by a long circular driveway that ended in broad steps leading to the front door. The color was enough to draw the eye, not the gaudy pink he'd first imagined when he heard the word, but a rose limestone that was soft on the eye.

Mueller raised his binoculars and scanned the grounds. Below the mansion there were tennis courts, a soccer field with patches of brown showing through the melted snow, and a covered swimming pool. Dull green privet hedges bordered paths that meandered through bare gardens on their way to the water. There was no one out. Too wet. Too cold. Mueller saw one black car parked in the driveway with stanchions, Soviet ensigns whipping in the wind.

Mueller biked to the town of Centreville, the nearest community that served that part of Chesapeake Bay, a small place, hardly a town at all, but there was a bank, a church, a Main Street, and a liquor store. Mueller dismounted across the street and studied the two black sedans parked in front. Same make and model as the car he'd seen in his binoculars. He recognized the diplomatic license plates. He saw several men in suits inside the store's plate glass window and he followed them when they emerged, talking among themselves, joking. He watched them closely, but wasn't sure he recognized the man he'd come to find.

•   •   •

Mueller could feel the cashier's eyes follow him while he browsed the shelves of gin. Their eyes had met when Mueller entered. The doorbell clanged when Mueller stepped in and the cashier had looked up from his Saturday newspaper.

Mueller put a pint of cheap gin on the counter. "How much?"

"Three bucks."

He was a stocky, older man in a cardigan sweater buttoned over a shirt and tie, and his gray hair was parted on the side. He wore wire-rim glasses and a wide smile, and Mueller knew that he wasn't getting out of the store without having to listen to some story about something. Mueller looked to see if he had exact change, but he did not. The cashier held the five-dollar bill hostage.

"You here for the races?"

Mueller nodded. *Why stand out.*

"A lot of folks come down early to fit out their boats, you know."

"I didn't know."

"You're not from here, are you?"

"No."

"I haven't seen you here before."

"I'm not from here."

"I know most of the folks from around here, even the weekenders. Small town. You get to know everyone. I even know some Russians."

Mueller looked at the cashier.

"That was them who just left before you came in. . . . I'm short on ones. Quarters okay?"

Mueller nodded. "They come in a lot?"

"Oh, yeah." The cashier rolled his eyes in an exaggerated expression. "It's a funny story, you know. The first owner of the place out on Pioneer Point started the winter races. He gave a party for all the skippers, but his wife—she's from New York—got bored down here and wanted nothing to do with the place. She finally divorced him. She called the place a pink elephant. He wanted to make a killing dividing the estate into lots, but the planning board turned him down. He sold the place to the Russians out of spite. We weren't happy. Communists right here in Centreville? I'm still not happy about it. But don't get me wrong. They don't bother me. The neighbors got upset at the chain-link fence. And their guard dogs. They bark a lot."

The cashier pushed Mueller's change across the counter.

"They're good customers," he continued. "They park outside and come in groups of five or six. Buy Schmidt beer, Smirnoff vodka, and sometimes they get Jack Daniel's. Don't speak good English. Half the time I don't know what they're saying. They point a lot. They're pretty quick with their embassy IDs and remind me they don't pay tax. Nice about it, but the extra paperwork is a hassle. Seem like regular folks. Just don't trust their driving."

Mueller pocketed his change.

"When I see them come barreling down the road I give them plenty of room. What's your name?"

"George."

"Nice to meet you, George."

Mueller took his pint of gin in its brown bag and slipped it in his deep overcoat pocket.

This became his routine. Each day that week he sat on the bench across the street from the liquor store and waited for cars from the Soviet compound to arrive. He read the newspaper or a novel, or sat in the sun. When the Russians arrived he made a mental note of the license plates, and he recorded their faces in memory. A few women got out of the cars, but it was mostly middle-aged men, usually in hats and heavy coats, often loud, and Mueller got to know who was the driver, who the passenger. When they entered the liquor store Mueller crossed the street to buy his pint of gin.

"You again," the cashier said.

Mueller intervened the third day. The driver of one car was pointing to a shelf and having a hard time getting his meaning across to the cashier. The Russian was polite, but became exasperated at the cashier's slowness, and he pointed excitedly, yelling out a string of words, which entertained his companions, who laughed.

"He's looking for cognac," Mueller said, helpfully.

After the Russians left, Mueller went to pay for his pint. "You speak Russian?"

"I understand a bit."

"What else did they say?"

"They called you a few names."

On the fourth day Mueller saw the forest-green Buick. He recognized the driver. He was the same man who insulted the cashier. Heavy, thick neck, stubby fingers. Mueller knew what he had to do.

He crossed the street, walked up to the driver, and said something he knew would provoke the man, a little hostile, certainly insulting. Words were exchanged. There was some shoving. A fist thrown. The driver's Russian companions were outside the store in a moment restraining their agitated colleague. Mueller's pint of gin had broken on the sidewalk in his fall, and the Russian driver bled heavily on the hand where glass had opened a gash. A few townspeople gathered around the scene, but no one had seen what happened, so no one knew if the incident had been the fault of the Russian or of the stranger who'd crossed the street. No one heard what had been said, although the cashier vouched for the stranger. This all happened in the afternoon that day.

The oysterman's cottage Mueller had rented sat two miles outside of Centreville on a cove. He biked back there after the incident. The house was a small, quiet place with a gently sloped roof and a screen porch. Wind, rain, and sun had leached color from the shingle siding and the place fit into the colorless winter landscape. A second nearby building held an old canoe, discarded crab cages, rusted parts of gasoline engines, and an old pickup. Mueller got the cottage for a good off-season price and in the first week he'd found a way to engage his mind with all his free time. He read in the sun, cooked a bit, found time to contemplate the lengthening daylight, and rehearsed the quiet life he planned for himself and his son after he resigned.

He didn't wait long after returning from town that afternoon, and he again set out on his bicycle. He made an incongruous picture—grown man, in office shoes and a car coat, pedaling his rickety bike on the narrow road in blustery weather.

He passed low-lying fields of pussy willows left over from the previous season, and further on he veered left on the dead-end street that ran alongside a chain-link fence topped with razor wire. Yellow signs warned trespassers to keep out. The road ended at a locked gate with a red plaque adorned with hammer and sickle.

Mueller straddled his bicycle and looked through the iron bars. The land was drained of color and trees were bare in winter undress through the patch of forest. He made out the rose limestone mansion. There was no one to speak with at the gate, no one to engage, and he began to wonder why he'd come. They had to come to him, he reminded himself. This wasn't going to work.

On his bike ride home he saw the green Buick. The car came into view when it swerved around a curve at high speed, straddling both narrow lanes. With a tight grip on the handlebars, Mueller aligned his bike's front wheel along the road's edge. He had no room on his right where the thin strip of shoulder fell into a culvert. He narrowed his eyes on the small world of white paint. He moved deliberately, but not slowly, and he was very aware of the automobile speeding toward him. Mueller thought he'd be safe, so he angled slightly but suddenly, taking up more of the lane. The car swept past. Wind slapped his body, jostled the rickety front wheel, causing him to lose control. The bike jumped the culvert and Mueller was thrown off.

It was a few moments before Mueller was able to put his mind around the fact that he had been run off the road. He was on his back in wet earth. He looked at his hands. One ached, but no blood, just bruises mixed with clay and pebbles embedded in his palm. He moved his neck without feeling pain and then saw his bike. It lay on its side against a boulder that erupted from the side of the ditch. Two spokes had popped from the front rim, bent and unridable. He stood and that's when he knew how badly he was injured. A horrible pain shot up his thigh. A dark wetness seeped from a tear in his trousers. On the ground there was a pointy stick that had snapped from a sapling.

Mueller limped to his bicycle and he confirmed his initial opinion. It couldn't be ridden. But, in a way, that didn't matter because he didn't think he'd be able to work the pedal with his injured thigh. He'd have to walk the bike to town, and that inconvenience, even more than the injury, irritated him.

"Idiot," he said, under his breath.

He remembered the cashier's advisory, and Mueller admonished himself for not being more careful, but then dismissed his part in the accident. The car was too big. The road too narrow. Its speed too great. And it had all happened in a split second. The driver, the one he'd had words with, was entirely to blame. "Idiot," he said again.

Mueller had walked a few steps when he saw a small sports car approach from the direction of Centreville. The red convertible slowed and Mueller saw the driver, a young woman in dark glasses and colorful scarf tied under her chin. Her hair whipped behind in the wind. She must see the incongruity of a bicyclist walking his bike, Mueller thought, and he considered whether the two-seater would be able to hold him and the bike. It was getting on to dusk. Better to get a ride and he could always come back for the bike.

Mueller signaled as she passed, and he thought, *No, she isn't going to stop.* He glanced back. *Stop lady. Have a heart.* Surprisingly, he saw her pull over a short ways down the road. Mueller pointed his numb foot in the right direction. He wasn't aware how much he'd bled until he felt the blood slosh in his shoe. His hand went to his thigh wound and there was a fierce tenderness. He became aware that the young woman was speaking to him in a loud voice, asking a lot of questions, standing there beside him, trying to get his attention. Somewhere in his struggle to provide answers he felt an overwhelming dizziness.

6

BETH ENTERS THE PICTURE

MUELLER BECAME aware that he was in an unfamiliar room. His long groggy dream tapered off without an ending and vanished in the lifting fog of a fevered sleep and the bright light that seemed to be everywhere. He blinked. There were only sensations at first. He opened and closed his hand, feeling his fingers. He did not comprehend the large canopy that spread over his bed, or the pillows under his head, or the many shelves of children's books in the room. He became aware he was breathing. Then came the questions, one after the other. Where was he? How did he get here?

He heard a woman's voice outside in the hall. He couldn't see anyone through the half-open door, but there was no mistaking her loud instructions.

"There will be twelve tonight for dinner, Lizzy. I want the linen tablecloth, and the nice glasses, and Mother's silverware.

It's an event and I want it to be festive. Do you think anyone has flowers this time of year? Will you remember it will be twelve? I want the extra place setting in case he is well enough to join."

Mueller saw a shadow move in the dark hall, and suddenly a young woman came through the door and approached the bed. She wore dark glasses and a soiled work coat over scruffy blue jeans. Her hair was long, whiskey-colored, windblown, and her face was red from sun or cold and streaked with dirt where she'd wiped the back of her gloves. She removed the gloves one finger at a time and gazed at Mueller.

"So, you're alive," she said.

Mueller nodded.

"How do you feel?"

Mueller had to think. "I'm okay." His voice was hoarse.

"Better okay than not okay." She answered the question that she saw in his expression. "This?" she asked, displaying her dirty clothing. "The garden. My father can't plant bulbs, but he tries. Mother always did them. I've redone them. So . . . here you are." She gazed at him.

Mueller made an effort to smile. "Where is here?" He tried to sit up, but lancing pain made him reach for his leg.

"Yes, you're okay, I see." She helped him lean against the headboard, tucking a pillow under his head. "This is my father's home. You passed out. Do you remember that? I was asking what happened and you fell over. One minute you were standing there and the next you fell and struck your head. You were quite a mess. The driver of a passing van helped get you in my car. I called the doctor in town. Stitched your leg. Fixed the ugly gash on your head."

Mueller felt the bandage above his ear. He lifted the comforter and saw cotton gauze wrapping his thigh. A spiderweb of purple colored his skin.

"You'll live," she said, unsympathetically. "What happened?"

"I was on my bike. A car went by."

She looked at him skeptically. "A car went by?"

"He tried to drive me off the road."

"You're very lucky."

"Who are you?" he asked.

She cocked her head. "Your fairy godmother, it seems. When was the last time you rode a bike?" She put out her hand. "I'm Beth. Is there someone we should call?"

The office? His secretary? "There is no one to call," he said. "I've rented a cottage." She was a plain woman with a pretty face and her thick work coat gave her the appearance of wide hips. These observations came to him all at once, as he was trained.

"You're alone?"

"Yes."

"You're welcome to stay for dinner." She threw out, "You were talking a lot in your sleep." She put her hand on his forehead. "You're cool now, but the fever lasted all night."

Mueller was surprised by the calming touch of her palm on his skin. He wasn't accustomed to kindness from strangers. Cautious. "What did I say?"

"Gobbledygook." She looked skeptically at him. "You think I'm joking? I couldn't understand a word. I take that back. There was one word. 'Stop.' You kept saying 'stop.' There you have it."

It never occurred to Mueller that he might talk in his sleep. *Stop?*

"Your pants and shirt are there. We washed them. And there's your wallet. We put you in my brother's pajamas. I didn't undress you." She said this in response to nothing. "Lizzy had that pleasure." She said that without an ounce of irony. "So, you'll join us?"

Mueller nodded. "Yes." When she was gone Mueller shifted his legs to the side of the bed and tested his footing. He could stand without pain, but his thigh was tender and swollen. He hobbled to his clothes and took his wallet from the back pocket of his pants. Driver's license, State Department ID, insurance card, cash. Nothing missing. Tradecraft had taught him a trick to know if his wallet had been violated. The trick was simple. Place a human hair in a folded note. Imperceptible to the careless meddler, but he would know the note had been read if the hair was missing. He unfolded the paper. The dark strand was gone.

He sat on the chair and considered his situation. What was next? The Russians would show up sooner or later. The police would ask questions, and probably already had, and the lines would begin to converge. Someone had washed his clothing and mended the tear in his trousers. He went through contortions to place his left leg inside the trousers, grabbing the end of the bed when he wasn't able to balance on one foot.

At the window, he pulled aside the drawn curtain and looked out onto a wide lawn of spring snow melting under the furious heat of a noon sun. Farther along a small dock jutted into the bay. He leaned forward against the glass and saw a gravel driveway that curved around the front of the house. A black Cadillac was parked there and a silver-haired man in a European suit stepped out onto the driveway and greeted Beth. They hugged. Mueller was surprised at the emotion on display. He leaned into the window and saw she was crying. He had an odd sensation in the moment. Curious and impatient, those opposite feelings existing in him at the same time.

His thoughts turned to the green Buick that had run him off the road. He would have to deal with that. And then he thought again about his restless night and his fevered talking. He felt his face. It was shaved, but he hadn't done it. Beth came to mind.

An hour later. He was at the front door of the house about to step into the bright day, when he heard a woman scream.

"You don't want to do that!"

A stout, jolly maid came out of a dark hallway waving her arms in the air. "You stay in the house, Mr. Mueller."

His name. *They had looked*. He smiled and nodded. "I'm just getting some fresh air."

"The air is fresh in here too. We don't have stale air inside this house. We don't want you falling down those steps."

"I'm fine with walking."

"You're good with biking too, I'm told. You don't know how lucky you was. She was so upset. You was in a fever, talking and going on and on. She was up all night. Worried sick. I don't want you go down those steps and fall on your damn fool head."

· · ·

Dinner. Mueller sat at one end of the long table between two talky, well-dressed women, but he was silent and could have been sitting by himself. He was the outsider among the lively guests who whispered to each other or debated loudly. Mueller looked at his plate, picked at his entrée, and rubbed his thigh, which throbbed in sympathy with his boredom.

The table was festively set with flowers, wineglasses, bone china, silverware, and serviette rings empty of their cotton napkins. A huge crystal chandelier hung over the table, bathing the twelve guests in warm, flickering light. Two loud ones at the end of the table talked over each other, voices emphatically rising to argue a political point about totalitarianism. The hideous din gave Mueller a headache. He listened, smiled if smiled at, said little.

A stylish older woman in turquoise shawl and strapless gown glanced at Mueller twice before she leaned toward him, eyeing him intently. "You're awfully quiet."

"Listening," he said.

"Oh." She continued to look at him, waiting.

"He's the one I found on the road," Beth said.

Mueller felt like some kind of charity case.

Beth quickly rose from her place and took the seat beside him, empty because the occupant had gone off. She smiled at Mueller. "Are you bored?" she asked.

That obvious? Dinner parties with strangers were low on his list, as were other people's home movies, and he had little tolerance for shallow conversation about politics. People no longer talked civilly. They argued. "No," he said. "But I hate politics."

Beth opened her eyes wide, laughed. She whispered, "I hate these dinners."

Her comment surprised Mueller. He remembered dirt streaking her cheeks, but the dirt was gone, as was the red flush of sun, and she was transformed. Perfumed skin, wavy chestnut hair, and a black strapless gown that set off her bare shoulders. Without dark glasses her eyes were a startling blue and looked at him with an eagerness that made him want to lean away. Her string of pearls and a giant gold pin that glittered starlike on the dark fabric made her look less ordinary, less chubby.

"They're all his friends," she said, nodding toward the head of the table, where a gray-haired, older man with thick eyebrows listened intently to his neighbor. His head was bowed and the other man whispered something. They were in deep conversation on some urgent topic. "He holds this dinner every spring in race week. Mother died a year ago. He is still living the life they had together, but it's a big house and he hasn't gotten used to being alone. That's why I visit. Bad things happen in pairs." She looked at him. "Red baiters want to make him a target."

She nodded at a couple at the end of the table. "Republicans. A banker from New York and that's his third wife, half his age. I shouldn't gossip, but we all do it, don't we?" She added earnestly, "He's come out in support of the hearings on Capitol Hill and that's what makes me angry."

Mueller resisted the impulse to look at his watch.

Beth turned to another couple. "My father's partner. Collects art, likes opera. He smokes cigars. You can smell them on his clothes. He thinks he is open-minded, but he is hopelessly conservative. My father puts up with him somehow."

She paused. She contemplated the table of well-dressed guests. "Everyone in this room is worried about something. Anxious about something." She nodded. "He's a Jew who got out of

Germany, his last name is Fried, and the woman next to him, with the black hair, well, she goes on and on about pesticides that leach into the water table when farmers spray for mosquitoes, and her name is Worthy. Has it ever struck you how some people have names that suggest what they do? Veterinarian named Woolf, or a banker named Nichols. Mueller?" She looked at him. "What do you do?"

"State Department."

"My brother works there."

Mueller turned to her and lingered on her face, its lines, and slowly the similarity of brother and sister shaped itself into a certainty. Surprise is a funny thing. It only lasts a second. He remembered the remark, so odd in the moment of telling, how Altman had said it and laughed: "My sister is there, old boy. In her is the end of breeding. She would like someone to speak with and you may be just the one to commit that act of bravery."

Mueller considered the possibilities that might play out, the danger. The line he could not cross.

The stylish older woman suddenly leaned into Beth, her expression exuberant. "So, how did it feel? Opening night? The reviews were kind. They called it a comedy but I have always thought *Measure for Measure* was a tough knot to untie. Pride. Humility. The most righteous character turns out to be a lust-addled hypocrite. I'd say that's a good description of what is happening in Washington today. 'Some rise by sin. Some by virtue fall.' You, my dear, were a magnificent Isabella."

Mueller turned to Beth. *An actress?*

Dessert was being served when the argument began. The

outspoken woman had wrapped her shoulders in her turquoise shawl and curtly addressed the man directly across the table. He had a crew-cut, thin tie, and a military sternness to his clenched jaw.

"On what evidence?" she snapped. "How can you say we're better than the Russians? They have show trials. We have show trials. How else can you describe the ridiculous hearings that are going on in the Senate?"

She became aware that the guests around her had stopped talking. She looked around for allies. "We are talking about the hearings on Capitol Hill," she explained. "I disagreed with the idea that some people find popular that there is a thing that the senator calls moral degeneracy, that he says is why Rome fell, and will doom us, which equates communists and homosexuals."

The room was silenced. The word had jumped from her lips and hung in the air like a bad smell. Guests looked at each other, but no one spoke. The lady looked at their host. "Arnold, they've even got you testifying."

"I'll be fine," he said. He nodded at one guest, then another. "It's all a misunderstanding. A few questions about things I did years ago in Vienna. Politics shouldn't spoil the evening. We're here to talk about sailing."

"But we haven't talked about sailing," the lady said.

"I will talk about sailing," he said. "In the den. Shall we go? We have liquor, coffee, wine, tea, whiskey. Out the window you can see the Soviet navy's cadet training ship, the *Sedov*. It has four masts. Just arrived from Buenos Aires on a goodwill tour."

Mueller left the group and found his way outside. He sat on

a bench with a view of the dark bay. A vast night sky of stars stretched across the water and, in the distance, the dim lights of Washington. Pine scents from evergreens mixed with the ambiguous smells of the warming earth. He heard a noise behind him and turned to see Beth approach.

"The police came by today," she said, sitting.

He looked at her.

"I said you were recovering. I told them I'd bring you by when you felt better. Tomorrow if you like. You can stay here another night."

"Who came?"

"The sheriff."

"From Centreville?"

"Yes. I had called and said you had been run off the road. He was concerned. He asked if the driver was Russian."

"How would he know?"

"You were by their compound. They drive fast on these roads. I said he might be. Was that wrong?"

"No, he was Russian. Nothing is wrong."

They sat in silence. Neither of them knew how to carry the conversation forward. Finally, she said, "What brought you out here in the off-season?"

"The quiet. I don't like crowds."

"It wasn't the biking?" She laughed.

Was she making fun of him? Her eyes were open wide, but her expression wasn't mocking. Perhaps she was unsure of herself. He laughed with her. "I haven't biked since college. I had the wrong shoes."

"How long are you out for?"

"I'm not sure."

"How long have you rented the cottage?"

He'd been too vague. Certainly he should appear to have some idea. "A week. Maybe two. I'm taking time off to enjoy the quiet. Catching up on my reading."

He threw out a few authors he'd read in the last two years, still contemporary enough to suit his purposes, and authors he'd enjoyed so he wouldn't have to fake a commentary if asked. But she didn't.

. . .

It had been arranged that Beth would pick up Mueller at the courthouse when he was done with his interview with the sheriff. It was raining again and the blanket of low clouds deepened the green of the scrub pine and darkened the mood. They drove in silence most of the way.

"What did he say?" she asked, finally.

It had been a short meeting. "He said they're orderly folks. It was a strange conversation. He said things that I think he wanted me to reject."

"What do you mean?"

"He said they stick to themselves, they don't cause trouble. They even put nickels in the parking meters when they don't have to because their diplomatic plates exempt them. I got the sense he was provoking me to disagree. I told him I didn't want to press charges. It was an accident."

Mueller paused. "He doesn't have jurisdiction. He said drivers aren't diplomats. They don't have immunity. He's already interviewed the driver. The man doesn't speak English so another Russian translated. It irritated the sheriff. The man was on an American highway and he couldn't read English street signs."

"Did he say you were in the middle of the road?"

Mueller looked at Beth. "Who said that?"

"When he talked to me, he said the driver said you were in the middle of the road, and he had to swerve to avoid you."

Mueller frowned. "I don't remember it that way."

She walked him to the cottage's front door. She held her umbrella high for both of them and took his arm. He thought it was to help him walk, but he was surprised when she pulled him forward. He unlocked his door. Before he stepped inside he thanked her. She smiled. She gave him the faintest breath of a kiss on the cheek and a quick hug. She seemed to be a little embarrassed, but added in a whisper, "I'd like to see you again."

He nodded. "Me too."

"What are you doing tomorrow?"

· · ·

Mueller spent the next afternoon in the back of the cottage, by the bay, watching movements at the Soviet compound. He had not perfected the patience needed to wait for something to happen when there was no certainty that anything would. Time was the enemy of his restless imagination. He thought he saw something, but when he looked closer it was the same car he'd seen earlier in the day, and the routines at the compound were just that, ordinary comings and goings that had no bearing on his task. Mueller put away his binoculars when dusk arrived. He'd made his play. Now he had to wait.

He entered the cottage's back door and threw his overcoat on a kitchen chair. When he flipped the wall switch light filled the room. That's when he saw the front door ajar. He remembered that he'd closed it because a raccoon had gotten into the garbage he'd put in the shed. Muddy shoe prints crossed the kitchen and went into the living room. Quietly, Mueller removed his Colt service pistol from inside an old sock in his duffel bag, and undid the safety. He was alert to sounds, eyes scanning for clues, senses heightened to danger. A sound behind him, a quick movement, and suddenly he turned, gun out.

"So you *are* here," Beth said, startled. She stood at the bathroom entrance. "I knocked. No one answered. I wondered where you could have gone without the bike."

Then she saw the pistol.

He lowered the gun and placed it on the kitchen counter. "I was in the backyard. I'm not used to people walking in unannounced."

"We agreed I'd come over and cook dinner."

He'd forgotten.

"I found a key above the door. I bought chicken and asparagus. It's the first of the season." She pointed at two bags of groceries that sat by the sink. She nodded at the pistol. "What are you worried about? It's safe here." Then, "At least it's safe if you're not on a bike."

He found a way to smile, but he didn't offer an explanation. She began unpacking groceries and very quickly she was preparing a meal.

It was the first of several nights that she made dinner for him. She offered to come and he accepted. They established a little routine. She arrived in the late afternoon with a bag of groceries and before dinner they took a walk along the beach. They didn't talk much, but she pointed out the large homes along the cove and described who lived in which house, offering gossip about the town. And then she would run ahead, or skip rocks across the cove's calm surface.

On the fourth night she arrived with a bottle of wine and the morning paper, which she'd gotten into the habit of bringing when he said the only thing he missed about Washington was the *Post*. Winter's gloom was already beginning to recede and the days were getting longer. He didn't resist her efforts to brighten the drab cottage with daffodils and a plate of homemade cookies. She brought fresh ones every afternoon after he complimented her first batch. He'd given her an extra key so she didn't have to ring the doorbell and wake him from a nap.

She had a glass of wine with the pot roast she'd prepared and he'd allowed her to pour a glass for him, but he barely touched it. They talked more easily now. She invited him to share his background, and to encourage him she talked about herself and her childhood. As was the case in most conversations then, they turned to the war.

"I was a nurse."

"Where?"

"The war ended before I was sent overseas." She stood and approached Mueller. "Let me see your stitches." She parted his hair and looked at the small head wound.

He felt her fingers part his hair and massage the scalp around the injury.

"Relax," she said. "You're so tense." She went back to the wound. "I think it's healed. It wasn't deep. I can save you a trip to the doctor. Shall I remove the stitches?"

"That's not necessary."

"I know that. I'm offering. It will take one minute."

He was discomfited by her kindness. "Okay," he said.

He winced when she pressed alcohol-soaked cotton around the wound's three stitches, and she patted his shoulder, soothing him, and whispered, *Relax*. It surprised him how the touch of her hand calmed him. It was a feeling he hadn't had—hadn't let himself have—for a long time. She snipped the sutures with a penknife scissors and removed three black threads with her eyebrow tweezers. She massaged his scalp when she was done and he let her go on for a while. He allowed himself to close his eyes and enjoy her touch.

He was glad neither of them was good at flirting. It was a kind of game, a deception. He preferred not to have that responsibility.

Should he sleep with her? He wasn't someone who was easily aroused, but he found her desirable that afternoon on the beach when she burst out laughing at him. She was not someone who would turn his head on the street, but she was attractive, and she had lots of other good points. She was lively and witty, and smart, and respected his privacy. She laughed impulsively without thinking, and he found that her spontaneity made him comfortable. She was easy to be around. He didn't know when it started, but he found himself getting fond of her. It was affection, and with it came a great need not to hurt her. But it wasn't passion. He didn't want that, or perhaps he did, but he was afraid of it. Or maybe he was afraid he'd ruin it—hurt her, hurt himself, make a mess of it. That's what his wife—ex-wife—had told him. "You don't know how to be close. You pull back. You say you want to be close, but you live inside yourself." He'd protested that she was wrong, but divorced and alone, he'd come to believe that she was right. He had listened to her complaints, even tried to be the vulnerable man she wanted, but nothing had been enough. They had only made each other miserable. He hadn't seen her betrayal coming. She had turned on him and taken the boy.

. . .

A car's headlights pulled into the driveway and filled the kitchen with blinding light. It idled momentarily outside the cottage and then the engine was cut.

Beth opened the back door on the third knock and saw a tall man, with a prominent jaw and a big chest, standing in the dim glow of the kitchen's light. He wore a wide-brim hat and a long gray overcoat.

She found Mueller in the living room where she'd left him.

"There's a man at the door asking for you," she said. "I think he's Russian."

"Show him in," Mueller said. "Then if you don't mind, would you close the door behind you? I'll see him alone."

Mueller ushered the Russian to the far end of the enclosed porch by the wide bay window that looked onto the cove. He didn't know this man, but he knew his type in the hierarchy of the rigid Soviet system. A trusted man, but not a senior officer made to stoop to being the messenger boy. He was glad they hadn't sent the driver, thinking they could end this with an apology. There was no greeting, no handshake, no false cordiality. Mueller didn't offer the man a seat or a smile. It was a brief conversation. The Soviets had come to Mueller, so they would be agreeing to his terms.

• • •

Beth couldn't make out what was being said behind the closed door. She leafed through the newspaper she'd brought, but it quickly bored her. She found herself glancing at the closed door until she could stand it no longer. She opened a book he'd left on the counter. A photograph stuck out like a bookmark. It was a black-and-white photo of a young boy in lederhosen by a farm-house and on the back, in child's handwriting, *Daddy*. She gazed at the boy and thought she saw a resemblance. She studied the smile on the face and the look of surprise of a uniformed man in the background waving the camera away.

She knelt at Muller's duffel bag, anxious at the prospect of prying into his private life. She listened for a shift in their voices, or the scraping of a chair on the floor, to detect if they were wrapping up. She vigorously wiped her sweating hands on her apron and slowly undid the bag's zipper. Her hand touched rolled cotton socks, starched shirt collars, a belt, shoes, and deep in a corner she found a tennis ball. *Odd*, she thought. *Where is his racket?* The pistol was there too, and she was careful to set it aside. A camera, a book of poetry, but nothing that would reveal his life, or compromise it. No diary. No letters. Then a small envelope inside the book and in it more photographs of the boy. There he was at a birthday cake. And there he was in Prater Park, the boy and his father standing at the Giant Ferris Wheel. The photo was a closed surface, unsatisfying, and it didn't open up. The unguarded moments were the best. The boy waving at the camera while riding a bike with training wheels.

The door handle turned and Beth sat bolt upright. She returned the photos, stuffed everything in the bag, and zipped it shut. Back at the table, she smiled when the men entered.

She let the guest out of the house, just as she had let him in, without a word of greeting or farewell. She stood in the open door and felt the evening breeze lift her hair, and she wrapped her arms on her chest against the chill. She watched him get in his sedan, a big man with dark eyes that gave her a cold look.

• • •

Mueller was at the dinner table Beth had set. He watched her fill their bowls with noodle soup and set a basket of bread between them. Neither spoke.

"I hope you don't mind leftovers," she said. "I took yesterday's chicken and added a few vegetables. How does it taste?"

"It's good."

They sat together without speaking. There was the sound of eating, spoons dipped, soup tasted, and a heightened sense of quiet. Mueller raised his eyes and saw her staring at him.

"Who are you?" she asked.

Mueller was surprised by his vague urge to tell her where

he'd grown up, who his parents were, how he'd gone off to war and seen things that no young man should have to see, but this urge passed quickly. "We don't need a past to enjoy this moment, do we?" Then, "I'd prefer if you didn't ask."

She head-cocked slightly, contemplating that thought. "Then who is he?" She nodded to where the stranger had walked out. "He is in our moment."

"He works in the Soviet embassy." A hint, he thought.

"That's all?"

"He was involved with the car that hit me. It will all be worked out."

She frowned, unsatisfied by his answer. She broke a piece of bread she'd baked, placing it on his dish, and taking another for herself, which she dipped in her soup.

"You have a son, don't you?"

Mueller raised his eyes.

"I found his photograph." She pointed at the book on the counter. "How old is he?"

"Six."

"Does he live with you?"

"His mother has him. It's a long story." Mueller wanted to say more but stopped himself. "He is growing up without me. I didn't think it would matter. . . ." He saw her eyes grow curious and he considered how much to share, how much to hold back. Then he told a story. He spoke without emotion, as if he were speaking about someone else, and his voice became quiet, his tone guarded. He didn't see his son often because the boy lived in Austria, out- side Ratz, and his travels to Europe had been reduced since coming to Washington, so he'd seen the boy twice, and even when he did visit, his relationship with the boy's mother was terrible. The boy spoke German, little English, so Mueller spoke German to his son, and that fact, he knew, as he thought about how their lives would diverge, made it hard to see what sort of attachment the boy would have—and who he would be to his son. And what did the mother tell the boy to turn him against Mueller?

"In my last visit I was inside the farmhouse I'd been given for the visit and he was outside by the woodshed. We were in the mountains. December. Cold had come. We needed firewood for the stove, and he was eager to help so I let him take the axe. He was at the chopping block turning little logs into kindling with one-handed hits on a log he held in position with his other hand. I watched him from the window without letting him know he was being watched. It was dangerous, of course, but he'd insisted, and what could I do? I wanted him to appreciate our brief time together. 'No' is a difficult word for the guest parent. And I admired how he tried to imitate my style of one-handed chopping. Suddenly I jumped from the table and cried, 'No!'

"I burst out the back door. I saw blood on his hand and fear in his eyes. 'Let's see,' I said. He was crying, but he put his hand out. The finger was cut below the tip. I took him to the house, washed the wound, and applied a bandage to stop the bleeding. The cut was shallow, but he was mortified. I said the bandage would do, but I asked if he wanted to go to the clinic. He shook his head defiantly. 'It's only a little cut,' he said tearfully. Of course, he didn't believe that, but he wanted to show me that he was brave. He got in my lap and I comforted him. He asked me if I'd ever cut myself as a child when I chopped wood. I knew he was comparing himself to me. We are God to our children at his age. I could lie to him to make him feel better. The right thing to do was to lie—and sometimes a lie is required—but I had promised I would never lie to him. It was a promise I made to myself to earn his respect, so I said 'No.'"

Mueller said the last word and was suddenly quiet, almost moody. He broke a piece of bread from the torn loaf and twice dipped it in his soup, then ate. He looked up at Beth, eyes fierce. "There. That's a story about my son. Does it tell you what you want to know?"

She looked at him for a moment. He'd slumped in his chair. Her voice was sympathetic. "You love him, don't you?"

"Yes." He cleared his throat to hide his emotion. "I do."

"I'm glad that I'm here," she said. "I'm glad that we met."

He was surprised when her eyes reddened. She reached across the table and put her palm over his hand. Neither spoke. The moment lingered, each looking at the other, each understanding he had a world of hurt that she would never know. A part of him that was inaccessible. She withdrew her hand and wiped her eye with her knuckle. She smiled kindly.

"I'm sorry," she said. "I don't mean to get emotional. I didn't know what to expect when you collapsed on the road. I couldn't just leave you. And here we are. I've enjoyed this week. Ever since I was a little girl I've woken up in the morning with a dread that everything good in my life will go away. I live today's regrets for tomorrow's disappointments." She looked around the little cottage that she'd brightened with flowers. "This will end. You will leave."

"Not tomorrow."

"Soon enough."

He didn't answer. Nor did he avert his eyes. He nodded.

She washed the dinner dishes, handing them to him to dry. He stacked plates in an orderly row in the drain rack. When they finished she went to the bathroom and then joined him in the bedroom.

He was under the blanket, his clothes draped over a chair. He watched her undress, first removing her sweater and then reaching behind to undo her bra. He felt her slip under the covers beside him and he felt the startling intimacy of her nakedness lightly touching his body.

"Come closer," she said.

He considered the request. Considered how he should show her that she was a desirable woman, and that he was attracted to her. And he considered the wrongness of what they were about to do. Realized they were doing what she had said not to do, creating tomorrow's disappointments. He turned to her. Her breath was close, warm, and he could feel the faint beating of her heart. Did every good beginning have to end in disappointment?

She reciprocated his touch, gathering his hair, bunching it, and affectionately messing his combed look. She moved her fingers to his face, finding his nose, touching one eye, then the other, and drew her fingertips across the seam of his lips. Her touch released a riot of sensation in his skin. Their arms wrapped each other and their bodies entangled in a slow unfolding of flesh. She drew her hand along the inside of his thigh, moist with sweat, and reached into his boxer shorts. Her tongue moved to his mouth and she pressed her lips on his with hungry kisses that he was returning.

She slept with him again the next two nights. They spent their days walking along the beach with lunch basket and blanket, and one afternoon she got him out onto the bay in a small sailboat. They sailed on the bay to an island of scrub oaks and made love on the beach under a blanket. On the last day she inspected his leg wound and opined that he was recovered, and she removed the sutures. When they were eating dinner that night he said he had to take care of something the next day. He would be gone for a little while, he said. He'd be back. She nodded. She smiled and said, "You don't have to lie to me. We've had something. It's enough. If it's gone, that's okay. We had it. You can't take that away."

7

RECRUITMENT

H E'S WAITING for you." The maître d' at Harvey's took Mueller's coat and pointed to a corner booth in the rear of the bustling restaurant. Mueller glanced in the bar's large mirror to consider the people who sat alone nursing a drink.

"I'm not late, I hope."

"You know him, Mr. Mueller. He's always early."

Mueller appreciated how the maître d' knew to ease the anxiety of the late-arriving customer. Mueller kept his duffel bag and made his way through the restaurant packed with a lively lunch crowd, drinking Capitol Hill staffers, voices rising to compete with louder voices at adjacent tables. No one he knew.

Mueller slid in the rear booth beside the director. He nodded at a third place setting. "Anyone else joining?"

"Just us." The director fingered the stem of his half-finished martini, no ice, three olives. He looked at Mueller. "Well?"

"They made contact."

"Who did they send?"

Mueller gave a name. "I asked for Vasilenko."

"You're sure it wasn't him?"

"I'm sure. We knew each other in Vienna."

"I understand Altman's sister found you on the road."

"The long arm of coincidence."

"What happened?" the director said.

"I wanted a scratch on the hand. I misjudged. Got too close. I was thrown."

The director looked at Mueller. "Keep her out of it."

"She's not in it."

"Her father is an old friend." The director waved over the waiter, who collected the extra setting. The director gave his order without looking at the menu, choosing from memory, and Mueller repeated the order to save time.

"Oysters?" the director asked. "They're fresh. In season."

"If you are."

"Cocktail?"

Mueller shook his head. "Water, no ice."

"Still set on leaving?" The director threw back his drink and ordered a second. "No second thoughts?"

"No. I'm out."

"You're not out. Not yet. I need you until this is done." The director leaned back. "You're good at this, George, because you have the right kind of intelligence. Teach for a year. You'll get bored."

The two men talked shop until the oysters arrived. Soon

after, a waiter carried in the two main-course dishes and placed them on the white tablecloth. The director tucked his napkin into his loose collar, making a bib for himself, and took the grilled baby back ribs in his hands. Mueller laid his napkin on his lap and eyed the greasy meat. "Use your fingers," the director said. "It's barbecue. Best goddamn barbecue in the city."

"They made a mistake," Mueller said. He had the director's attention with that comment. "The driver had no driver's license. None of them do. They are embarrassed. We came to an arrangement."

"What arrangement?"

"Vasilenko has agreed to meet. I got their attention. It's a start."

"Tell Coffin. Keep the Council in the loop."

It was a short lunch. They cleaned their hands with lemon water and warm towels, but skipped dessert. On their way out they passed a large round table in the center of the restaurant occupied by a loud, smoking, drinking bunch, jackets off.

One man stood. He was average height in a double-breasted suit, fleshy-faced, a bead of sweat hanging on his upper lip. His graying hair was combed back over a receding hairline and he'd loosened a canary tie around his thick neck. He blocked their path.

"Senator," the director said, feigning surprise.

The senator thrust out his thick hand with the practiced movement of a man who sought votes for a living. "Good to see you."

"And you."

Mueller also got the courtesy of a politician working the room, and he received the man's muscular handshake. Mueller nodded at the four seated junior staffers, but none rose.

"Good speech at Wheeling," the director said. There was no enthusiasm in his compliment and it hung in the air like day-old fish.

"We look forward to your testimony next month," the senator said. His cheeks had the warm blush of gin. "You are not immune from investigation, you know. Some of your men are on a list. We've got questions for you."

The director stepped around the senator with a brusque maneuver and smiled savagely. "You'll have your questions. I'll have the answers."

Mueller and the director were at the restaurant's front door waiting for their checked coats, out of earshot of other customers. The director leaned toward Mueller and lowered his voice. "Godawful speech. Demagoguery at its worst. Baseless defamation. Mudslinging. He does bare-knuckle politics with his sleeves rolled up. He is a danger to us, make no mistake about that. He'd start a goddamn witch hunt if he knew what we know."

The director added with a sly wink, "A fat worthless bastard. Rude and unhousebroken."

8

COLLATERAL DAMAGE

EARLY THE next morning, Mueller got an urgent call to go to Mrs. Leisz's apartment. Mueller flashed his ID at the Metropolitan Police officer standing guard outside and he passed through the lobby to the stairs. A skylight over the stairwell let in morning sunlight, which held the dusty air in suspension, and he was a fly caught in amber. His footsteps on the stairs excited squeaks in the wood treads and upon reaching the first landing he felt himself observed, but when he glanced at the apartment door, it shut. He heard the greedy hush of whispers.

Yellow police tape blocked the open door of Mrs. Leisz's apartment. Mueller tried to duck under, but he was too tall, so he pushed down on the tape, lowering the threshold, and lifted one leg, then the other, to clear the barrier. He found a chaotic crime scene inside. Two police detectives with latex gloves crouched on the rug talking over each other, or at each other, in the shorthand of workingmen coordinating evidence collection. A short beefy man in a gray fedora snapped flash photographs, careful each time to include a six-inch ruler in focus to provide a sense of scale, and with it, a chalk slate marked with time, date, and place.

Two other men stood together in the center of the room, backs to the door. They turned when Mueller entered. The shorter man, smoker thin, wore a loose-fitting suit tightly cinched with a belt several sizes too large. His sucking cheeks drew on a Lucky Strike and he released a steady stream of smoke when he spoke. His eyes were enormous above sunken cheeks and they bulged when they caught sight of Mueller. "The hell are you?"

"My colleague." This from James Coffin, who wore his black mackintosh and had not yet removed his gloves. "The one I called. George, this is the coroner."

"Coroner, no. Medical examiner. We're medical examiners in the District." The medical examiner extinguished his half-finished cigarette, saved the butt end to his shirt pocket, and looked Mueller over with the authority of a man exercising his claim to the room.

Mueller nodded politely. He stood near the two men, but kept his distance. He was by them, but not among them, close enough to hear what they said, but far enough away that he could ignore their comments while he glanced around. It was easy for him to recognize the signs of a burglary. The bureau in the living room, as well as the one visible through the open bedroom door, had ranks of drawers tipped fully open. Burglars open bottom drawers first so they don't have to waste time shutting one to get to the next. Shirts, underwear, pants, and embroidered linens spilled out of the open drawers or lay in a heap on the floor. Bureaus were an obvious place to search for jewelry or cash, so Mueller was more curious about the books taken from the shelves and flung to the floor. He glanced at loose papers littering the pile, and then reached down for a torn manila envelope. It was the one he'd left behind with Alfred Leisz's death certificate, release form, and the police report.

"Hey, put that down," one detective snapped. "Don't touch anything."

Good, he thought. He had a story to explain his fingerprints on the documents. A story if he needed one. Mueller moved to the bedroom door, peering in, and then returned to the living room. His calm face, clear eyeglass frames, and combed hair gave him the expression of a man who could see or hear anything without surprise. He listened to what the medical examiner had to say about the corpse on the floor under a bedsheet. Mueller saw telltale bloodstains on the white cotton. He gazed at the sheeted form and lifted his eyes to the medical examiner, who continued in a staccato tenor.

"We found her lying here where she is now, on her stomach, when I arrived. I could flex her fingers so the body wasn't in full rigor, which means she'd been dead at least eight hours, but not much longer than that. I would put time of death around midnight. There was pronounced purplish discoloration on her stomach from postmortem lividity and she was at room temperature, which at three degrees an hour—what you'd see in a slight woman—confirms midnight.

"Cause of death is strangulation. Manner of death, murder."

The medical examiner lifted piano wire turned into a garrote with toggled wood at either end. "Neck lacerations match the spiral pattern on the wire."

Coffin turned to Mueller. "Would you confirm that it's her, George, if you don't mind? I think you're the only one who actually met her."

Mueller slowly came off the doorjamb, face expressionless, manner accommodating, but his mind was in revolt. The medical examiner lifted a corner of the bedsheet, enough for Mueller to see it was Mrs. Leisz. Someone had closed her eyes, so he was spared that discomfort. The angry purple laceration on her throat was a necklace of blood. There was no pain in her face to haunt his imagination, and that too made his quick glance tolerable. Her lips were bloodless and she had the cold void face of death. He nodded.

Mueller stepped back when the sheet again covered the body. He said to Coffin, "Where are the children?" There was a beat of silence. "She had two children. A boy and an infant."

A detective, rising from the floor, removed his latex gloves. "Human services got them. The boy found her in the morning. He knocked on a neighbor's door and they called the police. That's where they are. They'll be there until they find a relative."

There was more conversation and more questions, but nothing further was learned, nothing important shared, and the two CIA officers left shortly afterward. Mueller and Coffin did not talk as they descended the stairs, keeping a deliberate silence against inquisitive eyes peering from cracked open doors. When they were finally seated in Coffin's parked car they allowed themselves to talk candidly. Coffin had rolled up his window in an act of extreme caution.

"It wasn't burglary," Coffin said.

Mueller turned his head to Coffin.

"It's convenient to let the police think it was a burglary. That keeps it a local police matter." Coffin added, "No one will link it to her husband's death, except as a bizarre coincidence. He died in an office accident. She the victim of a burglary. We will be helpful if they call us, but we need to stay away."

Coffin paused for a long moment. The two men sat silently in the small cramped English sports car, imported, so Coffin sat on the right behind its lacquered wood steering wheel. Coffin spoke at last. "Everything begins and ends with the right application of methodology that allows us to see things that we might not wish to see. It's our wishfulness, George, that blinds us to the facts." He turned to Mueller. "The Soviets think Leisz found out who Protocol is. They thought the wife might know. I doubt she knew anything. That's what you said in your report. Why would she? But if you want to keep someone from talking, you don't concern yourself with whether or not they know something, you just make sure they can't talk about it. Collateral damage, George. They will go to great lengths to protect Protocol. We have our work cut out for ourselves. Have you advanced things?"

"Tomorrow."

Coffin started his sports car, completely unsuited for a real winter, the floor drafty and cold. His bespoke leather gloves clenched the wheel. "Altman didn't show up. Wasn't he to come too?"

"No."

"Oh, my mistake. I thought you'd asked him to come along so we could get his take." Coffin threw out, "I think of him as sitting on the porch while the help toils in the garden. It's symbolic of his attitude. He can be so condescending sometimes. Born into privilege with a silver spoon. I call him the Instant Enthusiast. He has an idea, like the one he came up with in our meeting, and then he loses interest. He forgets it was his idea. He says, 'Where did that terrible idea come from.'"

Mueller recognized the new tendency to gossip about the man not in the room. He didn't know where Coffin had developed his grudge against Altman.

Coffin added, "Altman recruited Leisz. Is that right?"

"No, I did."

"Oh! I didn't realize. Good to know."

Too much surprise. Mueller looked at Coffin, tall frame hunched over the diminutive steering wheel, neck craned back checking for traffic as he pulled away from the curb. He thought: *Too much surprise for Coffin's ignorance to be convincing.*

9

COLONEL YURI VASILENKO

MUELLER WAITED at the stoplight. Rain came in a cold steady drizzle and pooled in the street. He'd left his umbrella in the office, optimistically thinking the weather would pass. He lifted his coat's collar and suffered getting wet. When the light changed he made a long-reaching stride over water backed up at the clogged gutter and ran past cars stopped on Pennsylvania Avenue. He glanced at the faces of drivers behind windshield wipers, confident he didn't know them, and confident too there was no one he should worry about.

Mueller reached the Carlton Hotel's sidewalk canopy and shook the water from his coat. He entered the revolving doors that the porter set in motion, and he was ejected into the lobby, crowded with guests waiting out the storm. He made his way across the room, coat over arm, eyes alert to anyone he might know, and slipped into the Whiskey Bar. There was a raucous din in the dark, mahogany-paneled room, thick with cigarettes and eager drinkers kicking back after a day's office drudgery.

Mueller had no problem spotting Vasilenko. The Russian was alone in a booth. A large man, well over six feet, big chest, thick hands, and the appearance some big men have of bulk without weight. He'd stretched one arm leisurely across the booth and the other was on the table, fingers caressing the stem of a martini glass.

Mueller acknowledged Vasilenko's quick wave and crossed the room. He slipped into the booth, leaving a wide space between them.

"Well, well. Good to see you." Vasilenko signaled the waiter.

"I'm late. The rain."

"Of course. Always shitty weather here. Sweaty in summer. Damp in winter." Vasilenko smiled without amusement.

"Worse than New York?" Mueller followed the Russian's eyes.

"We're not alone," Vasilenko said. He nodded at the bar. "He must work for you. The short one with moustache. He sits in a car outside the embassy. Where do you get these amateurs?"

FBI, Mueller thought. Walker's man. He wasn't happy about that. He ordered a beer when the waiter arrived. He turned to Vasilenko. "Well?"

"The driver is going back to Moscow. It was an error of judgment. He had no qualifications, but he knew someone." Vasilenko drummed his fingers. "A stupid mistake."

"And you?" Mueller asked.

"Me?"

"Things good?"

"I can't complain." He fingered his martini glass and then threw back the drips that remained. He signaled the waiter for a refill. "My wife is in Moscow with our son. Good kid. You met him once. Fifteen now."

"I remember. Smart. Like you."

Vasilenko looked away, disgusted. "And you? Married still?"

"Divorced."

"Long?"

"Couple of years."

There was a beat of silence. "I liked her. Charming. Young. Too young maybe. This life is hard on a marriage."

"Yes. It is." Mueller wasn't ready to share the many other faults of their work. This was as close as he was going to get. Anything more personal had to be a lie.

"What will it take for you to come over, George?"

Mueller gave a husky laugh. He knew where this was going. "What are you going to offer me?" He looked at the Russian. "Four hours in a bread line, ten square meters of living space in an apartment block in Moscow? One of your cars?"

"We pay for information."

"I'm doing fine."

"You'll have a dacha. A girl. Two girls. Or a boy if you prefer."

Mueller sipped his beer. A habit. "You work for your country and I'll go on working for mine."

"You'll see. We will show the world that communism is inevitable. The West is filled with self-righteous intolerance and I have found that intolerance destroys the intolerant. We are about worker equality and human dignity."

"How do you measure that?" Mueller asked. "The empty shelves in your stores? Vodka rations?"

Vasilenko smiled, drummed his fingers, and looked directly at Mueller. "Our shelves are empty sometimes, yes, but what does all this materialism get you? Huh. At least we can laugh at ourselves, which is more than I can say about you. Here's a joke. A man walks into a food store and asks, 'Do you have any meat?' 'No we don't.' 'What about milk?' 'We don't sell milk. Across the street is the store where they have no milk.'"

Mueller smiled.

"So you like that I make fun of what you think of us. Here is another one. A judge walks out of a courtroom laughing loudly. A colleague asks, 'What's so funny?' The judge says, wiping away tears of laughter, 'Ah, I just heard an excellent joke.' 'A joke. Tell me.' 'Are you crazy?' the judge says. 'I just sentenced a man to ten years for that joke.'"

Vasilenko laughed. "You are bound by the rules of civilization. We don't have that problem. That's why we will win." Vasilenko ate the last olive in his empty glass. "We know who our enemies are. I don't think you can say the same thing." He nodded at the FBI agent at the bar. A second man had joined him. "They follow both of us."

A waiter gently set down a fresh martini and Vasilenko leaned forward to sip the overflowing glass. "Let me know what I can do for you, my friend. We owe you a favor."

"You still hunt quail?"

"Of course."

"I know someone with private land. We should go. Will they let you out?"

Vasilenko smiled. "A weekend perhaps."

Mueller reached under the table for a long black leather case he'd carried into the bar. Opening it he displayed a magnificent Winchester shotgun.

"What's this?"

"You admired mine in Vienna. Remember, in Baden by the bombed monastery? The cold day." Mueller presented the gun. "I thought you'd like it. It will help international relations and improve your aim."

Vasilenko left the gun in Mueller's hands. His smile vanished and a dark shadow clouded his face. He looked tolerantly at Mueller. "Are you trying to get me sent back to Moscow? I would love this, of course. But how would this look to the *rezident*? I appreciate your effort to put me at risk."

He stood abruptly. He shoved one arm in his bulky overcoat. Before leaving he looked at Mueller. "If you want to meet from time to time to be friendly, that's fine. We have many interesting things in common. A lot to talk about. But let's not play silly games."

"Sit down," Mueller said. He patted the seat. "Let's finish our drinks."

Vasilenko frowned, but then removed his coat and slumped against the back of the booth. Mueller took a salted peanut from the bowl and popped it in his mouth. He pushed the bowl at Vasilenko, who grabbed a handful.

"How is the leg?" Vasilenko asked.

"Stitches are out."

"The driver swore he was on his side of the road. He didn't

know you were hurt until the police came to the compound. It was an embarrassment he didn't have a license. We respect your laws."

Mueller nodded. "What have they got you doing?"

Surprise. "Me? The usual. Trade mission. A few conferences. I focus on high-temperature alloys."

"How's Chernov?"

Vasilenko shrugged. "Same as he was in Vienna. He has a job to do and now he has supporters in Moscow. That gives him privileges. Some power."

"Colleagues, or do you work for him?"

Vasilenko smiled. "Don't press your luck, my friend." Vasilenko finished his martini and slid the empty glass to the middle of the table. He nodded at Mueller's hardly touched beer. "Not drinking?"

Mueller took the beer in one long draft. His stomach was in revolt. He put ten dollars on the table. "On me."

They met again the next week, and then again the week after that. Each time it was at the Whiskey Bar in the Carlton Hotel at the end of the workday, and each time Vasilenko appeared mysteriously out of nowhere. The Russian drank heavily and Mueller abstemiously. Mueller brought technical journal articles on bioweapons to give Vasilenko something to take back to the embassy. The articles were publicly available if you knew where to look, so they were of modest intelligence value, but the information provided cover for their meetings.

"This," Mueller said, putting a shopping bag at Vasilenko's feet when he slipped into the booth, "is the May 1947 *Journal of*

Immunology you asked about. It reads like science fiction. Aerosol bomblets dropped from helium balloons that are designed to spread bacteria clouds over cities. We find clever new ways to annihilate each other."

It was a sunny day, late afternoon, but Vasilenko was gloomy and he ignored the comment and the shopping bag. The Russian ordered a second drink and sipped when the waiter served it.

Mueller watched Vasilenko, said nothing.

"My son is a good athlete. Good student. He has set his mind on this high school. Perhaps you have heard of it. Bauman Moscow Higher Technical School. It's the most prestigious engineering school in Moscow. Already he has ideas about better-performing machines, devices for mathematical calculations. His future is good if he gets in."

Vasilenko lit a cigarette and drew on it deeply. His face was flushed from alcohol and his fingers impatiently drummed the table. Vasilenko looked at Mueller without pity. "We are different, you and I, but our countries share one thing. Corruption." He spat the word like a poison.

Mueller sensed his companion's agitation and he was alert to the man's confessional tone.

"He's a good student. His mother pushes him. He passed the entrance exam, which few do. It's university level. They take fifteen boys, but there are more suitable candidates than slots—so they must choose."

"Who chooses?"

"Well, that is the point." Vasilenko clenched and unclenched his fist, and then clenched it again, knuckles turning white.

"Party members review the candidates and make the choice. So you need to know who can help. There is one party member, my wife's uncle, who knows one man on the admissions committee. He can help, but it will be expensive."

Vasilenko looked at Mueller. "You have a son. You understand. If you were me with a talented boy who has set his mind on this future . . . what would you do? How far would you go?"

Mueller watched Vasilenko draw deeply on his cigarette. Mueller felt this was one of those moments in life that seemed like a cruel joke, but it was hard to find the humor, or discern the wit, if you suspected, as he did, that the joke was on the man sitting opposite. *A quiet pool. The right lure.* "I have a friend who can help."

"A friend?"

"It can be arranged."

Vasilenko looked skeptically at Mueller. "I don't think so. Stalin was a disgrace, but Marxist Leninism is inevitable." He said this without irony. His foot tapped the documents under the table. "Keep your shopping bag full of shit."

• • •

Rain broke hard and steady—exceedingly hard and steady— while Mueller stood alone in the empty third-floor conference room in Quarter's Eye. The downpour had let loose all at once, and daylight turned swampy green. A low rumble of violent rain pounded the lawn and the parking lot. The conference room darkened and he stepped up to the window's view of the storm, excusing the act to himself by looking at his watch. It was 5:00

p.m. There was only rain and the promise of more rain—the cold rain of winter.

The agreed time of the Council meeting had passed and Mueller was still the only one in the room. He hated to wait, or to be made to wait. He fingered a No. 2 yellow pencil, rolling it across his knuckles, a silly trick he'd perfected at a drunken freshman party at Yale. The wind had picked up and he had an anxious flutter of excitement that the blowing storm would snap a branch or flood the street. There was no room to worry about himself. All this—the scope of the storm, the absence of sun, the tremendous noise, and the suddenness of it all—made an impression on him. He was aware, in the weird way that strange occurrences trigger unsettling thoughts, that he had already lived half his life and had nothing good to show for it. He couldn't even tell a stranger what he did for a living. Secrets consumed him. The sense of mission that had drawn him to the work was long gone—corrupted—along with his naïve, younger self.

He saw a young woman out in the storm hurrying to cross the lawn. Her umbrella bent under the pounding rain. She moved urgently, leaning into the wind, running through puddles. He thought of Beth. Where was she right now?

"George?"

Mueller turned. Altman stood patiently in the open door and it was obvious he'd been there watching Mueller for several moments.

"You look lost in thought. Where is everyone? Just you and me? We'll have to do this by ourselves."

Instant Enthusiast. Coffin's glib observation about Altman had been funny when he heard it because it was just slightly true, and the label crystalized an impression he'd had about Altman that he'd never been able to put into words. The new label settled in like a stubborn grievance.

The other members of the Council arrived shortly, first Coffin, in tuxedo for an evening gala, purposeful with a dossier clamped to his chest; and Downes, smug and heavy, like a bulldog. They joined Altman, whose jaunty mood defied the weather, and the three men settled at the table opposite Mueller. He felt the outsider again. The meeting started at once. Coffin gave an update on the Leisz matter, which was hardly an update at all, for there was no information on the burglary, but he threw out the news the FBI were involved. Apparently the Hungarian embassy took the children and asked some questions.

"Should we be worried?" asked Coffin.

Mueller could practically hear the cogs of his colleagues' minds whirring. The question was simple enough, but the answer was braided in a complex tapestry of cover stories. Mueller gave thought to a flaw in the fabric and said something vague.

"That's all you can come up with? 'Time will tell.' I don't need to know that. That's quite obvious." Coffin opened his dossier. He looked up, addressing Mueller again in a rising tenor voice. "So, if it's not money Vasilenko will take then we need to try something else." Gloom on his face reflected the long hours he'd pondered their dilemma.

"My report doesn't rule out money," Mueller said, "but he would have to be desperate. He is a hard-line Communist. Believes in the system. Greed doesn't motivate him."

"Everyone has a price," Downes snapped.

Mueller stared. "You're frustrated. I'm frustrated. I don't want this to go on. If I thought money would turn him I'd say give him what he wants. It's not money. He can't spend money without attracting attention."

"There is something, I'm sure," Coffin said. "There always is. Any suggestions?" He looked at Downes, smug face slightly dyspeptic, and at Altman, who leaned toward Mueller, probing.

"How is his relationship with Chernov?"

"Tolerable. We didn't get into it. He steered the conversation away."

"Competitive?"

Coffin answered. "We believe that Beria is making a play. As you know, from what's come to us since Stalin died, GRU doesn't like the power NKVD is taking. Long knives are out. It's King Lear. Vasilenko, the earnest hard-liner he is, can't be happy."

Mueller snapped, "That's not enough. His family is in Moscow. He won't put them at risk. Not for that."

There was a beat of silence.

"George, calm down." Altman closed his manila file and solemnly folded his hands.

Mueller stared at Altman. "What?"

"How long has his wife been in Moscow?"

"Six months. With the son."

"What does Vasilenko do for companionship?"

"He goes to Moscow Center a few times a year and visits his wife." Mueller added, "We haven't found a girlfriend."

"He drinks?"

"No more than the usual." He looked at the men around the table. "No more than anyone here."

Coffin allowed himself to be slightly amused.

"I think we should try it," Altman said. "This doesn't have to go through Operations. They'd have to clear it through FBI Liaison. David can arrange it."

"Freelance."

"We have the authority. Let's not get bogged down in stupid bureaucratic formalities. The stakes, gentlemen, are too high. We have an asset in place. She is a maid who was cleared by their security and she cleans apartments for several of the Soviet embassy staff. She speaks Russian. A good case officer. She cleans Vasilenko's apartment. We've spent a year putting her in place waiting for the right job."

Mueller watched Downes remove a file from his briefcase. He laid out the details of what they would now call the dangle. Date. Time. Safe house location.

• • •

A fine, misting rain fell through the fog as Mueller darted across L Street toward a gray, sooty apartment building with a mansard brow and ugly fire escape. More rain. When would it end? Car headlights suddenly appeared out of nowhere and drove toward him. Mueller's only choice was to jump out of the way. It sped by, splashing him. The darkness, the fog, the car's reckless speed, all made it impossible to see who was behind the wheel.

He pulled his hat down on his forehead and stepped into the

cover of the first doorway. He waited a few minutes just to be sure. He looked but saw no one. The car had been its own freak thing. That was the conclusion he came to. He left the overhang and continued on, walking quickly, but not so quickly that he would attract the wrong kind of attention. His clipped footsteps echoed without provenance.

He buzzed the apartment once. He held a key but he didn't want to arrive unannounced, startling her. On the third floor he approached the farthest door and used the agreed-upon three knocks.

"I brought you coffee," he said, when he was inside. He handed her a lidded paper container. "You alone?"

He looked around the tiny apartment. Little had changed since the time when they'd brought up the Bulgarian. There was a lace negligee draped over a chair as there had been the last time, but someone had made sure the glossy fan magazines on the coffee table fit her cover of aspiring actress making money on the side cleaning apartments—*Photoplay, Modern Screen, Movie Life.* Tolerably neat, he thought, but charmless—some man's idea of a single woman's apartment. Shades drawn. A few romance novels. Chairs you'd find in a budget hotel. Gold-framed mirror picked up at a flea market. He saw nothing that stood out, or drew attention to itself, that would compromise the job.

"Who sent you?" she asked.

"I'm the handler on this."

She was younger than Mueller had been led to expect by

Downes. Black-frame glasses dominated her face, her red hair was drawn into a ponytail, and she wore blue jeans and a carnation-white turtleneck sweater. Pretty enough.

"Is that how you'll dress?"

"I'm his maid." Her voice had a tone of rebuke. "There are other clothes in the closet if I need them."

"How well do you know him?"

"He doesn't suspect. I'm in his apartment Wednesday afternoons to clean. He works at home while I'm there and I hear him on the phone. He doesn't know I speak Russian. We talk sometimes. He's a big fan of Rita Hayworth. He is very proper. But he's a man. I've seen him look at me. He's got an interest."

He followed her into the bedroom. It was small with one window looking onto the fire escape without a view of a neighboring apartment. A fan magazine on the night table was open to a double-page spread of the just released *Salome*. Rita Hayworth lay in repose, gowned in diaphanous garments with the come-hither look of a famous glamour queen. There were framed family photos on the dresser, a lucky charm bracelet, and a box of costume jewelry. He lifted one photo of a middle-aged couple with a child, and then drew it closer, studying the likeness.

"There's even a family resemblance." He looked at her. "Your name? Your cover name?"

"Jane. Is there anything I need to know?" she asked.

"About him?"

"The job?"

Mueller wondered what she'd been told. Probably nothing.

Too many people in responsible positions who didn't know what they were doing.

"We will be behind that wall." He pointed to a large mirror on the bedroom wall. "Next door. There will be two of us. Me. A photographer. Two other men will be outside for security, to help calm him down if there is a need for that. It's impossible to know how he'll react. You'll have to continue cleaning the embassy staff apartments for a few weeks and then you'll be taken off. Operations will give you a new assignment."

He removed an envelope from his sports jacket that contained two marijuana cigarettes. "Offer this to him. If he tries it, so much the better. The threat of a drug arrest would seal it."

"How far do I take it?"

He averted his eyes. *No one had told her anything.* "Clothes have to be off. He has to be compromised. We need photographs that are unambiguous. You'll have to judge when you're uncomfortable."

She nodded.

"Gesture to the mirror when you get to that point. We'll come through the door."

Mueller knew it would be worse than that. It always was. These situations were always chaotic, yelling, screaming, a lot of nasty things said, and they could also be dangerous. The john directed his anger at the thing nearest at hand. Not always. Some men resigned themselves. Others hit the girls.

"We will be right here," Mueller said.

Taking down a man. The doomed animal thrashed against its binding ties when it saw the butcher's knife.

"We will be in when you give the signal." He looked at her face and was suddenly struck. "Have you done this before?"

She shook her head. "No."

Idiots. "It will be okay. We will be in here as soon as you give the signal."

A prostitute was the normal way this was done, but it was agreed that Vasilenko would see that coming. He was too smart, too clever, too wary for that type of obvious trap. Something in his world that he trusted—young and innocent. That's not how she was described to Mueller, but she fit the profile. Young and poised.

Mueller walked to the living room and made a final inspection. All Vasilenko needed was one false note to sense a trap and he'd be gone. The job compromised. Mueller's eyes swept the titles of the paperback books, the dates on the fan magazines, the ashtrays, looking for cigarette butts that would not be hers. He opened the refrigerator. A bag of sprouting potatoes. Save or toss? "Do you eat out a lot?"

"Yes."

He closed the door. He looked at her. "Where are you from?"

She looked confused.

"Where are you from?" he demanded.

"Me or her?"

"Her . . . Where are you from?"

"Maryland."

"How old?"

"Twenty-four."

"Ambition?"

"Acting. Saving money to go to New York."

"Gilda?"

"Rita Hayworth."

"Orson Welles?"

"Second husband."

He studied her composed face. "You'll do fine."

10

TRAPPED

THE CALL came after midnight. He'd gone to bed after a long dinner with Altman at the F Street Club and he'd felt good staying away from the booze. Drinking alone hadn't stopped Altman, who had two vodka tonics and then wine with dinner. Mueller found himself restless to be sober in the company of a man boisterous with too much alcohol. Old acquaintances, once close friends. He could complete the stories that Altman felt a need to tell at great length.

Mueller sat bolt upright when his bedside phone rang. He reached for his glasses without which, by some vagary of concomitant senses, he couldn't answer the telephone properly.

"Hello," he said. Half-asleep.

"They left the bar in a taxi."

Bar? He was on his feet, bare soles on the cold floor, and he pressed his fingers to his forehead to concentrate. *Think*. His body was alert like a prey animal. He looked at his wristwatch.

"Where are they coming from?"

"Georgetown."

He had twenty minutes, tops. "FBI?"

"No. She brought him out the back to the alley. They're clean."

Mueller had the taxi drop him two blocks away on a side street, a precaution, and he hurried along the sidewalk, staying away from the streetlights. His breath plumed in the night air. He'd left quickly, and he regretted leaving home without his gloves. He wondered what else he'd forgotten. He went down the mental list of things that could go wrong. This had been his life for too long. The cold reminded him of mist on the Danube. That one night of fog. Weeks of waiting, long periods of drudgery punctuated by a harrowing moment of acute tension. It was all about the plan, the actions they had rehearsed, which if followed, kept the mistakes of poor judgment in the moment to a minimum. Trust the plan.

The photographer was already in place when Mueller quietly let himself into the neighboring apartment. He'd seen two Agency officers in place in the hallway. There was no need to give them any sensible cover, so the plan risked a neighbor calling the police on two loitering strangers, but it was a tolerable risk at that hour of night in a quiet apartment building. It was either that, or have no security to manage a bad outcome.

Mueller draped his coat over a chair and peered through the two-way mirror into the empty bedroom. The narrow twin bed was made. A negligee hung from the open closet door. Family photographs were arranged on the dresser. Drapes drawn. Light entered the darkened room through the open door that led to the living area, lit up, bright, and he could see the legs of a tall man stretched onto a coffee table.

"How long have they been inside?" Mueller asked, whispering.

"Fifteen minutes."

There were two 16mm film cameras. One ready. One backup. No light stands.

Vasilenko would be wary. He would have his eyes open, ears alert, even as passion planted its talons. Prey animals knew to move cautiously near the bait—drawn by hunger but looking for the trap. He and Vasilenko were alike, Mueller thought. Drawn to risk, tired of the young man's game but good at it.

The bedroom looked bare, Mueller thought. Too bare. Not lived in. Where was the accumulation of useless stuff that came with ordinary living? Twice Mueller's eyes passed over the bedside table before he spotted a man's ring. He leaned forward, nose almost at the dark glass. It was heavy, gold with a crest, like a college fraternity ring.

"Shit," he said. Someone had used the place and not swept it properly.

The couple rose from the living room sofa and Mueller saw them pause, drinks in hand, taking a moment to talk about something. Familiar, but negotiating the situation and the temptation that brought them together.

There was a faint *whrrr* of film traveling through the camera when the couple entered the bedroom, but Mueller knew it couldn't be heard through the glass. She turned the overhead light on, but Vasilenko turned it off. She glanced sideways at the mirror, but stopped herself.

Mueller saw her face, worried in the moment, having been told to leave the light on, looking for an instruction. *Improvise*, Mueller whispered to himself.

Vasilenko placed his drink on the night table and he spotted the ring. He turned on the bedside lamp to get a better look, studied it for a moment. He said something. She said something. Their lips moved, but the sound was lost. She shook her head, laughed, and then removed her sweater over her head in a single motion. He put the ring back where he had found it.

She got out of her skirt without removing her heels, and then sat on the edge of the bed and undid one ankle strap and then the other. It was all performance, Mueller thought. A dance for an audience of one.

Vasilenko removed his shoes, shirt, and trousers and stood by the bed in white cotton underwear and black socks, pale, fleshy, a big man who had thickened at the waist. Mueller had a flicker of sympathy for this man whose life was about to crash and burn. He was a decent sort. Probably a good husband, a caring father. What was his mistake that set him apart from any other man? Boredom? Loneliness? The attraction of young flesh? Mueller didn't let himself give in to pity. He knew the Russian would easily, vigorously, do the same to him if the circumstance required it. They were in the business of deceit, high-stakes lies. Vasilenko had been quick to reject a trophy shotgun and some helpful cash, but they'd found his weakness.

The couple sat on the edge of the narrow bed in their underwear, sharing the silly intimate nonsense that the presumption of privacy permitted. He was vulnerable, she was coy, and Mueller saw the steel jaws of the trap ready to snap. Vasilenko took the marijuana cigarette she handed him, and he inhaled with a first-timer's awkward hesitation, then coughed. She glanced at the mirror.

Don't look! "Shit," Mueller muttered.

She reached behind her back and undid her bra. Small breasts. How much more did he need to seal the case?

Mueller watched her draw her fingers across Vasilenko's tufted chest hair, the romantic girl exploring her new friend with patient touch.

"You're getting that?" Mueller asked.

"Yes," the cameraman said.

"We need to see the whole room."

"How long do we go on?"

"How long has it been?"

"A couple of minutes. Maybe more."

"A little more. Is the exposure good?"

"High-speed film. It will be fine. The faces are exposed. He turned on the night lamp. You'll have what you need."

"What other jobs do you do?" Mueller asked.

"For you?"

"Anyone."

"Weddings mostly."

Mueller wanted to laugh, and he looked at the cameraman to confirm that he wasn't joking. Mueller turned back to the view of the bedroom. She had gone onto her back, naked, and Vasilenko was moving his hulking figure over her. He was putting kisses on her lips that she was returning. Sad, Mueller thought. He tried not to think about the man's son. It was hard to take someone down. He'd done it before. It didn't get easier. The naked man and woman were wrapped in each other's arms.

"We've got him." Mueller turned to the cameraman before he left the room. "Keep filming. If he gets violent I need that too."

Mueller assembled the two agents in the hallway, lined up behind him, coordinating with eye contact and a nod. Hand gestures. He slipped a key in the door lock, turned slowly to confirm they had access. On hearing the click of the bolt he raised a signaling finger.

Three men burst through the apartment door. They arrived in the bedroom to find Vasilenko standing bedside naked, his face a mix of surprise, embarrassment, and the deep flush of anger. The two men stared at each other.

Mueller motioned for the girl to leave the room. She had wrapped herself in the sheet and slipped out quickly, wordlessly.

"Get dressed," Mueller instructed Vasilenko. "This doesn't have to be difficult. I think you know what we want." He nodded at the mirror. "There's a record of this. No one will see it, or even know this happened, unless we don't get the right type of cooperation."

Vasilenko glared. He shook his head, disparaged himself, his mistake, his stupidity. He spat the word *"Govno!"*

Mueller waited for Vasilenko to dress. The two men sat opposite each other in the living room, adversaries, one with a new advantage, the other cautious, wary, glum, but also restless and impatient. There were new rules of engagement between them, and it didn't matter who they had been, or pretended to be in their previous meetings. The old game had taken a turn.

"What do you want?" Vasilenko asked.

"A name."

"Who?"

"A man. He is with us, but he works for you."

"I wouldn't know. I'm not in counterintelligence."

"How do I know?"

"I'm telling you. I will report this. They'll send me back to Moscow Center. So what. We'll see what happens. I'll take my chances."

"No one has to know," Mueller said. "We can keep this quiet. Protect you. It's a name we want. You'll be kept out of it."

Vasilenko emitted a gruff, sarcastic laugh. He lit a cigarette from the pack on the coffee table and drew deeply, relaxing himself. He stared at Mueller with disgust.

"We will pay," Mueller said. "When we get the name, you won't have obligations to us. This"—he gestured to the bedroom—"forgotten."

"No one forgets."

"We can be generous too."

"How much?"

"How much do you need?"

Vasilenko drew on the cigarette and contemplated Mueller. He threw out a figure.

Mueller looked skeptical. "Why fifty thousand?"

"I don't need that much, you're right. And if I spent it, how would that look?"

"Why fifty thousand?"

"To reassure myself that you think highly of what I will give you."

Mueller acknowledged how Vasilenko could bargain even when he had no leverage. It was a confidence that Mueller respected. It suggested that Vasilenko knew there was an endgame that had yet to play out.

In the pause that followed, and in the body language spoken, Mueller knew he had an understanding.

"I will give you instructions," Vasilenko said. "Where to meet. When. I will come to you. Don't approach me anymore." Vasilenko gave the ground rules and set expectations. He said he'd see what he could discover. For security reasons everything was compartmentalized. He was NKVD, so he didn't see cables or messages from GRU counterintelligence. He might hear something, get a hint, circumstantial information, a fragment that he could provide that might add to a profile. At the door he turned. "I will contact you when I know something."

• • •

Mueller informed the director and the Council that Vasilenko was turned, but he cautioned against quick results. If nothing else, he would confirm the Agency had been penetrated. Not everyone was convinced of that. Mueller's report on the meeting was "eyes only" for the Council. It didn't go into the file that was shared weekly with FBI counterintelligence. There was an interagency arrangement that all contact between CIA and Soviet staff be shared with the FBI liaison. This formal reporting of meetings was the way FBI distinguished authorized contact from potential recruitment of double agents. Mueller's reports had described Vasilenko as an expert in metallurgy who was able to discuss advances the Soviets had made in high-temperature alloys for ballistic missile parts. Vague stuff. But enough detail to convince Walker. Mueller had made most of it up reading *Popular Mechanics*.

He met Vasilenko again a week later. They'd worked out a way to communicate. A vertical chalk mark on a mailbox in Georgetown was the signal. Mueller had come alone to the safe house on L Street. Two knocks followed by a third. Mueller let Vasilenko in and made sure there was no one in the stairwell. Habit.

"Here is what I have," Vasilenko began. An aluminum moon filtered through the gauzy curtain illuminating his face. His expression was grim, serious, but defeated too. A compromised man. Mueller took notes.

"My first suspicions came in the fall, 'forty-nine. I was in Vienna. Everyone in Moscow Center knew the CIA was mounting a campaign to recruit a network of spies inside the Soviet bloc. We saw evidence of one incident after the other. Hungarians hijacked a C-47 on its way to Munich and then diverted it to the Carpathian Mountains, landing near Lvov with a dozen paramilitary troops. You call them freedom fighters," Vasilenko said with disdain. "We tracked a ship that left Malta and went to Rome and Athens with a handful of volunteers—criminals mostly—and mercenaries who were put in small craft to land off the coast of Albania. Then we got intelligence you'd recruited Albanians in Trieste and put them on planes piloted by Poles and sent them to parachute near Tirana."

Vasilenko paused. "All the missions were neutralized by us. Some men were killed when they landed, and we captured others. A few radios got working and sent out a report, but they were eliminated quickly. They had no chance." Vasilenko wiped one palm against the other, theatrically. "Finished."

Another pause. "I heard about these failures from colleagues and we were all pleased. But we knew we weren't that good to eliminate every mission, or the CIA was that sloppy to run operations and have them all compromised. You lost three hundred men. Maybe more. No one survived. There was only one answer. We had penetrated the CIA. Our luck could not be so good. There had to be a source. That's what we all suspected.

"I was Directorate K working in the Second Bezirk, by the Prater Park in the Leopoldstadt district, the European Division. There were rumors, but NKVD was compartmentalized. My wife and I were transferred to Moscow Center a few months later. I didn't know anything else. You don't talk about these things with colleagues. You ask questions and then Counterintelligence comes to you and says, 'Why are you asking questions?' So that was that. But I had a friend. Let's call him Vladimir."

"What's his name?"

"Is that necessary?"

"Yes."

Vasilenko lit a cigarette. The red end glowed in the dark room. "He had nothing to do with any of this, but fine. Vertov. Alexie Vertov. He was ambitious. He was a GRU lieutenant in his forties, when you need to be promoted to colonel or it means you are passed over, your career is finished. Vertov confronted his superior and asked for a promotion and this man said, 'Alexie, you have a lot of nerve. Do your job. Do good work. People notice. Don't push it.' So Vertov's promotion was rejected."

Vasilenko looked at Mueller. "Why am I making a big deal out of this Gogolian incident, trivial at first glance?" Vasilenko leaned forward. "It was motivation for his anger. He got drunk with me and he said he'd read cables from our embassy in Washington that talked about a double agent. Moscow Center gave him the name Sasha. You call him Protocol. His handler has the code name Nightingale, but Vertov knew the code, and he knew this was Chernov. Vertov continued to talk too much."

"And?"

"Arrested." Vasilenko drew a cutting finger across his neck. "We all take risks," he said in a voice that drifted off. When he continued his voice was quiet, and he spoke in the rush of words of a man wanting to finish up an uncomfortable confession. "I found out more when I was transferred to Washington. There is a room on the top floor of the embassy that has been sealed with lead in the walls so FBI across the street can't listen. The room is off-limits, but one day I was called in to see Chernov. There is a map on the wall with flags pinned to the designated locations around the city. These are Protocol's dead drops. This is how information is conveyed. A post office box in one neighborhood. A chalk mark. Same as us. The exchange is made. He takes the shopping bag of money and leaves a shopping bag of secrets. They don't meet here. Too dangerous."

"Where?"

"Once in Istanbul. Berlin twice."

"Why?"

"Change procedures, arrange banking. Coordinate communications. Make human contact. Each side tests the mental state of the other."

"Rome?"

"Perhaps. This is what I've heard. You asked what I know. This is what I know."

"How is he paid?"

"I said, cash in a shopping bag."

"That's all."

"There is an account in Bern. A dead drop there with cash deposits that go into a numbered account." Vasilenko added with sarcasm, "For his retirement."

"Which bank?"

"I don't know."

"Dates?"

"I don't know."

"Hotels?"

"I don't know."

"So, it's someone from headquarters who's been to Bern in the last five years. That narrows the field," Mueller said sarcastically. "What good is this? It's vague, general. We can't use this."

"You've been to Bern."

Mueller stared at Vasilenko. "I'll pass that along to my colleagues in case they've overlooked it." Mueller twirled a pencil on his knuckles and considered the man slumped opposite him. "Let's back up. Tell me about Chernov."

"He has two lives, like the philanderer Gurov, one known,

open, seen if you want to see it, and the other hidden, a secret. He is GRU and *rezident*, and a protégé of Malenkov. He joined the Soviet Army, fought at Stalingrad, and was in the first unit to enter Berlin in the last days of the war. He was put in charge of ex-Nazis."

"How do you know this?"

"I know. If you don't believe me, fine. We're done." Vasilenko leaned forward. *"I know."*

Mueller considered the story. "Go ahead."

"He took charge of all the files Goebbels kept on Jews, American spies, bankers with ties to the black market, all the information he could use against people. Chernov took it all. He is a ruthless man. He took all these Nazi and Abwehr files, everything the German military left behind, including the inventories of art taken from Jews in Berlin and Vienna. He took everything to GRU headquarters in East Berlin. That is what I know."

Vasilenko's cigarette had burned down and he tapped the fragile ash on the saucer he held in one hand. There was a long silence.

Mueller put aside his pen and notepad. What was true? What was false? How much was rumor, worthless? How much was bad information planted to take the investigation down a rat hole? Mueller didn't think it worthless or false. Vasilenko had too much at stake—either way. A man with a family whose future was at risk. Mueller felt empathy for him—a man reduced to looking out for himself, for whom ideology was now a luxury, country an accident of birth, who saw his life through the focused lens of survival. He was at the beginning of his betrayal. The easy part was the talking, and the sudden blows would come afterward, and with it would come regret for the moment of weakness when the easy choice to speak showed its terrible consequences. That's when the other blow hit, coming quietly from within. The slow realization that he'd never have a country again. The first breakdown happened quickly in the chaos of a desperate moment, and the second kind happened slowly over time, as invisibly as dusk.

"Tell me about this man you call Sasha," Mueller said. "What do you know? How did he meet Chernov? How was he turned?"

"I don't know his name," Vasilenko said. "I know they met in Vienna in 'forty-eight. How was he turned?" Vasilenko glared at Mueller. "A stupid question. How was I turned!" He snapped his response and slumped into his chair, sullen, lip quivering.

Upset, Mueller thought. *Good*. "Who ran him?"

"Chernov."

"From the beginning?"

"From the beginning."

"Was he part of a network?"

"No. Alone. He was too important to put in a network. Risk being exposed?"

"His first success? In Vienna?"

"There were no successes in Vienna. There was only hunger everywhere, in all the zones. The French zone, American zone, British zone, Soviet zone. Misery and hunger and cold. The old Vienna was gone and there were only food lines and rusted tanks no one had moved from the streets. Each side handed out cheap money to buy votes of wild political parties. The terrible winter of 'forty-eight was followed by a disastrous summer. Bodies of the starved floated on the Danube. Then there was May fifth. I remember that day. The terrible food riots that started at the Prater Park Ferris wheel in the second district. Mobs moved to the Innere Stadt." Vasilenko paused. "Successes? No. Currency manipulation. Starving children. Streetlamps smashed. Who gained? We did. The Allies were blamed."

Mueller was quiet. "I remember."

"Of course. You were there."

Mueller picked up his pad and pen. "Let's back up again. What do you know about him?"

Vasilenko was silent again. He looked out the window at the moon hanging in the sky. When his eyes turned to Mueller he was once again calm, deliberate, contemplative. "The thing you most need I don't have. What have I found? Write this down. I won't do this again. Fragments. Hints. His real name has an *L*. That I know from sloppy encryption. He is American, but that you could have assumed so I am not surprising you. Parents or grandparents are German, or maybe Austrian. That's it. You have everything."

They stood. Mueller moved to the window and stood to one side, hidden from view, and looked down into the street. There was a car parked where there hadn't been one earlier. It idled. Lights on the dashboard illuminated the driver.

"Your people?" Mueller asked.

"Yours," Vasilenko said.

FBI? Mueller hesitated. "We'll go out the back."

The alley was narrow and dark, cluttered with garbage cans. High up on the walls were small apartment windows. A woman raised her voice at a child. Somewhere a radio played. Their clipped steps on the concrete echoed between the buildings. At the street, Vasilenko looked left, then right. He raised the collar of his bulky overcoat and hurried toward K Street. Mueller watched a minute before he stepped out of the alley and headed in the opposite direction.

II

DOUBT IS CAST

A LL THIS is good," Coffin said, "but it's vague. Helpful? Yes. Actionable? Perhaps. We can't take anyone off the list with this."

Mueller had gotten a call from the director's secretary to come to a meeting. He'd arrived to find Coffin, but not Roger Altman or David Downes, and that had surprised him. The director sat in his high-backed leather chair and struggled to relight his pipe, flicking a butane lighter low on fuel. Mueller was on the sofa opposite Coffin, and the three men made a triangle.

Coffin continued. "We are being led to believe Protocol's last name has an *L*. Why so precise and yet so incomplete? Are we being played? *In offering commend it.*" Coffin paused. "Let's stipulate it's true. *L* appears in half the names on the list. Heat on a couple of officers has gone up, but not much. And we're looking at who went to Austria and Switzerland after the war. Well, everyone did. We were headquartered in Bern." Coffin looked at

Mueller. "We've learned one thing: there is good reason to add your name to the list."

Mueller nodded. The late-afternoon sun streamed in the window, shading Coffin's face and deepening the circles on his eyes. His beaked nose gave him a predatory visage.

"Vienna is the key," Coffin said. "Our first loss was there, and now we know Protocol was turned there in 'forty-eight. Helpful? Yes. It's one of two new facts we got. I have a list of questions we need answered that flow from these facts. What was the date? Where did it happen? What was his motive? The circumstances? The bait? We lost Hermann Weisz in June on the train. We never knew how he was compromised, but now we know it was Protocol, so he started working for the Soviets before that. May or April. Not before that. They wouldn't have waited long to test his usefulness."

Mueller could feel Coffin's mind work through the logic of his speculations. Mueller didn't like Coffin, but he didn't go out of his way to show that, and he had come to have a grudgingly settled tolerance for his lecturing way of explaining the theory of intelligence. Parsing the text on a page. Was it interesting? Was it true? Mueller knew Coffin's world was a dark place of labyrinths, puzzles, and trapdoors. He looked for patterns and goals, and he studied motives—the rationale behind a man's impulse to act out treason. He looked at language allusively, like a critic, seeking the hidden meanings and the subtext. He understood the importance of a startling detail that could be lost in the surrounding drama of an incident but which drew attention to itself, and Coffin could keep it in the back of his mind for years until he made sense of it. This memory for detail and a deeply questioning intellect were a useful brace of skills for the head of counterintelligence. Mueller knew all this, respected it, tolerated it, but he also knew that Coffin's flaw was his intensity and single-mindedness. Thinking became doublethink and at its worst careened into the gravitational pull of boundless conspiracy.

"What if Vasilenko is a plant?" Coffin said. "Leading us to the wrong man."

The director lifted his leg and massaged his swollen ankle. He smiled tolerantly. "That's possible, James. It's always possible." He looked over to Mueller. "What's your view, George? Have you got an opinion on that? You're the one closest to this Russian."

"It's always a risk," Mueller said. "He hasn't led us to anyone yet, so I can't say we're onto the wrong man." Mueller contemplated Coffin and the director. "I find it hard to believe he's a plant. Twice I gave him bait that he rejected. He wasn't easy to land." He addressed Coffin. "You can go down that wormhole, James. I'm not going down with you." Mueller didn't hide his impatience.

Coffin's eyes were drawn inward, his forehead furrowed, a champion chess player considering his opponent's move. "George, you're right. It's a reasonable reading. Perfectly reasonable. Perfectly reasonable . . . I have a larger concern with security generally of which the list is the most obvious threat."

"What?" the director asked. "What's on your mind?"

"Men came over from the OSS. We didn't do background checks. We assumed that they were safe."

"What makes them security risks except that we didn't do backgrounds?"

Coffin jumped off the sofa. "Jesus, how can I say it? They're homosexuals. Just like goddamn Ritchie, the one they picked up in the park. If we know about it, then I guarantee the Soviets know. And the FBI. If they know, it's only a matter of time before the senator finds out and he'll raise it when you testify. You'll stand accused. That's what he does."

The director stared at the head of counterintelligence. "Sit down, James. We don't need this drama. I get the point. I know the risk. Sit down." The director lit his pipe and drew twice. A hint of tobacco and licorice drifted among the three men. "Your note this morning said we should add someone to the list. Who?"

"I'm not sure this is the right meeting for that."

"Of course it's the right meeting."

"With all due respect—"

The director kept his patience. "What's his name?"

Coffin avoided Mueller. "Altman."

"On what basis?"

"He's homosexual."

"You think he is, or you know he is?"

"People talk." Coffin looked at Mueller.

Mueller snapped. "Why are you looking at me?"

"You've known him the longest. He's your friend."

Mueller felt anger begin to corrupt his thinking. He waited until he had mastered his irritation and then he spoke. "He is an acquaintance. An old acquaintance whom I trust, who has never acted against this Agency. I am offended—no, that's not strong enough—I am appalled that you use this slander against him."

The meeting was over. Coffin laid his list of questions for

Vasilenko on the coffee table like an offering. Mueller stood at the same time as Coffin, two adversaries locked in a draw, and he grabbed the typed page.

The director waved Mueller to sit. "Stay for a moment." The director waited for Coffin to leave the office.

"There is no room here for that kind of attitude. Is that clear?"

"No." Mueller snapped his response.

"What don't you understand?"

"I've known Roger since college. He is a friend."

The director paused a long moment. "People show you what they want you to see, George. It's not wise to have friends in this business."

Mueller suddenly knew everything that was wrong with his life. *Stand up. Quit. Walk out.* "I would be surprised."

The director asked, "Anything else on your mind?"

Mueller met the director's eyes. *It's no way to run a spy agency.* Mueller shook his head. "No."

"We are alike, you and I," the director said. "Academics at heart who find ourselves in the thick of things in this nasty world. They'll fire me one day. We all make mistakes and we pay for them. A new president will come in and I'll be out. We're all expendable." He paused and mused. "I'm thinking of promoting Roger." The director lifted a copy of the morning *Post* that lay on the coffee table. "Sometimes a newspaper is just a newspaper."

· · ·

Two weeks passed. Vasilenko had more information to provide. They used the agreed signals to indicate the next exchange. A chalk mark on a post office box near the Episcopalian church southeast of Union Station let Mueller know to make his way to a busy clothing store downtown. He found the manila envelope Vasilenko left between the radiator and the wall in the men's room, and Mueller left an envelope of cash in the same spot. It didn't surprise Mueller that once Vasilenko tasted money, his appetite grew. What he'd given was only the beginning of what he was willing to offer up, but the new material was of little use. Volume without value. Five thousand dollars a pop. Human nature. The line was crossed once. All that followed was greed and fear.

12

BETH PAYS A VISIT

MUELLER FOUND Beth lying in the hallway outside his walk-up apartment. He'd stayed late in the office and then had dinner alone at Harvey's. He trudged up three flights with his laundry and a bottle of milk, and he found her curled on the floor. She wore a wool overcoat, boots, and her fur hat had slipped off so her hair fell on her face. She was asleep. Soft light from the ceiling fixture made her skin pearly white. Her mouth was open in an exhausted expression.

"Beth." He gently shook her shoulder.

She stirred, eyes opened. She sat bolt upright, embarrassed and speechless.

"Come inside," he said.

"What time is it?"

"Late."

Mueller made tea for her on a hot plate. She sat in her coat on the sofa, boots off, legs curled underneath, and she arranged her tousled hair as best she could. She took the tea with both hands and gingerly sipped from the steaming cup. The room was cold.

"This is where you live?" she said, astonished.

Walls were bare. Repeated coats of paint thickened the molding and gave life to the ghosts of tenants past. An upholstered Chesterfield sofa was squeezed beside a mahogany breakfront; a round dining table with two matched chairs held the center of the room. It felt like the contents of a large apartment had been stuffed into a small one, and everything was the wrong size. A bedsheet covered the window. Cardboard moving boxes were packed with books. His large library, which represented a cornucopia of happy times dedicated to pure thinking, was grouped by topic, and then alphabetically. His jewel among the romantics was a Hawthorne first edition, and the grouping of popular fiction had an old Eric Ambler, which he admired for its wisdom within a vulgar yarn spun to showcase a clever plot.

"It's temporary," he said. "I'm moving in a month or two."

She looked around. "How long have you been here?"

"A while." *Too long to mention.*

"I didn't mean to be found that way," she said, sipping her tea. "I must have nodded off. Do you always stay out late?"

"Work."

"What time is it?"

He sat opposite her in one of the chairs. "After midnight."

She nodded, but said nothing.

"How did you find the place?" he asked casually.

"Roger told me."

So, brother and sister had talked. He contemplated how this link closed a circle among them and made it possible to lower his guard.

"I came in for the hearings. Father is testifying tomorrow. He's nervous, but he won't admit it. They will try to demonize him. And for what?"

Mueller had an impulse to say something kind, but a false reassurance felt wrong, and there was no way to put a positive light on the red-baiting spectacle in Congress. He nodded.

She took a tennis ball from her bag. "You left this in my car. I thought you'd want it back, although I don't know why." She stepped to the bureau and a porcelain china bowl filled with tennis balls. "Do you play?"

"Not anymore. In college."

"Oh, well, they do make a good display." She toyed with the ball and suddenly threw it at him, which he caught midair with his fist. She looked around at the cramped apartment and made her judgment. "Art on the walls would brighten the space. A rug would help too. And flowers."

And a different mood, he thought. The monastic cell suited his suffering after he'd returned divorced from Vienna and his life was turned upside down. He'd moved in on a temporary basis, but one month became three years with the deceptive ease of a film dissolve.

"Do you have a lot of girlfriends like me?" she asked.

He was confused.

"Girls who pick you up on the road and nurse you back to health. And sleep with you?" She laughed self-consciously. "No.

This place would scare them off." She looked at him. "Have you ever cooked here?"

"Dinner?"

"Anything."

He didn't answer right away.

"I didn't think so," she said.

"I haven't answered."

"You don't need to answer. The fact that you had to think about it means you haven't, or if you have, it's milk and a bowl of cereal. I like to cook but not alone. If I lived here I'd eat out too."

He looked at her. "Why did you come?"

"Do I need a reason?" she asked. "Isn't it reason enough that I'm here?"

Silence lingered. When she looked up from her tea, their eyes met. "I didn't want it to end like that at the cottage. We don't have to be disappointed, if we don't want to be. Do we? We don't have to be people in a dry month waiting for rain."

Mueller smiled at the poet she'd chosen to quote. "*Tenants of the house. Thoughts of a dry brain in a dry season.*"

"Yes!" she said emphatically. Her voice was almost giddy and then she became moody and looked at him. "I have a confession. I did something once that I don't tell many people. I worry they will think I'm eccentric, which is the polite word people use when they actually think you're loony.

"I was a Salvation Army volunteer. I stood in Rockefeller Center in a scarlet uniform with the matching cap, bell in hand, which I dutifully rang. I needed a job to get out of the house and away from my mother. So I volunteered. I had seen these Salvation Army people banging their bells in front of Saint Patrick's and I always wondered who they were in real life. I wondered why they did it. So I joined them. To find out.

"I stood at the corner of Fifth Avenue that Christmas and rang my bell in front of the bucket. Men walked by and dropped a quarter, or a dime, or a nickel. I would give them a button and some eye contact. If they didn't take the button, I gave them an expression of kindness and gratitude. They would walk away. So, I had the most profound encounters with people, especially with poor people who didn't have a job. Once, I got this beautiful moment of prolonged eye contact from a young man, homeless probably, hardly a teenager standing in front of me in his torn coat. He looked at me and he reached into his pocket for a penny. My eyes said thank you and his eyes said *nobody knows what it's like to be hungry.*

"And sometimes I'd get ignored all day, or they'd take pity on me and strike up a conversation, thinking I needed companionship, or another job. It made me uncomfortable sometimes because I felt I was doing something unjob-like. I had no idea how perfect an education I was getting for finding people whose stories I could tell. I saw these people on the street and a gesture became a word, their clothing a sentence, the expressions on their faces a whole life. And I wanted to share that. So I wrote about them."

"I didn't know you wrote," he said.

"Because I haven't told you. Sketches for the stage. I have a diary too."

He pondered her. "Am I in it?"

"Don't flatter yourself." Beth folded her arms across her chest, a protective reflex, and gazed patiently at him. She leaned to him and was curious. "Why didn't you tell me you knew Roger?"

"Remember," he said, "don't ask." He relented. "We met in college."

She continued to look at him with a puzzled expression. "What else haven't you told me? Is it the same with your feelings for me?"

He rose and took her teacup, and then he walked into the tiny kitchen without answering.

"That's how you like it," she called after him. "Secret. Like your work. Well, I too can keep things to myself. Would you prefer me that way?"

He returned to her side with more tea. "Don't."

"Don't what?"

His eyes were averted, but they met hers and he lingered on her face. His voice was almost a plea. "Don't think ill of me. Be patient."

She touched his collar and loosened his tie. "Let's see what happens. May I take a shower?"

What Mueller hadn't expected was that he could feel attached to a woman again, and feel something furtive and heady, as it had been in college with his first girlfriend. The feeling startled him, and he was reluctant to give in to it. He could see the course of things, the strings that would begin to attach, the mornings of rushed pleasure before work, and the building responsibility for another person. He thought too that there was a kind of relief in only wanting her body, and having her willing to give it, keeping the rest of their lives out of it. How long would that last?

He saw her face unadorned, fresh from the shower, wet hair

fallen to her bare shoulders. She wasn't wearing glasses. Her eyes were an intense blue and sparkled in the water that clung to her face, falling down her cheeks. Her towel wrapped her chest, but there was a place between her breasts that drew his eye. She was vigorously drying her hair with a second towel and standing at the bathroom door a few feet away, without any false concern for how she looked. She stopped drying, and then her eyebrows were up, with a question.

He realized he'd been staring.

"I want this too," she said. She undid her towel for him and waited for him to come close. She took his face in her hands and drew his lips to hers. She guided him through the open bedroom door to the narrow unmade bed that was pushed against the wall. She lowered the window blind to get privacy from the couple moving about their living room in the apartment just across the airshaft. Then she turned to Mueller. He was nearby in the center of the tiny room, bathed in moonlight that came in another window. She lifted his T-shirt over his head and dropped the cotton garment to the floor. Her fingers worked to undo his belt buckle and when she had succeeded she lowered his trousers to his knees, and he stepped out, one foot, then another.

"Take your socks off," she said. "And your watch."

Together they lowered themselves onto the twin mattress and looked into each other's faces. He put his hand on her hip, and then let his hand fall to the moist skin and dense hair between her legs. She adjusted his hand and lay back on the pillow, looking up into his pale face. She closed her eyes to concentrate, but then opened them wide.

"Why have you stopped?"

He gazed at her.

"Tell me. There is a reason. Are you sorry I'm here?"

He lowered his head so it hovered close over hers, kissed one eye, then the other, and when he pulled back he drew his finger across the seam of her lips. "I'm nervous," he said.

She looked in his dark eyes, astonished. She laughed. "Nervous? About what?"

"Where this is going."

They looked into each other's faces, eyes searching the other's eyes for a clue to what lay ahead. The silence lingered and with it came the eagerness of their breathing. He lowered his mouth to her breast, its nipple wrinkled like a walnut, tasting the fresh perspiration. No woman had spent the night in his apartment, and he remembered the many evenings he'd gone to bed alone thinking about this moment, wondering if it would ever come. He was uncertain how he felt about her being the first to share his solitude.

He moved his mouth to her lips and he kissed her now with deep kisses that she returned. He suggested that she turn over, but she said no, she wanted to face him. He entered her slowly and together they acted as one flesh surrendered to urgent sensation. Afterward, they lay side by side, separate and not touching, looking at the moonlight rippling across the ceiling, listening to their beating hearts.

Mueller was up early the next morning and had already showered and dressed when Beth emerged from the bedroom wearing his pajama top. It fell to her thighs. Her hair was a wild nest of curls. She stumbled past him in a groggy daze without saying one word and entered the bathroom, closing the door. He heard water running, a cough, and then the sound of the toilet flushing.

It was a grim apartment, he thought, suddenly self-conscious of the spare furnishings. He looked out the makeshift curtain to the apartment across the air shaft, window cracked open, where a couple from the Deep South lived with four young children. Somewhere outside he heard the mother's shrill voice rail at a child, and suddenly, he understood how he'd used their loud arguments as a way to rationalize living alone. They were the cautionary example of a romantic beginning that became unhappy family life. If life were only that simple, he thought.

Mueller unfolded the morning newspaper and flipped to the classified advertisements, his fingers traveling down the column of babysitters seeking work, looking for "Dorothy A"—Vasilenko's signal to check for his chalk mark.

"You need a babysitter?"

Mueller found Beth standing over his shoulder, absentmindedly drying her hair.

"I'm good with children," she said. "I can babysit your son. I have time."

"This isn't for him." He saw her confusion. "He's in Austria with his mother."

They ate breakfast together. She ate slowly, a spoonful of cereal at a time, elbow propped on the table without false concern over how it would look or what he might think. She stopping eating and cocked her head. "Will you come with me to the hearing this morning?"

The first string, he thought.

"It would mean a lot to me. There will be press and a crowd wanting to be entertained by the spectacle of the senator vilifying a man for his beliefs." She looked at him. "This country has lost its soul."

Beth carelessly stirred the puffed rice, playing with her cereal. She looked up. "Whatever it is that you do, I don't care. It's your business. I don't meddle in other people's lives. I wouldn't want you to meddle in mine. We go about our lives, and if we're lucky we find someone with whom we can share the loneliness. You don't have to be miserable in a relationship, you know."

She reached across the table and placed her palm on his hand. Her expression was caring, almost sad. "Giving famishes the craving."

Her eyes met his. "Eliot," she said.

• • •

Room 357 in the Senate office building was thick with spectators and national press. There was a carnival din of voices waiting for the hearing to start, and a few eager faces looked to the front of the room, where a solitary white-haired man sat at a witness table before the high curved dais. Sober senators huddled with aides, or waited for the chairman of the Permanent Subcommittee on Investigations to bring the room to order. The chairman wore a gray flannel suit, starched shirt with a garroting tie, and his thinning gray hair combed to the side. His cheeks were heavy with a drinker's flush. He cocked his head to receive a brisk whispered instruction from a young aide.

Mueller was making his way through the aisle, crowded with late arrivals seeking a seat, when he heard his name called. He saw Beth in the middle of the row, arms raised, waving to get his attention. He begged his way past seated men, who drew in their knees, and he continued down the row, apologizing to the bigger men who were forced to stand to let him pass.

"I didn't think you were coming." Beth removed the coat she'd used to save a seat. "What held you up?"

"Traffic." A sort of truth.

"You know my brother," Beth said.

Mueller nodded at Roger Altman, who nodded back. They assessed each other—acknowledged one another like secret conspirators, eyes signaling a private recognition no one else observed. It was a knowing glance they exchanged under the cover of a casual greeting. "Good to see you old boy," Altman said. "Here in these circumstances."

Altman leaned across his sister, who sat between the two men, and whispered to Mueller. "It feels like *Julius Caesar*." He nodded at the senators on the dais. "The best in us attracts the worst in them. That is who we have become."

The chairman brought a gavel down hard, then a second time, and a third time, getting attention of the restless crowd. The chairman trained his withering gaze high over the bright lights, reproving spectators furthest removed from his authority. "Ladies and gentlemen," a voice boomed.

Mueller was seated obscurely in the middle of the room, but he was nevertheless conscious of being visible. Unwelcome enough in any circumstance, this exposure was not at all what he had in mind when he'd agreed to attend the hearing. He hadn't thought of it in advance, but his presence there, among the room of people glancing about to see who else had come, made him uncomfortable. He too scanned the room for a face he'd want to avoid. In fact, no one looked at Mueller except when they pretended to look at him in order to take in a person sitting in the row ahead, or behind him.

There were the formalities of the hearing—the opening statement, the swearing-in, and the sergeant at arms's instructions to the crowd to keep order and abstain from talking. Mueller didn't see anyone from the Agency, and he hadn't expected to, but he couldn't say the same for the FBI. He recognized two agents at the chief counsel's table—calm, crew-cut, confident—seated with Committee staffers.

And then the hearing began. Arnold Altman gave his name, age, his addresses in Maryland and on Park Avenue, and he recited for the record his work in banking and then briefly as secretary of the International Monetary Fund.

"We are here," the senator said in a stentorian voice amplified by the hearing room's tall ceiling and wide windows, "to ask some questions, Mr. Altman. The Committee heard testimony of two former officials of the Economic Cooperation Agency that the exchange rate fluctuations of the Austrian currency in 1948 worked against the country's financial stability and in favor of the Soviet occupation forces. Funds were moved from Soviet satellite Czechoslovakia to Swiss banks through IMF accounts and were used to drive down the schilling. These are the facts we have from the testimony of two former employees."

The senator looked out at the room and then at his colleagues. His voice was firm and accusatory and it went on with
the great rolling cadences of a man more accustomed to inciting
a mob in a stadium. "This is the Austrian incident. That's how we
refer to the currency manipulation that devalued the schilling,
ruined the economy, and led to the food riots. Men and women
and children died. For the purposes of this hearing today, I will
summarize the situation in May of that year. The only mention of
you, Mr. Altman, was in a cable sent to Austria and Washington
indicating that the Czech delegation to the IMF was objecting to
the devaluation of the schilling. The objection was transmitted
by the office of the secretary of the Fund through the State Department to Austria, and I believe the wording of the cable from
the secretary advised that the Czech delegation objected to the
devaluation and questioned how IMF's classified currency support was compromised."

Arnold Altman leaned forward to the microphone and spoke
in a respectful tone. "Was there a question?"

The senator looked over the top of his glasses. "Whether you
have any recollection of the protest that the Czech government
made in the action your office took."

"I do not. If I could see the documents I might recall."

"So your testimony is that you don't recall?"

"Yes."

"And do you know how the information got to the Soviets?"

"I don't know that it did."

"But member governments took monetary matters through
the secretary."

"No, that isn't correct, because you say monetary matters. As secretary of the IMF it was my duty to report discussions of the Fund to governments."

"Sir, that wasn't my question. My question was, did you communicate this to the Czechs?"

"To the best of my knowledge, I don't recall."

"At this time you have no recollection that the schilling support was leaked?"

"That is right."

"Did you work for the Czech delegation to the Monetary Fund?"

"Yes, technically, assuming you mean the executive director. He was a Czech national on the board at one period of time when I was secretary of the board."

"So," the senator said, leaning back, "you worked for him, as you say, technically."

"Yes, technically."

"And you listened to him?"

"Yes, he was on the board."

"And he listened to you?"

"We talked. I suppose it would be natural to assume that if one man is talking the other would listen." The crowd stirred, and a few in the audience laughed.

"In the fall of 'forty-eight," the senator said, "the Czech representative, or executive director, or whatever you call him, was a Communist."

"I don't know."

"He represented the Czech government, did he not? The fall

of Czechoslovakia was in 1948, was it not?" The senator took a note handed to him by his young counsel.

Mueller whispered to Beth, "Where is this going?"

Brother and sister had moved closer together in the bond of family threatened by the senator's intimidating power. She clutched her sibling's arm. Mueller saw the difference between power and authority, the former on display, the latter a weakly cloaked performance. Beth's face was drawn, color had drained from her cheeks, and there was a sad, helpless expression on her face. Her mouth was open almost as if she'd stopped breathing, but she shook her head in a vague way. "I don't know."

Mueller looked across at Roger Altman, who had covered his sister's hands with his own. His jaw was set, eyes fixed and flinty, and Mueller thought Altman gazed at his father with something that was not quite compassion. It was so startling and unexpected, Mueller stared. Only the senator's voice took Mueller's attention back to the proceedings.

"You're an American citizen?" the senator asked.

"Yes," Arnold Altman replied.

"Born here?"

"No."

"Where were you born?"

"Sudetenland."

"That's Czechoslovakia, correct?"

"Now it is. It was Austro-Hungary when I was born."

"And when was that?"

"The date?"

"Yes, the date."

"July twenty-fifth."

"You still have family there?"

"I was brought here as a child."

"Do you speak Czech?"

"A few words. We spoke German at home."

"Now let me go back to something. The Communist Party, its front organizations and its controlled unions, has sought, since its inception, to plant within our democratic institutions its individual members, including espionage agents. I'd like to clarify one thing. The record shows that you admitted friendship with two IMF employees identified as communist sympathizers. Isn't that a fact?"

"I have a problem with that question, Senator, on several levels. Which men do you refer to? What do you mean by communist sympathizer?"

It surprised no one that the hearing dragged on through the morning and reconvened after lunch, and with each hour the hectoring questions became more hostile, the lapse from fact to innuendo more obvious. Mueller stayed until the end, but only because he'd said he'd stay, and he felt it was wrong to abandon Beth, who took each badgering question as a blow to herself. She suffered badly. There was nothing civil in the proceeding, nor was there anything that Mueller could call productive. It was a small sideshow that seemed to have no point except to make Arnold Altman look bad, and the sideshow wasn't over. Adding to the indignity, he was told he would be called back for a second hearing.

Those who knew Arnold Altman were not surprised by his impatience, nor were they surprised by his final statement, which all agreed was a direct indictment of the Subcommittee's tactics, and did him no good. He denounced the senator's methods, the unsubstantiated accusations, the abuse of its solemn responsibilities. His brief little speech quoted President Madison to the effect that you first enable government to control the governed, and next you oblige it to control itself. He said this in a firm, clear voice. Then "These hearings, sir, have lost all sense of decency."

The sympathetic applause from a few people in the room was met by boos from others, and in that moment the audience of right-wing fans of the senator and their indignant opposite on the left together formed a tarnished throng that was a version of America.

Mueller followed the Altmans as they made their way down the mobbed aisle toward the exit, being shoved and shoving, blinded in the glare of camera flashes, and badgered by reporters' shouted questions. Beth had her father's arm and guided him through the crowd, making a path where there was none and wielding a stiff arm against hostile people who stepped forward. It was chaos.

Mueller walked a few steps behind the Altmans, but still close enough to be part of the family group. His tall, thin frame, his clear plastic eyeglasses, and his sour expression made him a target for the hecklers. He ignored the whispered epithets spat by respectable-looking folks, and he kept his eyes on the goal, the exit door up ahead. He heard a fat woman accuse him of being a communist sympathizer, and he wanted to stop, shake her, shout in her face, *No, this country has lost its soul.* It was only a supreme act of self-control that kept him from engaging the woman in an argument. And to what end? He'd make himself feel better if he shouted what he thought of her, but no purpose would be served. It would only feed her ill-tempered accusations. This too made him yearn to be away from it all, cloistered in an ivory tower.

Mueller pushed past the big woman, closing the gap that had opened between himself and the Altmans, who waited for him at the guarded exit. FBI agent Walker held back the heaving spectators and protected the family. "Through here," he said.

Walker inserted himself between Mueller and the hecklers and provided the opportunity the family needed to slip away. Mueller met Walker's eye as he passed, and he acknowledged the help with a polite nod. "It's not over," Walker whispered. "Choose your friends carefully."

Mueller stared at the FBI agent, but the man didn't explain himself, or elaborate, and the crowd behind them crushed forward.

Mueller followed the Altmans through a winding maze of narrow hallways that led outside. They stood at the top of the Capitol's terraced marble steps and there, once again, they were just ordinary citizens. Beth accompanied her father down to a waiting black chauffeured limousine. She held his arm in a charitable way while he went down the long flight of steps. Mueller remained at the top with Roger Altman. The wind had picked up and with it the cold. The afternoon sky was a merciless, brooding gray. Altman wore dark glasses, a cashmere overcoat, and a delicate white scarf, its ends dying into the neckline. He was putting on his tan gloves one at a time, stretching his fingers deep into the leather.

"He brought it on himself, you know," Altman said. He turned and met Mueller's confusion. "He chose to testify. To clear his name. The next round won't be pleasant. They're calling me to testify against him."

"You?"

"I was there when the schilling tanked. They think, somehow, I can shed light on the whole episode, but all it will do is focus attention on me. He didn't think about that. He is naïve."

And so, again, Mueller heard the son's stubborn grievance against his father. Altman's voice was a pleasant tenor, but it acquired a throaty bluntness when he talked about his father, which added to the impression of fractiousness.

"Beth appreciated that you came," Altman added. "So did I."

Silence lingered. Altman looked at Mueller. "How's the leg?"

The leg? Mueller gave a brisk smile. "You got the report?"

"Her report."

"What did she say?"

"She's fond of you . . . who would have guessed."

The two men considered each other on the broad steps. Mueller was uncomfortable, perhaps embarrassed. A part of him regretted that he had not found a way to tell his colleague that he was intimate with his sister, and that Altman had to find out from her. Mueller said nothing. It would be wrong to apologize for there was nothing that required apology. Apologize for what?

"She doesn't know I'm with the Agency," Altman said. "And she shouldn't know." Altman smiled at Mueller. "She wouldn't understand. She has a different view of the world. My father's view of the world, a little romantic, a little naïve. The world needs people like her to protect it from people like us."

Altman suddenly stretched his right arm out and shoved his hand into his glove. Gruffly he said, "I suppose you'll be coming out to the house next weekend for the races."

"Am I invited?"

Altman hesitated. "If she hasn't invited you, consider this your invitation."

13

A WEEKEND PARTY

J AZZ FROM a band on the lawn of a big house farther along the cove drifted on the calm evening. The bay's water had settled for the night and the glass surface brightened the music. Unseasonably warm weather and the urge to escape the Capital's nasty politics brought life to the weekend homes tucked comfortably into coves and inlets.

Mueller was alone. He stood in the garden under a night sky clotted with distant stars. Amber headlights moved along the ridge and then, at different points, one by one dropped down driveways that led to the glowing homes. Voices and laughter carried across the water, clear like struck crystal. A motorboat sliced through the water on its way to somewhere.

Suddenly he had company. The soft click of a footstep on the stone path, then Beth was at his side. She had a cotton shawl over a strapless dress and stood self-consciously in heels on the un-

149

even surface. Their eyes met. She acknowledged him, and he her, and then he returned to his vigil. Neither said anything for a long moment, and they were surrounded by the evening's soundtrack of laughter, jazz, and the laboring motor of the boat.

"Did you hear?" she said at last.

"Hear? What?"

"Our windshield was smashed." There was fresh worry in her voice. "We had crank calls yesterday and the day before. Someone got our number. They would call and hang up. They'd call again and say the most awful things. Terrible things. I didn't know there were people like that." She was calm, but her arms wrapped her chest in a protective embrace. "More than rude. Threatening. Yesterday morning we found the car. Someone climbed the gate, came down the driveway, and threw a rock. The police were helpful, but out here"—her arm made a wide arc of the bay—"we're outsiders. To them I'm the daughter of a communist sympathizer. I mean, it's crazy, stupid. Ignorant! Oh, it makes me mad. I don't have all the words to express my anger."

"Will you go back to New York?"

"I would when my play's run is over. Father won't. He says he won't be intimidated. That's all well and good, but it means he goes about his life and I'm left to worry. I worry for two."

Suddenly she cupped her hands to her mouth in a makeshift megaphone. "Stay away," she shouted. Her voice resounded in the quiet night and startled a bird nesting in a nearby tree, which alighted in flight. "Stay away."

She looked at Mueller. "That should do the trick, right?" She laughed. She clutched his arm, startling him, and he felt her lean on his shoulder. "Let's go inside," she said.

"Go ahead," he said. "I'll come in a minute." When she stood fixed like a statue, he snapped, "Go ahead."

She was puzzled. She glared at him before abruptly saying, "I will."

When she was gone he looked back at the dark cove. The motorboat had no lights, but it was visible in the moonlight. He was curious where the boat had gone, only now to return to the dock at the Soviet compound. The moon hung like a lantern in the sky and illuminated the four-masted barque moored mid-channel. Its spindly mass fused with the dark water and tiny bulbs ran stem to stern like Christmas lights.

The evening chill drove Mueller up to the grand Victorian home. He approached the driveway, where arriving cars were met by valets and couples stepped into the evening to join the party that overflowed the open doors. A festive rumble drifted toward him. He made his way up the dark path, a moth drawn to sparkling light.

Inside the front door he found himself in a noisy, chaotic scene. The racy adventurous feel of the party washed over him like a cleansing bath, and his restless eye found satisfaction in the constant lure of strapless women and boisterous men. He moved through the crowd, his shoulder opening a path where there was none, thinking that he'd know someone, but he didn't, and he was self-conscious that he seemed to be the only guest not working the room. He looked from one glowing face to another, and sometimes a woman he saw returned his glance with a generous smile, but none of these single women was Beth. He sought her like a sailor sought a beacon, but the crowd was dense, the smoke thick, crews of the sailing yachts big and tall, and the party overflowed the vestibule into rooms along the hallway.

And then a hand came down on his shoulder. Arnold Altman's eyes were alive with enthusiasm. He wore a single white carnation on his black tuxedo. "The hearing was a success, don't you think?" He beamed. "I made my point."

A success? Mueller kept his opinion to himself.

"Someone needs to stand up to that man. Pompous, but smart, and that's what makes him dangerous. I saw those tactics in Germany. People were afraid to speak up."

Mueller took his eyes off the happy woman looking at him and gave his full attention to Altman.

"My good friend Leo Bendel," Altman said. "He owned a tobacco business and collected art. Wonderful man. He was forced to move from Munich. He and his wife were hounded, expelled, arrested, and sent to one of those camps. I remember their friends, their German friends, said nothing. They were silent while this decent man was arrested for being a Jew. No one spoke up. No one. I have seen the evil of intolerance. When I spoke out in the hearing it was for my good friend Leo Bendel." Altman looked at Mueller. "You were good to come. How is the leg?"

His leg again. Everyone remembered. "It's fine."

"I want to introduce you to someone," Altman said. The host reached across a narrow opening in the crowd and pulled over a slight woman, plain to look at, in a simple pattern dress and flats. Her eyes were wide with surprise and discomfort.

"This is Roger's fiancée," Altman said, proudly.

The girl shyly put forward one hand and Mueller shook it, surprised it was limp.

"I'm George."

"Nice to meet you." Her voice was a soprano whisper. She had a frail, homey look, with freckles, and she was wary. She wanted to retreat from the introduction and return to her anonymity, but the older Altman put his arm on her shoulder to keep her from fleeing.

George heard his name called and he looked off in the direction from which he thought the sound originated. Roger Altman had been with a group of friends, but he'd pulled away, and was coming straight to Mueller, eyebrows raised in an excited approach. Drinking, Mueller thought, but not yet drunk. He wore a tuxedo and a jolly expression flush with whiskey. His voice was exuberant and louder than usual, alive with alcohol.

"George, I didn't see you arrive. Glad you could come, old boy. We're celebrating the Greek holiday of winter racing. Haven't you heard of it? Well, neither have I. This is Emily, my fiancée. Have you met?"

"Just now." Mueller saw the girl plead for something, but what exactly, Mueller could not tell. She clutched her small cloth purse with both hands.

"What do you do?" Mueller asked Emily.

Roger answered. "She's not much for conversation. Or for crowds. And we've outdone ourselves this year, don't you think? Who would guess that putting in to fifty-degree water was so popular?"

Nothing more was said. Roger Altman tugged his fiancée's hand and led the docile, wide-eyed girl away through the room of drinkers.

"A nice girl," Arnold said. "He doesn't treat her well. He might lose her."

Lose her? Mueller shook his head. "I don't think there's a chance of that."

• • •

Mueller searched for Beth. The party was raucous and lively with old acquaintances who were at turns loud and foolish, and he steered clear of these groups. Liquor flowed freely from a bar in the dining room served by two men in bow ties. A waiter in sailor uniform passed a tray of champagne flutes and he was followed by a waitress in mermaid costume offering crudités and deviled eggs. The waiter wore white gloves and the waitress was in a sequin dress with a long dorsal fin. Mixing among the guests was a man in a pale pink chiffon toga carrying a great horn of fruit.

This was the "casual drop-in" that Roger Altman had mentioned was their way to celebrate the start of winter sail week. Only daredevil men of the adventurous sailing community, committed to folly, earned bragging rights for braving the frigid water. It was an Ivy League crowd. Mueller recognized a man from his class at Yale, and then another, and there was a clutch of Yalies smoking in the garden.

Mueller spotted Beth across the room. He was glad to see her face among the strangers. It was only as he pushed through the crowd that he saw two men hovering around her in animated conversation. She responded to whatever was said by throwing her head back, laughing brightly. The two men were almost twins, handsome sailors in identical uniforms, eager faces with the same predation—and it was their intensity that made Mueller jealous.

"Beth," he said, inserting himself, "I've been looking for you."

"For me." Her smile vanished, eyes fierce. "Well, it was you who sent me away. And now I'm in the middle of a conversation."

Mueller felt slapped. He looked at the two men, his height, but strong to his thin stature. "I'm sorry," he said. Mueller's fingers wrapped his water glass like a chalice and he stood awkwardly, rebuked. Mueller nodded to her and to the men. "Excuse me."

"I will find you," she yelled to his back.

Momentarily, Mueller stood in the crowded hallway among lively strangers whose upbeat mood mocked his hot burn of embarrassment. Did he care that he'd offended her in the garden? It was too easy to pretend that he didn't. He still had not perfected a polite way to have a companionable evening with a woman and not have his attention hijacked by work.

One drinking group of Yalies came down the hall and carried the sullen Mueller into the next room, where a group of singers was gathered around a grand piano. Women stood around the edge of the room in brave dresses, their hair puffed in bizarre shapes. They looked at the singers and the room was alive with interest in the pianist as his fingers danced on the keyboard. The pianist was short, bald, with glasses, and he got the room's attention with up-tempo music and bawdy lyrics. He welcomed new couples to the room with his tenor spoof of "Falling in Love

Again." He targeted Mueller holding back at the door, watching from his observer's perch, with a mocking version of "Ten Cents a Dance."

Mueller nodded, acknowledging this attention. He had never been close to these men at Yale and saw no reason to be close now. The bald pianist kept up a monologue between songs that held the room's attention. Floating rounds of floral-colored cocktails passed among the crowd. A momentary hush. The pianist struck a chord and held a falsetto note in his lungs for a breathless minute, and the crowd took his cue. All at once the room joined in singing the hit tune "Road to Bali." Men and women took up the chorus: *We're poor little lambs who have lost their way . . . we're little black sheep who have gone astray.*

Mueller slipped out during the closing verse. He found it tiresome to be sober among a room of drinkers. The foolishness of alcohol wasn't amusing to the observer who stuck with soda water. He saw it all, and would remember it all, but the evening would be a dull hangover for the others.

It was too late to find Beth to apologize, too early to return to his cottage, and too cold to wander the gardens alone. He found himself in the front hallway by a closed door. He tried the handle and found it unlocked. Mueller stepped into a book-lined study and was happy to leave behind the raucous party. There was a ponderous carved wood desk, a brass stand with a globe of the earth, a whiskey-colored leather sofa, and bound volumes on book shelves that rose to the high ceiling.

Mueller's eye caught a framed oil painting the size of a serving tray leaning against the lowest book shelf, and he knelt to look. The portrait was of a nursing mother, her hand guiding her breast to her child's mouth. She gazed lovingly at the innocent thing in her arms.

"It's a Schiele."

Mueller turned. Roger Altman was standing just inside the open door, which he closed.

"It's a portrait of Stephanie Grunwald. She was the daughter of Schiele's best collector. He painted her as a memory for the father. He also did that painting."

Roger pointed to a landscape that also leaned against the bookcase. "It's titled *Birch Forest*. The Nazis called it degenerate art. We call it modernism, and some of the other work you see here on the floor are good examples of cubism. After the *Anschluss* the Jews of Vienna needed cash to buy their way to Paris or Switzerland. They sold their work. Sometimes for a pittance."

Altman nodded. "I like your expression. The owner of this painting who sold it to me said, 'You'll be able to judge whether a man has taste or not if you see that he is able to appreciate great art.' You have taste, George. I can see that in the way that you look at her hand. Remarkable, isn't it, the mother looking at her child and gently holding her breast to feed him with such love in her eyes." Altman paused, reflected. "For the artist there is nothing better than to know that his work is in appreciative hands."

Altman turned the painting so it now faced the wall. "Each painting is unique. One of a kind. Irreplaceable. A woman is unique too, but a woman's beauty fades. A painting's beauty is eternal." He turned to Mueller. "Do you know of Egon Schiele?"

"I do."

"I see. It's good to know. You always surprise me with the things that you know."

There was a pause. "Do you have plans in the morning?" Altman asked. The question surprised Mueller. "To go sculling. It's been years since we did that. How is your technique? Are you still the chaser you were in school?"

It was agreed.

•   •   •

Dense fog. Dawn light came through the cottony gray that blanketed the bay. A buoy clanged somewhere. Visibility was nearly zero and sound had no provenance. Mist was heavy with moisture over the cool surface of the water.

Two sculls sliced the calm green, moving side by side, bows sharing the lead. Oars dipped in a steady pace, and with each pull the oarsmen grunted, voices lending strength to their arms. There was no one to see them. They traveled in a bubble of visibility that was just an oar's length of water, but they saw each other, competed with each other, straining to gain the advantage. Oars entered the water in a quickening pace. They were dressed in sweatsuits for the dawn chill, but the exertion of their race drew sweat to their foreheads and stained the gray cotton.

Suddenly a monstrous four-masted barque rose straight out of the water and loomed through the fog. Waves slapped the hull. Beads of sweat channeled their eyes, smarting, then blurring eyesight, but neither wanted to risk surrendering the lead by losing half a stroke to gaze at the ghostly mass that slid past.

The finish line was suddenly upon them. A clarion red buoy

bobbed in the wake of their sculls. And then only the sound of air being gulped and labored breathing.

"You lost," Altman said, gasping. His head rested on his hands, holding his stilled oars.

"I won," Mueller said. He too gasped for breath and he too rested his forehead on his oars.

Then quiet. The sleek sculls continued to glide the surface still powered by the last great heaves the two men had put into their effort. All around there was only dense fog and the strange silence of water.

"I won," Altman reiterated, rising to sit upright. "You had nothing to drink. It was my handicap."

Mueller shook his head, exhausted. He filled his lungs with a mouthful of air, and moved his arms to shake out the tension in his shoulders. "You lost."

"You've never beaten me," Altman said.

The two men were still youthfully fit in spite of desk work and job stress, and they grinned at each other, proud of the ambiguous result, each pleased to be spared an obvious and embarrassing loss—neither conceding.

"Will you be crewing in the race today?" Altman asked.

"No. You?"

"Father's boat. The one at the dock. It's old, slow. Work?"

"It's Saturday."

"That's never stopped you."

"Reading. Thinking. A bit of work."

Altman threw out an opinion. "You think too much, George. You're too self-absorbed. The tedious life of perpetual self-examination is a bore. You're moody, dark, always preoccupied. I'm not sure what Beth sees in you."

Mueller stroked to keep his scull even with Altman's.

"It's not a race," Altman said.

"I'm not racing."

"Life, George. Life is not a race. I meant life is not a race. It's a journey with surprises and unexpected twists. Who would have thought you'd be seeing my sister?"

Mueller wondered. Question or observation? He stroked harder to pull away. His bow cut through the murky water.

"You and Coffin met the director last week," Altman said, voice raised.

Question or observation? "Yes."

"What did you discuss?"

The two boats were alongside each other at matched speeds. The two men had picked up their pace and their oars overlapped in the narrow gap separating the boats, oars synchronized, dipping to avoid the other. Mueller spoke in staccato bursts between oar pulls. "Coffin has another theory. He lives in a gloomy castle brooding about all his doubts. In his mind everything—*everything*—is a security risk. I'm a risk. For all the reasons you know." Mueller looked across the water. "And you're a risk." Mueller slowed his pace. "I defended you."

"He's good at that. Talking behind one's back. You defended me? Well, jolly good for you."

Mueller stopped. He detected offense in Altman's voice when he had instead expected gratitude. Mueller had gone out of his way to protect Altman. It was the right thing. Mueller respected

the choice Altman had made in his life and he knew the burden
it placed on him in the hostile, frightened gossip that passed for
intelligent conversation in Washington's social circles. Nobody
in Mueller's life—not at home, in school, at work—had ever spoken of homosexuality except as a disorder that would destroy a
career. Lost in the excited prurience of the conversations by ones
who weren't homosexual about someone who was, was the person, the man, the human being. Mueller felt an obligation to defend Altman because he knew Altman, knew the man.

Mueller arrived at Yale from the Midwest with limited experience, and none of the sophistication that the graduates of New
England boarding schools brought with them to college. He was
naïve and curious. He didn't understand the social fear of affection between men that rose to drama and, at its worst, hypocrisy.
Mueller had found Altman attractive in a way he couldn't put into
words—the quick smile, his intelligence, a passion for athletics,
and a shy vulnerability. Mueller was curious about the tall, lean
boy with hair that fell over his forehead and pushed back with his
hand, and that made him open to "bonding." That was the word
they used to describe the things they did together, the crewing, a
cappella singing, and it was a different type of relationship from
the more formal dating on weekends with Vassar coeds. The end of
their friendship came one day after crew practice in the boathouse
when Altman emerged from the shower. Mueller inserted his arm
between their bare chests, blocking Altman's advance. "It's not going to happen again," he said. He was respectful, but firm.

Neither of them brought up the incident. They never discussed what happened, and as far as Mueller knew, it was some-

thing that stayed between the two of them. They were part of the same social set, but they were no longer close friends, and Mueller blamed Altman for that. In time, enough other things filled their lives and the incident was lost in memory. Here they were, twelve years later, the same men with the same competitive spirits, the same fit bodies. Except that Mueller had married and Altman never had.

Mueller's recollection emerged from its past in that moment on the water. Perhaps it was Altman's offhand comment, which Mueller didn't understand, or the fog, or the sculls, which were like the ones in the boathouse, or the tone of Altman's smug self-confidence, *Well, jolly good for you.*

Mueller's oar came out of its saddle and traveled in a long arc that struck the surface and sent a stream of spray Altman's way. Suddenly, a crack. Mueller felt the hard contact of the end of his oar and he saw Altman slump and go underwater. He emerged a moment later, gasping for air, wet hair flat on his forehead. Blood came from an inch-long gash above the eye and the crimson flow washed across his cheek. He clung by one hand to Mueller's scull and drew the other across his forehead and then inspected his palm.

"I'm okay," he said.

"My fault," Mueller said. Mueller put out his arm, and Altman clamped on, so the two men's forearms were coupled by their wrists, and Mueller hauled Altman onto his boat, legs dangling over the side. Altman removed his cold, soaked sweatshirt and shivered. Mueller went to strip off his shirt, but stopped when Altman waved off the offer of dry clothing. Instead, Altman wiped his hand across his chest and displayed a crimson palm to Mueller.

"This is how I'll die. On the water. Struck by someone I thought was a friend."

Altman laughed, a short laugh, a self-conscious laugh, then a longer laugh. The two men found themselves laughing, laughing at nothing, looking at each other and laughing more, an infectious laughter fueled by an understood absurdity that neither could put into words. In the midst of the laughter, Altman slipped.

Mueller grabbed his arm and kept him from falling. A touch. Altman's hand took hold of Mueller's chest in his effort to keep his balance. His hand lingered a moment. Eyes met. Altman slipped into the water and in a moment he had climbed into his boat and was pulling hard toward the boathouse.

Mueller started after him, but he let himself fall back and then he found himself alone in the cloaking fog. He yanked on his oars, drifted, pulled again harder, and with each stroke his anger rose. He felt good about striking Altman, and that made him feel uncomfortable.

14

A PERSON OF INTEREST

MUELLER WASN'T prepared for what happened next. When he later reconstructed the chain of events, he convinced himself that he could not have foreseen the danger. Even the regular exercise of caution is a poor defense against the diligent working of an intelligent adversary.

It was a quiet week in Washington and he'd made a few short visits to the office, but he kept his time there to a minimum to avoid seeing colleagues and having to answer questions about his time, or lack of time, at the sanitarium. On the fifth evening he passed the post office box on L Street and he saw Vasilenko's double chalk mark. Two lines. *Something is up.* Mueller looked at his watch. He had half an hour to reach the agreed drop point. It wasn't just the time he worried about. There were documents inside his briefcase that he should have left in his office safe, but how was he to know that he'd see Vasilenko's mark on his way home? He rejected returning to Quarter's Eye, or going home. There wasn't time.

Dense fog laid its false peace over Union Station. The limestone façade was bone-white in evening spotlights, and traffic sped around the fountain on its way to drop off or pick up passengers. Mueller waited for the green-and-white trolley to pass and then quickly crossed the tracks. He gained the sidewalk and entered the loggia, glancing down the hall of pendulous iron lamps chained to the ceiling. Passengers from a late-arriving train hurried through the corridor in bulky overcoats on their way to taxis queued at the end of the portico.

Mueller entered the great hall with its vaulted ceiling rising high above the marble floor. He observed men whose backs were turned, and when he confirmed they weren't Vasilenko, he moved to the next. Mueller saw two Metropolitan police at the far end of the hall strolling among the wood benches. A barbershop was shuttered, and next door the cashier of a newsstand was locking up for the night. The shoeshine stand was empty. A bar that catered to soldiers heading back to base was the only spot where convivial men and women gathered for a drink before boarding their train. A few of these tipsy commuters gawked at one wall where a giant electric locomotive jutted into the hall through a shattered wall, its black brow dusted in white and dented from impact. A month before, brakes on the overnight train from Boston had failed.

Mueller looked up at the mighty clock that dominated one end of the hall. The six-foot arm traveled around the dial, once gilded, now darkened with soot and grime. Trust the plan. How long would he wait? Maybe the Russian had been held up. There was always a crisis somewhere, or a last-minute request to work late in the embassy. Spies weren't like trains, they didn't operate by the clock. Things happened. Even to trains things happened. He glanced at the huge locomotive that looked like a mechanical mole broken through an underground wall. Mueller had never gotten used to the waiting. You can't train for that. The hardest part was not knowing.

How many times had he stood here? This exact spot. There was something illusionary about time and space, which is why whenever he came home from a trip and paused by the exit under the giant clock he felt like he'd never been gone. Past trips came back to him as he stood there, all existing at the same time in memory. Mueller saw the huge arm jerk forward a notch, slicing off a minute of the future, and come to a quivering halt. 9:05 p.m.

Where was Vasilenko? Mueller's eyes went to people standing behind the police tape, eyes moving from one man to the next, looking for a big man in a floppy fedora.

There! Their eyes met. An acknowledgment. Vasilenko had emerged from the men's bathroom and crossed the great hall to the second exit, avoiding Mueller, but the doors were locked due to the late hour, and he was forced to approach. As he came to the doors he stepped quickly to the side, joining Mueller in the shadow of an overhang.

"This isn't right," he hissed.

What wasn't right? "I'm here."

"You're late." Vasilenko glanced back and let his eyes search the faces of people moving along the far wall under the frieze of stone escutcheons displaying iron ties, hammers, and protean workers in symbolic celebration of progress. Passengers from the just-arrived *Silver Meteor* pushed from the gate into the waiting crowd. A name was called out. A cry of excitement, the quick race across the vast floor, the two people stopping in a public embrace.

"We shouldn't be seen together. This isn't good."

"Is it inside?"

"What do you think?" Vasilenko nodded at Mueller's briefcase. "For me?"

"No, there wasn't time. I only saw the mark an hour ago. I can't get cash that fast."

"When?"

"Tomorrow. Noon. Inside the vestibule. The usual spot."

Vasilenko flicked his cigarette to the floor and ground it under his heel. "Don't be late."

. . .

Mueller entered the men's bathroom. Harsh fluorescent light aspirated the brightness of the white tile walls and the odor of mint cleaner mentholated the air. Mueller took the precaution to confirm there was no one in a stall. His only company was a middle-aged man in a business suit at the urinal. He leaned back from the wall, hand in crotch, and turned to Mueller, eyes urgent and signaling. Mueller looked away. *Jesuschrist*. A lousy spot for a dead drop. That damn fool Vasilenko picking a public bathroom. What was he thinking?

The man entered a stall.

Mueller removed an envelope wedged in the gap between cast iron radiator and the tile wall. The package didn't fit in his coat pocket, so he folded it in a newspaper he pulled from the trash and tucked it under his arm.

Mueller left the men's room with the brisk stride of a traveler anxious to get home. He repeated the mantra, *Stay calm*, but his legs moved like those of a man who wanted to get away from the spot as quickly as possible. Just beyond the door two men stood shoulder to shoulder, blocking his path. Trench coats, stern faces, and wide-brim hats pulled down on their foreheads. Mueller stepped to the right to avoid them, but they moved as he moved, then confronted him.

"Sir."

Mueller turned to the man who had spoken, stout, vaguely unpleasant, with wire-rim glasses that had the thickest lenses Mueller had ever seen. "Yes."

"FBI." He flashed a wallet with a badge. "Do you mind coming with us?"

Mueller's mind was in revolt. *Think! Think!* His eyes moved in the direction the agent had pointed to gain time. *Think!* "What's the problem?" he asked.

"We have a few questions. Right this way."

Mueller felt the man's grip on his arm and he allowed himself to be led through the train station. He was hustled outside and then a hand lowered his head and he was shoved into the backseat of a sedan. His briefcase and the envelope had found their way into the hands of one of his escorts. Mueller sat quietly between the two agents, but his mind was a turmoil of dread. What should he say, or not say, and how should he explain himself? The car sped through empty streets. Bright lights from intersection street lamps patterned the driver's face, but Mueller didn't recognize him either. He had nothing to say—not yet. He wouldn't be able to talk himself out of his predicament with these agents. Mueller's worry kept coming back to the sinking feeling that they'd known he would be there.

The next hour was unpleasant. He was made to wait in a windowless cell somewhere in the bowels of a temporary office building erected during the war to meet the needs of a burgeoning bureaucracy and never removed. They had taken everything—envelope, newspaper, briefcase, coins, house keys, wallet. They'd been polite but they didn't answer any of his questions. *What is going on? Why am I here?* He'd resisted the impulse to object—yell, actually. It would make him feel better, but it would not change things. They were following orders or procedures. When they took the briefcase, he said, "You'll have to pay for the lock if you break it."

Room 8 had two wood chairs and a small, battered table. He tried the doorknob but found it locked. Of course it would be locked, he thought, but sometimes people got sloppy. Vasilenko got sloppy. What else explained the error? The FBI had followed the unsuspecting new guy. It didn't matter how diligent Mueller was if the man on the other end of the bargain was careless.

The door to Room 8 burst open. Mueller had his head in his hands on the table, staring at nothing, and the door startled him. The muscular agent wore a tailored suit oddly formal for the late hour, and a loose necktie. Young, bright-eyed, slightly apologetic, arms akimbo.

"So you're the CIA guy. I'm Agent Peters. Good to meet you. Agent Walker thinks you're a pretty swell fellow."

Mueller arched an eyebrow. "He does, does he?" Mueller mumbled something meant to convey modesty. Gratuitous compliments bothered Mueller. Flattery held in its offering the possibility of an unwanted seduction.

"So what were you doing in Union Station?"

Mueller gave a story about the spectacle of the train wreck drawing crowds and he'd gone to see what the commotion was all about. Mueller saw skepticism crisp the agent's face. They both knew this was a game. Agent Peters placed things taken from Mueller on the table like an offering: his wallet, keys, loose change, a handwritten note from Beth, even the ticket stub from her performance at the National Theater that had stayed in his pocket all week.

Mueller looked up. "My briefcase?"

"There's another agent on his way. He'll have questions for you."

Mueller knew the danger he was in. A trio of missteps had put him in jeopardy. An unauthorized meeting with the other side. His briefcase had held classified cables, now in the hands of people not authorized to read them. It would get him a reprimand—another. Failure to lock his safe at night. Removing documents from the office. He was less concerned about that oversight. The danger lay in Vasilenko's documents. Information that suggested Mueller was doing the FBI's job would sound alarms, excite calls, raise concerns. Mueller didn't know how to evaluate that risk.

. . .

Midnight. The sound of his name. His leg had gone to sleep. He wished the rest of him would join it. It was excruciating to be awake on a hard chair, wanting the sedation of sleep but being too keyed up to succumb. Mueller opened his eyes. A man in the door. Mueller looked at his watch. An hour. It felt like an eternity.

"George Mueller?"

Who did they think was in the room? Insufferable underlings tested his urge to say something he might regret. "Yes."

"I'm Agent Colson."

The bright light revealed the man's ugliness. He was the one from Union Station. He had a fat neck, wire-rim eyeglasses that pressed into the flesh on his temples, thick lenses that made his eyes small and intense, like a bird of prey, and a single black hair sprouted from a discolored mole on his chin.

"Do you have anything to say?"

Mueller focused on the man's eyes to avoid staring at the mole hair. "About?"

"What you were doing in Union Station?"

"When did it become a crime to be in a train station?"

"You're not going to answer?"

"I just did."

"You can make this easy or you can make this difficult."

"Let's go with the easy. How's that?"

Agent Colson leaned forward and put his face close enough to Mueller to taste the foul breath of his growled words. "Don't fuck with me."

Mueller sat back in his chair and took a moment to consider the flash of anger on the agent's face. He knew the drill, the intimidation, the pressure to make a mistake that would be used against him. So Mueller relented to the interrogation. The agent's questions came at a staccato clip, one after the other, questions repeated as if his answer had been forgotten, and when he repeated his answer he got back hostile silence. No, he didn't know what was in the envelope. He had not opened it. No, he didn't read Russian. After an hour of this, Agent Colson walked out.

●   ●   ●

Early in the morning, Mueller was awakened from a fitful sleep that wasn't sleep at all but a recess from consciousness. His watch told him it was dawn outside, but inside there was only the incessant fluorescent light, the blank walls, his table, the empty chair opposite, the same ten square feet of cell. His neck ached from the long awkward position of his head on the miserable table, his mouth was dry, and his right leg had gone painfully numb. His clothes were clammy with body odor and his cheeks darkened with day-old stubble.

William Walker stood in the door. He came with a hint of cologne that perfumed the cell's stale air. Walker had the alert composure of a man who'd had a good night's sleep and was ready to greet the day.

Finally, Walker. They were getting themselves organized, Mueller thought. Each agent was a step up the chain of command, and a step toward a responsible conversation to straighten things out.

"I didn't expect to see you here," Walker said in his friendly drawl. "You in trouble?"

"I don't think so."

"You don't think so?"

It was the tone of Walker's voice that alerted Mueller. "I am available to be convinced, but, no, I don't think so."

"We're friends, aren't we? How long have we worked this together?" Walker turned the chair around and sat facing Mueller, elbows resting on the back. He leaned forward, exciting a crack in the wood joinery. "I'm going to ask you some questions. That okay with you? Then we'll take it from there. Try not to be too fresh. That's not helpful."

"Fine."

"What were you doing in Union Station?"

Mueller's surprise swelled in sudden laughter.

"What's so funny?"

They didn't know. He could count on Vasilenko for the usual caution. "Picking up an envelope. You opened my briefcase. You have the envelope. You've read what's inside, or gotten someone to read it. How's your Russian?"

"Picking up from whom?"

"You know who. You followed him. Yuri Vasilenko. NKVD. We recruited him in Vienna. His cover is trade. He was transferred here from New York and he continues to be useful." Mueller added. "Intelligence not counterintelligence."

Walker had no expression on his face, but he gripped the chair, and then released it and smiled. It was a smile that wasn't quite a smile. "You know the rules."

Mueller frowned.

"No one informed us."

Mueller waited to be lectured. "I have to be in the office."

"This isn't over, George. You're now a person of interest."
Walker stood. "There's a shower down the hall if you want to get
rid of your stink. I've alerted Coffin. He's on his way."

· · ·

Mueller met with his CIA colleague and the head of FBI counterintelligence in a second-floor conference room with a view
of the Potomac. A brace of flags surrounded a large portrait of
newly inaugurated President Eisenhower. Someone had merci-
fully found coffee and it sat on the table beside a tray with three
cups. Faint light from the dawning sun's corona fretted the tree
line and revealed fog on the river.

Mueller was alone for the first thirty minutes. He was restless, with the edgy, exhausted restlessness of a night without
sleep, head slumped on a table. He sat, stood, sat again, and fidgeted with a pencil he took from a container of sharpened pencils.
He twice glanced toward the closed door expecting the person
passing in the hallway to enter, but neither did. He was anxious
in a way that made him uncomfortable. His mind was drawn to
outcomes that he didn't want to consider. Bad outcomes.

Mueller stood abruptly when Walker came through the
door. James Coffin followed close behind. Coffin wore a dark
mackintosh and his homburg, which he hung on a stand by the
window. His thick black hair was flecked with gray and combed
straight back and he was fully alert at this early hour of the day.

His expression was flat, opaque, and his eyes followed Mueller as he walked around the table. He wore thin-soled leather shoes and a bespoke English suit. He nodded at Mueller, his only concession to the fact that they knew each other. Coffin lit a cigarette.

"Good morning," Mueller said.

"Yes, George. Here we are."

Walker poured himself a cup of coffee and sipped it standing up—his conference room, his territory, his command. Walker opened the meeting. He offered a mild rebuke for the lack of cooperation between the FBI and the CIA. He gave a short lecture on the law and reminded the two CIA officers that they could work together, as their charters required, or they could work apart, and in that case it was likely that things would come apart. The CIA, he reminded them, gathered intelligence. The FBI arrested spies and protected secrets. "Things don't end up well when we try to do each other's jobs. Do you understand? I'm reasonable, but I work for a man who has less tolerance for your swagger. Do you understand?"

Silence lingered in the room after Walker ended his little speech. Mueller squeezed the pencil to contain his impatience. Coffin held a filtered cigarette in long delicate fingers. "Understood," he said.

Walker paced the length of the table and turned to Mueller. "You met Vasilenko four times in the past two months." He threw a typed document at Mueller. "Our agents saw you together. Whiskey Bar on the fifth, then once in a parked car near the Carlton Hotel, and last night at Union Station. We're supposed to be informed whenever one of you guys meets a Russian.

We weren't. We got one report. We never got another. Did you write them? Or did we just not get copied? What's going on here, gentlemen?"

Walker looked directly at Mueller. "Tell me, George, are you the one we're looking for? Is that why he never showed up that night at Lafayette Park? Because the fucking Judas was right next to me? Am I the biggest fool in this town?"

Coffin tapped the fragile ash of his cigarette on the saucer. He didn't look up and he spoke in a perfunctory voice. "Calm down. We need proof we've been penetrated. Otherwise we are just speculating." He looked at Mueller and delivered an order disguised as a request. "George, would you step outside for a moment?"

Mueller waited in the corridor. He fidgeted with the pencil, fingers rolling it over his knuckles, and marked time. He paced the corridor traveling to a secretary's desk and then back, repeating this pattern until bored. He was tempted to put his ear to the closed conference room door, but secretaries who'd arrived in the office early had their eye on him. He didn't like the attention. It was a place of suspicions. A stranger in their midst. A secretary removed a file from her desk to hide it from view. Then other employees arrived, greeting each other in resonant voices until they saw Mueller, and then their demeanor became guarded and they spoke to each other in a conspiratorial hush. Harsh fluorescent light gave their faces a pasty hue. It was a cramped place, hardly ventilated, and Mueller caught the faint hint of a cigarette. Dawn and already smoking.

How long would they be? Mueller looked at the closed door,

at his watch, and then he glanced again at the diligent secretaries who typed, making an incessant clacking, while others stood at the water cooler gossiping. Fifteen minutes had passed. He had an urge to punch the wall.

Suddenly the door opened. Coffin nodded at Mueller to rejoin the group. Mueller sat where he'd left his coffee, and he looked from one man to the other, seeking a clue to what they'd discussed, searching for anything that would hint at his fate. Part of him wanted to be done with the whole charade.

"Well," he said.

"What happened in Vienna?" Walker asked.

"Vienna?" *Think.* "I don't understand the question," Mueller said.

"You were in Vienna in 'forty-eight. Correct?"

"Yes."

"You were in contact with the Soviets there, correct?"

"Yes." *What was in the papers? What had Vasilenko turned over?* Mueller looked at the two men. "Berlin had been blockaded. We knew they were running a network out of Vienna and I went there to find out what we could about their intentions in Berlin. It was unstable. Food riots on May fifth paralyzed the city. Berlin, Vienna, Bern. We were looking for agents disillusioned with communism, or wanting a paycheck. I was sent to build a network. I'm not sure I'm answering your question." Mueller looked at his interrogators. It incensed him to be questioned about the quality of his work. It was his worst trait, the self-righteous indignation he felt for the sacrifices he'd made, nights lost, marriage broken, health squandered—for what? They were all adults here doing their jobs.

"What's the point?" he snapped. "What are you looking for?" His fist hit the table harder than he intended. "Are you questioning my commitment here?"

"Calm down, George," Walker said. "We have questions and we need some answers. For the moment you can go. We'll be in touch. But don't leave the city."

The meeting ended. Mueller followed Coffin out of the building into chilly morning air. They drove to Quarter's Eye in Coffin's car in the light traffic of early commuters making good time on Pennsylvania Avenue. It was his English sports car with cracked leather seats and a quaint speedometer limited to the speed the car could actually reach. Cigarette butts overflowed the ashtray. This eccentric car was one of Mueller's only windows into Coffin's personal life.

Mueller turned to Coffin. "What did Vasilenko turn over?"

"I don't know. I haven't seen the material. Walker's got it and he says that he will keep it until he knows what's going on. I don't think we can risk a confrontation over this. We need to pick our fights, and this isn't a fight we are in a position to win, or perhaps it's better said that our chances are uncertain. He has something he won't share so he's got a trump card. There may be nothing. If so, he's playing us. It's regrettable that you were picked up."

"Very regrettable."

"Who picked the men's room?"

"He did."

"Why?"

"He doesn't give me his reasons." Mueller sounded more sarcastic than he intended. "The plan always had that risk."

There was a beat of silence.

"You left your safe unlocked."

That again. Mueller gazed out the window at a squad of marines jogging along the Mall. He resented the new order of things that substituted bureaucracy for the good judgment of men hired for their intelligence and initiative. Quit. Resign. He knew that it would no longer be that simple.

"I straightened one thing out," Coffin said. He leaned forward into the windshield, looking through the fog. "I said you were authorized to take classified documents home. I settled that with him." Coffin turned sideways to Mueller, dark eyes casting a judgment. "It doesn't look good at best. You had sensitive cables in your possession when you met with a high-ranking member of the NKVD. . . . Would you take a polygraph?"

The implications of the request settled in one syllable at a time. He was under suspicion. The oxygen of trust was sucked out of the air.

"What's your concern?"

"We just need to put this behind us."

• • •

Mueller's polygraph was conducted the next morning. He'd been polygraphed once, but not when he left the disbanded OSS to join the CIA as one of the Agency's first recruits. Those first officers who came over were all known to each other, soldiers who'd fought together against the Nazis, men of intelligence, class, integrity, men known for their willingness to set aside rules, particularly arbitrary rules, to accomplish their mission, but those heady days of lax supervision were gone. Calcifying bureaucracy had set in, and with it, the polygraph.

Mueller knew that the polygraph was designed, in part, to intimidate the subject. If the device was successful in detecting lies, it was because the subject thought it worked. The lie detector didn't actually measure lies, the choices a man made to conceal or prevaricate. It didn't measure free will. It recorded excitement. It recorded changes in breathing, blood pressure, heart beat, and sweat. Mueller understood the theory. All case officers did. When a person lied, the stress produced physiological changes that could be measured. And case officers knew the techniques of how to lie without detection. This was a popular topic of conversation at Friday vespers after the second bottle of Scotch whiskey had been opened. Officers shared tips on how to rehearse answers to condition a response. Squeezing toes in shoes before answering. Biting the tongue. Four hundred milligrams of over-the-counter meprobamate taken an hour before the test. All strategies for lying successfully. Everyone had advice, an opinion, a complaint about the process. Everyone also had a lie. Mueller knew there was no special magic. Confidence was the most important thing. Confidence and a friendly relationship with the examiner—rapport, where you smiled and made him like you. Simply not caring about the consequences was a strategy too.

Mueller met the operator at 10:00 a.m. Mueller didn't like the test, he didn't like the idea that he was being tested, and he took a dislike to the young man who was his test operator. He had a dull, military appearance—crew cut, narrow tie, dark suit, a big athletic build and an impassive face that Mueller couldn't approach, even if he had wanted to. Mueller tried to look happy to be there.

The operator went over the test procedure. He gave Mueller the list of subjects that he would ask questions about and Mueller looked up when he'd finished reviewing the long, single-spaced document that could have been a book.

"You've forgotten something," he said caustically, leafing through the long document.

That got the operator's attention.

Mueller bit his tongue.

The operator attached Mueller to the machine, taping wires to chest, thigh, arm, and hand.

"Ready?"

Mueller nodded.

"We're recording this, so a nod doesn't qualify as an answer. You have to speak. Understand?"

Mueller had never been good at taking orders or being corrected, and the operator's tone of voice deepened his aggravation that he had to be there in the first place. "Yes. Let's get on with it, shall we?"

He was asked his name, address, place of birth, parents' names—neutral subjects that produced a rhythm to the session. The second series of questions related to his early work at the OSS and the Agency.

"How long were you stationed in Vienna?"

"Nineteen forty-seven to nineteen forty-nine."

"Exact dates?"

"I don't have the day or week. Is that necessary? They're in my files. You can check there."

"The exact dates, please."

Mueller paused. "January, I don't know, second week of January nineteen forty-seven to December twenty-fifth, nineteen forty-nine. I resented flying on Christmas. That's how I know the date."

"What were your responsibilities?"

"Operations. I ran Soviet agents."

"How many?"

"Half a dozen?"

"Six?"

Mueller nodded.

"Speak the answer."

"Six."

"What can you tell me about Vienna?"

"Vienna? A divided city. Dirty. Cold. Rusting tanks still sat in the street. The Soviets were always looking to stir up trouble. I lived in the American sector near the Danube, which smelled terribly because the sewage plant didn't have fuel and buildings discharged waste straight into the water."

"Were you married at the time?"

"Yes."

"Czech?"

How did they know that? "What type of question is that?"

"Answer it, please."

Mueller was cautious. "Yes."

"Did you mention her nationality in your activity report?"

"No."

"Your wife worked with you in operations. It says here she was your translator. Is that correct?"

"Yes."

"Did the Russians approach you to work for them?"

"All the time."

"Did you work for them?"

Mueller looked directly at the operator. "No."

"Did they offer you money?"

"For what?"

"For any reason?"

"No. . . . I take that back. A Soviet colonel bought me a drink once. I let him pay," Mueller threw out. "I mentioned that in my weekly report."

The operator looked at his typed list of questions. "Have you ever taken classified documents home?"

"Yes."

"How many times?"

They knew of one. "Three times."

"You're lying about that."

"No, I'm not lying."

"You're nervous, aren't you?"

"You're making me nervous."

"Do you take drugs?"

"I did not take meprobamate this morning."

"Do you take drugs?"

"No." He snapped his answer and he glared at the operator. This is what they wanted. They wanted to get him agitated. Muel-

ler let his tension flow from his chest to his arms down his hands and then discharge from his fingertips into an imaginary bucket. Everyone needed a strategy to get through the polygraph. The morning session lasted four hours and broke for lunch. He had sweated through his shirt. He had been mostly calm, and he'd bitten his tongue when a stupid question provoked his desire to respond sarcastically. He stared out the window and kept coming back to the same nagging question. How did they know his ex-wife was Czech? Her family claimed to be Austrian to avoid being deported by the Soviets to the east. How did they know where her parents lived, her maiden name, and the background of her family? The end of one question in his mind became the beginning of another, and he found himself parsing the meanings of the operator's words, meanings that were overt and obvious but within each question were hidden consequences. His anger flared from the torrent of compromising words. That emotion was alive when the operator fixed wires to his body for the afternoon session.

"Do you know Yuri Vasilenko?"

They knew he did. "Yes."

"Who is he?"

"It's all in the file. Soviet NKVD. People's Commissariat for Internal Affairs. Father of a talented boy. I've met the boy. You can mark that down. Someone might find it relevant."

"How many times did you meet Vasilenko in the past two months?"

"Probably eight times."

"Did you write a report of each meeting?"

"No."

"How many reports did you write?"

"Five."

"When was your first meeting with Vasilenko?"

"Early March. Stalin was already dead. I don't remember the exact date. It was in Centreville."

"Were you alone?"

Beth. "Yes."

The operator looked up from his machine's dials. "Were you alone when you met Vasilenko in early March?"

Mueller felt his heart beat with his deception. Mueller saw the operator make a note. He snapped, "I was not alone. I was with a woman. Keep her out of this."

The operator stood and left the room. What bothered them was deception. One deception put all his questions in jeopardy.

15

QUAIL HUNTING

Y OU FAILED," the director said. It was a vague remark. He
could have been speaking about a bad opening night at the
National Theatre.

Mueller sat next to the director on an electric golf cart that
bumped along a carriage path that meandered through a field of
dry, clumped grass near Chesapeake Bay. Two shotguns poked
out of golf bags in the backseat, and a .22 caliber pistol lay on
the director's lap. The director pointed to a small blue- and gold-
flecked bird with white collar that ran on sturdy legs and disappeared into the brush. *"Sonofabitch,"* he cried. "She's running
from her clutch. Taking our eyes away from the chicks she's protecting. Patience, George, patience. We're close. We'll get one."
The director slowed the golf cart and put his hand on his long-
barrel pistol. The flush of excitement added to the reddening effect of the hot sun beating down from a turquoise sky.

"You failed," he repeated, to make sure he'd been heard. "You were sassy, but it wasn't that. The last question. Everything else was fine."

Mueller was silent. He stopped himself from saying what he wanted to say. Mueller knew it wasn't good form not to care about the test and the new rules.

The director glanced at Mueller. "Fine until he asked about the girl."

"I don't want Beth involved."

"You'll have to step off the Council."

"And onto the list?"

"You're on the list." The director cast a sideways glance. "Since Walker's men picked you up in Union Station. *Jesuschrist*, George, a men's room?" The director cast his eyes over the terrain for a likely habitat. "Take the polygraph again."

"It doesn't measure anything except excitement. You know that. He got me excited. I don't believe in it."

"Neither do I. But Coffin needs a clean pass. You can't talk yourself out of a lie. Even a silly lie. It colors the whole session. One deception brings on all of his paranoid speculations, and he's kept a list of every tiny detail of your sloppy work that he's turning into a goddamn project. We aren't a club anymore. Those days are gone. Pass the test. Let's move on. I need you on the Council."

Mueller gripped his seat against the bumps on the path that came faster as the director pushed the golf cart's speed. He was jostled and when he looked at the director, he was surprised at the pleasure he took driving fast, almost recklessly.

"We've known each other how long?" the director asked, speaking over the noise. Wind lifted his thinning hair. He had the flushed exuberance of a hunter. "I don't trust many people, George, but I trust you. I trust you because I know you. This town resents us, you and me. They resent that I get the calls from the president asking what's going on in Moscow. Well, you know, I don't have a goddamn clue what's going on, but I can't tell him that."

The director brought the golf cart to an abrupt stop. He looked at Mueller. "Pass the test. The FBI can't interfere if Coffin tells them you've passed. There are techniques, you know. A pill."

Mueller nodded.

"This is a good spot. The brush over there has got something. Grab a shotgun." Mueller took his and gave the other to the director, who cupped hands to his mouth and whistled, producing a clear, three-note call. He repeated it twice.

It was Mueller's nature to be cooperative and agreeable, and he found it difficult to reject a direct plea. He had discovered that the thing that got him in trouble in his adult life was his tolerance. With it came a willingness to accede to requests others made of him. He wasn't rude, or as rude as he could be. Senior positions were held by rude, impatient men who shouted to get their way, slammed fists in meetings, yelled at secretaries for the slightest scheduling error, or some other minor infraction. These men resented that Mueller's long acquaintance with the director gave him access above his grade. He and the director shared a quality of empathy. It was its own sort of club. Not good for espionage work. But good for living. They could sit in a crowded room with loud ranting case officers, and with a quick sideways glance, acknowledge each other like amused conspirators.

The director lifted his shotgun and pointed to clumped grass near the field's edge, thirty feet distant.

"Beria was arrested," the director said, splitting his concentration. "We got word this morning. He was arrested in the middle of a presidium meeting, right there in front of their top leadership. Grabbed at the podium. It's a rat hole in Moscow now. Impossible to know what's going on. I read all the cable traffic and you can't make heads or tails of the place. It's a power struggle. Purges are coming. Beria is the first."

The director sighted down the shotgun barrel at a low bush. One eye closed, sighting on the target, he added, "Malenkov had his picture in Pravda yesterday where the only other person visible is Stalin. Stalin's been dead a month. It's an old photo. This is what we're reduced to, George, speculating about who is going to succeed Stalin by looking at photos in the newspaper. What we need is our own goddamn Protocol."

The director lowered his shotgun and studied another clump of grass and evaluated its prospects for quail.

"It's a very unstable time. The Soviets have a hate-America campaign on. They are talking up their good friends the Red Chinese. I've got Eisenhower calling up every morning asking what I think is going on—*Sonofabitch*. Look over there."

The director fired his shotgun harmlessly into the air. The explosion of sound excited the grass and a covey of quail alighted, flying almost vertically like helicopters. The director whipped his long-barrel .22 pistol from his lap and got off three quick shots. One quail dropped straight to the ground.

"It mangles them a bit," the director said. "Tough to eat. But it's better sport."

The director turned to Mueller and laid down his pistol. Mueller felt the pause in the director's thinking. He knew they'd come to the point of the meeting.

"No one can know what we're doing. No one. We need to handle this ourselves. That's always been true, but now, today, it's urgent." He looked at Mueller. "What I am going to say has to stay between us. I trust Coffin, but he sees evil where there is only human error, and he will take us down a rat hole. I like Roger, but I don't trust him. He's someone they could turn. I agree with Coffin on that. So, that leaves you. Pass the test. When we've got Protocol you can go off to your ivory tower. That's our bargain."

The director started the golf cart and headed back to their parked car. "Does Protocol exist?" he asked in a singsong. He looked at Mueller, who gripped his seat against the bounding car. "What if there is no Protocol? What if the Soviets planted the idea of Protocol so we tie ourselves in knots looking for the Heffalump?"

There was a beat of silence between the two men.

"They're better at this game than we are, you know."

Mueller knew this was his test. "Protocol exists. They're protecting him."

16

WITHDRAWAL

MUELLER SAT in his cluttered office on the third floor of Quarter's Eye and gazed out the window. There was a mildew smell brought on by the humidity and cold in the underheated building; ventilation in the old barracks had never been properly installed, and this hint of mold was always there to remind him of the temporary nature of his office.

His mind was in turmoil. The thought of submitting himself to a second polygraph test was profoundly repugnant. For what? To be irritated again? They'd now focus on Beth, and he didn't want to go down that path. Of course, he knew that the point of it was to provide an objective measure of his usefulness—*Did I use the word "usefulness"?* he thought. He'd meant "truthfulness." He smiled at his unconscious conflation of words. Playing *their* game bothered him, because he no longer wanted in on the game, and his discontent surfaced and forced the error. What was the point of a second test? He would fail that too.

It didn't surprise Mueller that colleagues and secretaries seemed to know of his failure. Polygraph results stayed confidential, but the fact that you'd taken the test was not, and there was always gossip and speculation. Secrets were restless things. Secrets got out. When he got into the office that afternoon, he got a sideways glance from the receptionist, and he heard a secretary lower her voice conspiratorially as he passed her desk. Secretaries were always the first to know. He'd detected a vague reticence in the man who occupied the office next to his, a hail-fellow-well-met man who always offered a loud greeting. No one said anything, but everyone knew. Mueller had failed.

What surprised Mueller was that he hadn't seen it coming. He'd stepped around a privet hedge in his Alice in Wonderland world and fallen through a trapdoor. He felt like he was playing a walk-on role that someone had written for him. Things that had once been clear were now opaque and his options had narrowed. The motivations of men around him were suspect, and he no longer knew whom to trust. He no longer knew how much of what he knew he could believe. Yes, he had mistakenly taken his briefcase with him to the station, and that was an error, but that hid the deeper issue that infected his judgment. He just didn't care anymore and for that reason he hadn't seen this coming. He needed to get out.

Mueller opened his desk drawer and removed the envelope with the letter of resignation that he'd written but not sent. Three sentences. Short and to the point. He had already signed the letter, so in a sense he had resigned in his mind, and all that remained was to announce his decision. He considered a brace of doubts. Would he be blacklisted? Would he lose the teaching position he'd been offered? And how would the cloud of suspicion over him play out in a long tail of an FBI inquiry? His mind repeated the questions, but he had no answers. He sealed the envelope.

He called his secretary.

Dorothy was at his door promptly. A young widow of the war who'd moved to the capital from the Deep South, and stayed on after she got the grievous news on D-Day. She was polite, well educated, and smart beyond the needs of the office.

"Would you see that this goes to Rose, the director's secretary?" She stood alertly in front of his desk. He handed her the envelope.

"I'll take it now."

"Monday," he said.

"Not tomorrow?"

"I won't be in the office tomorrow," he said vaguely.

"Are you taking the day off?"

"It doesn't really concern you." He said this without thinking.

Afterward, it struck him that he hadn't needed to be brusque like that. She was only doing her job. It was up to her to manage his appointments and take his calls, and she'd need to know what to say if someone came looking for him. It would be a poor reflection on her if she didn't have an answer other than "I don't know." He should have thought of that.

These thoughts came to him on the Greyhound bus to Centreville. It was late. He was alone on the last bus out of town Thursday ahead of the first weekenders who would start traveling in the morning. He didn't want to worry about who might be on the bus to see him, so he'd gone at an off-hour. He needed time alone to consider his next steps.

He stepped off the bus at 11:00 p.m. Mist from the bay had rolled in and hung low to the ground between budding trees and the silence of the night. What struck him first was the quiet. The bus's growling engine had faded and there was only the mournful foghorn in the distance and somewhere along the street the tinny sound of a radio. He glanced up the street and then in the opposite direction toward the white church. There was no one out. Main Street was empty except for the sheriff's patrol car parked in front of the courthouse. He found his bicycle chained to the lamppost where he'd left it weeks before. A dog loped along the sidewalk but paid no attention to the stranger attaching a duffel bag to his bike. Alone and free. He wondered how long that would last.

He was a solitary bicyclist on the narrow road to his cottage. He had worried his leg wasn't healed well enough to pedal that distance, but found he had no difficulty. Fresh air filled his lungs and he concentrated on the small world that opened in front of him on the dark road. Out of nowhere a car came up from behind and illuminated a tunnel into the night, and Mueller suddenly gripped the handlebars tighter, preparing for the impact of wind. Terror squeezed his chest and then just as suddenly the automobile sped past and disappeared into the night.

Mueller entered the cottage with the key above the doorjamb. The kitchen was cold, but little had changed since he'd left. Beth's flowers had dried and their colors faded. He tossed them in the garbage and then went to the living room. He didn't turn on the light, but lay on the sofa. Moonlight entered the bay windows where the owner had closed in the porch.

Mueller put his head on a pillow and gazed at the ceiling. His shoes were on and so was his overcoat. He placed his hands on his chest, palms down. The moon hung in the sky like a lantern and washed his face in metallic light. The room was otherwise dark. He lay on the cusp of sleep, but sleepless, for a long time. His eyes gazed at the ceiling looking at nothing and seeing only shimmering shapes as clouds disturbed the moonlight. His mind drifted to the past, and to the moments of his youth and regrets for things done, or left undone, and his whole body filled with powerful emotion. His mind was a jerky kinescope of scenes from college, the war, and from Vienna.

It seemed to him that all the moments of his life occupied the same space, the past collected in the present, and future events already existed and were waiting for him to find his way to them—just as he knew what to expect when he got to the office and his secretary greeted him with her predictable cheerfulness. He knew what to expect tomorrow, and the day after, and the day after that. He simply had to wait in his loneliness for his future to arrive.

For no reason he thought of May fifth, Vienna, the night of the food riots, when he'd been stuck in the Soviet zone waiting for the turmoil to subside so he could return to the Innere Stadt. He remembered gangs of children racing through the narrow streets without shoes, desperate, hungry, moving in waves, disappearing and then reappearing. He was on his way to visit his son at his estranged wife's apartment, and he'd been making his way to an unguarded spot where someone who knew the city grid could slip in and out of the Soviet sector. He remembered windowless Soviet military vehicles racing toward the children, the city frozen in terror that they'd be detained and sent east to a camp. He waited at a corner, taking longer than he should to make his way to safety, as he worried these children were at risk. Young boys no older than twelve or thirteen, and many younger, desperate for safety, racing past barriers of smoldering car tires. No one knew how terrible it would be. Chaos had come suddenly from a single gunshot on the peaceful march, and then the noise, confusion, and desperate movements of children who'd been gathered together to show the world the face of a starving city. And he remembered seeing Roger Altman hard against a building seeking cover from the rampaging troops. He too was at the point of entry to the safe alley separating the American zone from the Soviet. That had surprised Mueller, and then he'd seen Altman risk his life for one of those children. A young girl had fallen, her leg cracked when she caught her ankle in a wide sewer grating. Altman ran out and took the innocent girl from the street just as a Soviet jeep bore down. He saved her life. Mueller came back to this uncomfortable recollection from time to time, and sometimes it would come to him out of nowhere, ambush him while he was resting, or reading, or waiting for the trolley. He'd look up at nothing and see that night in his mind's eye. He could be walking through a quiet neighborhood in Georgetown where nothing had changed in years, and he'd see the face of a girl, and he'd feel, almost physically feel, the memory leap out at him, and time would slow down in the gravitational pull of the past. He never asked Altman why he'd been there that night. He never wanted to know. He remembered only how he'd saved the girl's life.

. . .

Fiery noon. Mueller looked out the cottage's sunroom window at the bay. The day's fine weather was almost mocking. Molten sunshine bore down mercilessly from a blue sky. A light breeze rustled spring flowers budding in the tired earth and two gulls, carried on the wind, held a vigil above the cove.

Mueller lifted his binoculars and looked at the pink Soviet compound across the narrow stretch of water. The green Buick and black sedan he'd seen before were again parked in the drive-way. There was a strange quiet to the place. It was Saturday, but the tennis courts were empty and there was no sign of life. With the binoculars he saw that the second-floor curtains were drawn.

Mueller hadn't heard from Vasilenko and he was curious about that. He owed Vasilenko money for his last drop. News coming from Moscow was reverberating throughout the chain of command and the director had gotten it right that it was impossible to know whether Stalin had been dead for some time—murdered—or died in the way medical bulletins said he had. All signs pointed to a purge.

The loud honk of a car warned Mueller that someone had arrived. A car door slammed shut and he heard his name called, and then again. Then he heard the kitchen door burst open.

"So you are here." Beth stood in the open door, arms akimbo. "Are you okay? You look like you haven't slept."

"I'm fine," he said. "I took a late bus." He tried to smile to be pleasant, but the expression on his face was lost to a nagging preoccupation. Mueller stood slowly. It surprised him that he was touched she had come by, but he was at a loss for words, uncertain whether he should bring up the incident at the party. His eyes drifted as he searched for the right words.

"Your secretary didn't know where you'd gone. She said you'd taken the day off."

Secretary? He looked directly at Beth.

"I got your number from Roger. I wanted to invite you to dinner. To make up for being rude at the party. If I was rude. So, here I am, in person."

"I see."

"You missed the winter races."

His expression was blank.

"You know, people on sailboats trying their best to finish first."

He'd forgotten. "Who won?"

"A crew from the Naval Academy." She laughed. "Roger thought they cheated."

There was a beat of silence.

"How was your week?" she asked.

Mueller shook his head. "Miserable. About as bad as it could get."

"We have that in common, for what it's worth, but I expect it's not worth much. We had a scare when our dog disappeared, but then she came back. The threatening calls have stopped. Will you come to dinner tonight?"

Her hands were plunged in her pockets, and she stood awkwardly like a schoolgirl. "Will you?"

It bothered Mueller that he had the power to disappoint her. He wasn't ready for that responsibility. "What time?"

"Early if you want a drink. Say six. Roger will be there. Shall I pick you up?"

He nodded at a canoe that he'd pulled ashore earlier that morning. "I'll paddle. It's not far."

They stood side by side at her red convertible in the gravel driveway, hesitant, each waiting for the other to say a word, or make a gesture of separation—but neither did. She waited for him to say something, and when he didn't, she slipped into the driver's seat and slammed the door. She drove off.

• • •

Quiet dusk. Mueller sipped iced tea on the back porch of the Altmans' grand Victorian home and stared at a girl playing under a wide oak tree. He was alone at a table set for dinner. The little girl was playing by herself in the deepening shadows, only a child. Six years old, if that. From a low branch there was a swing made of rope and an old tire. The scrawny little girl was skipping rope. Her face was pale, hair wild, feet without shoes, and her dress too large. She looked clumsy each time she brought the rope over her head and made an effort to hop.

Mueller gazed at the girl, about his boy's age, he thought. He heard vague, excited voices in the kitchen. Then a woman ran out of the back door and swept the child into her arms. It was Roger's fiancée. She wiped dirt from the child's face and then carried her quickly in a protective embrace to the housekeeper's cottage that sat in the rear of the main house.

"The girl isn't Roger's, if you're wondering."

Beth had come up quietly behind Mueller and now stood at his side, wiping her hands on her apron. She nodded brusquely toward the cottage where the woman had disappeared with her daughter. "He helped her out of a jam. They have an arrangement. He gives her a little money each month and she plays along as his companion. It's good for both of them."

Beth looked at Mueller, suddenly appalled. "I'm telling you this in confidence. Do you understand? You must never repeat it." Her eyes had opened wide and were worried. "Roger would kill me if he knew I'd told you."

Mueller nodded agreement. He wasn't happy to have this obligation to her. A promise held within itself the source of its own disappointment.

She forced a smile. "We're almost ready to eat. Roger is finishing dessert. I think he's making a berry pie. He hates to cook, but he has one berry pie recipe that he makes when we have friends over. The kitchen here makes cooks out of all of us noncooks."

She sat beside Mueller in a cane chair and poured herself a glass of red wine from the decanted bottle. She leisurely sipped from the stemmed glass. They sat in the gloaming with a view of the dying twilight sun on the horizon. High up above the trees there was a remnant of blue sky. Slowly, Beth leaned forward. "How long have you known my brother?"

Mueller was tempted to pour himself a glass of the wine. Alcohol made it easier to speak in half-truths. He saw it in all his colleagues. Deception. Stress. Hard drinking. It was a bad combination.

"We were at Yale together."

"Roommates?"

"Different years."

"What was he like in college?"

"Like? Mixed up, like the rest of us. A little quiet, a deep reader. He impressed all of us with his intelligence. He read poetry. A lot of Ezra Pound. Shakespeare's sonnets. And then there was this other side of him—the political side. We said that he had the anticommunist fervor of an ardent socialist. If the Spanish Civil War hadn't just been lost, I think he would have volunteered. He was romantic about things like war and freedom and friendship. He liked to quote that line, I forget who said it, Kipling or Forster: 'If one had the choice of betraying one's country or one's friend, one should hope for the courage to betray one's country.' . . . Idealism is an illness that strikes young men. We found it easy to believe what we wanted to be true."

"You were like that too?"

"In my own way. I didn't have his passion."

Beth gazed at Mueller. "I never saw that side of him. I was twelve when he left home. He was the tall, handsome older brother who always had a group of friends around. A girl at his side, or a man. The men were all funny and clever, and the women were funny and clever too, but sexless. I remember thinking that he inhabited a totally different planet than the one I was on. I tagged along when I could, the kid sister who got in the car with these terribly smart people. I was in awe, really. I would look in their faces and give them imaginary lives, just like I gave lives to the people in front of Saint Patrick's who dropped a coin in my Salvation Army bucket." Beth's eyes had drifted off, but they returned to look at Mueller. "You know him pretty well."

"We've known each other. But I don't think you can say I've ever really *known* him."

"I'm not asking for an existential answer, George. No, that's not my point here. Of course, no one knows anyone really. You think you do until there is that one thing that surprises, and you reconsider their entire life in light of that new fact. Well, I know that, but that is not what I was asking. I was simply asking how close the two of you are. You *do* work together."

Mueller saw that Beth had taken her paper napkin and was tearing it in halves, quarters, and eighths. She tossed the shreds into the air. "Puff," she said. "The past isn't what it used to be."

They were quiet for a very long time. She stood and tossed her apron on her chair. "Let me get him. The food must be ready. Are you chilly? Shall we move inside?"

"No. This is fine. Thank you."

"How's the leg?"

Mueller couldn't help himself. He lowered his trousers and displayed the angry scar. "You could practice medicine."

•   •   •

Mueller watched a sturdy little motorboat plow through the bay's choppy water, waves splashing over the bow. The boat churned along without a signal light, and Mueller wouldn't have seen it except that the man at the wheel smoked. Even at that distance the lit end of his cigarette glowed like a tiny beacon. The boat made its way along the shore and then turned sharply to the jutting dock of the Soviet compound.

Mueller heard a creaking floorboard and turned just as Roger Altman and Beth came out to the porch. Altman carried a pot roast garnished with baked potatoes and she held a plate of steamed vegetables. Brother and sister placed dinner on the table.

There was quiet except for bustling dinner preparations and scraping chairs, and when that ended there was just silence. Mueller had gotten over his anger, but he made no effort to engage Altman in conversation. The two men sat opposite each other. Their eyes met.

"Good to see you, George," Altman said. "We wondered where you'd gone off to. Nobody in the office had a clue. They called the morgue. Can you believe that? Then Beth said you were out here."

"I hope it wasn't a secret," Beth said, suddenly concerned.

"No." Mueller nodded at Altman's forehead where a flesh-colored Band-Aid was stretched over an eyebrow. To Beth, "Did he tell you that I tried to kill him with an oar?"

She laughed, but Altman was only mildly amused.

"Three stitches," Altman said. "I was lucky."

Beth leapt from her seat. "I've forgotten the butter. We can't start without butter for the potatoes. Don't start. I want to say grace."

Mueller and Altman sat in silence after Beth ran off to the kitchen. Mueller had no reason to continue to talk about the incident—things like that were best forgotten, confined to memory.

"Bad luck with the FBI," Altman said. "Everything okay?"

"Bad week. I needed time by myself."

"Of course. We all do. Don't fret about the test. I flunked once. There's a pill, you know. Every one of us who is good enough to be worth the trust they place in us does something that doesn't fit into the new regime of rules." Altman nodded toward the cove and the small boat, which was now docked.

"Keeping track of the Russians?" Altman poured himself a generous glass of wine, which he swigged like water. "Something is up over there. Cars coming and going all day. I've got a telescope in the den. After dinner we can take a look."

Dinner was at turns pleasant and quiet, and loud and boisterous. Quiet prevailed when the conversation stuck to the books they'd each read and when they shared their common taste for the grainy black-and-white movies that were coming out of postwar Italy, but it turned raucous and argumentative when they debated the future of democracy. Altman denounced the spectacle of Senate hearings that were marching through its list of witnesses before his father was brought before the television lights again. "Once they get you on the stand," Altman said in defiant complaint, "they ask what they want, and smear you if you refuse to answer. It's bad soap opera. Everyone will be eager to hear what I know about Father."

"You can't let them do that," Beth said, leaning forward.

"Of course I can't, but they'll ask. They'll go on the attack."

Altman opened a second bottle of burgundy, which he drank by himself when Beth covered her glass with her hand. Beth became troubled with the conversation when it lurched to politics, and started to clear the table. She took the stacked dishes into the kitchen, leaving the two men alone. Mueller was sober and Altman not. The breeze off the bay was cool and brought with it the sound of laughter and voices from homes along the cove.

"This too is a question I've considered," Altman said.

Mueller turned his attention away from the bay and the voices. Mueller's thoughts had drifted, but "this too" got his attention and he was curious what he had missed. "This what? Did I miss something?"

"The whole question of—" Altman stopped himself from saying more when Beth returned. She plunked down in her chair.

"Are you still talking politics?"

Altman looked at his sister. "Would you excuse us? We have something we have to discuss. We'll be in for dessert in a moment."

Altman lit a cigar. Two men alone again under a starry night, cicadas all around. Altman blew a smoke ring and then a second ring inside the first. "Coffin isn't handling this well," he said. He looked at Mueller. "He's caught up in the theory of counterintelligence and he looks for proof with logic and analysis, but what he doesn't do, and this is why he will fail, is he doesn't look at the human factor. This is why he is wrong about you. You don't fit the profile of someone who would turn."

Altman enjoyed another draw on his cigar. "If you wanted to turn, how would you make the first contact? Have you thought about that? Would you walk into the Soviet embassy? Here? Overseas? Would you identify yourself with your real name?"

"Are you asking me?" Mueller looked at Altman.

"Yes. I'm curious. How would this have started? Real name to provide your bona fides? Or a fake name to protect yourself?"

Mueller found it an odd conversation. "Real name."

"Why?"

"You need to establish trust."

"I would never use my real name. That puts you in jeopardy. Trust is worthless in this business. Every one of our losses in Europe trusted Protocol." Altman paused. "How do you think it began?"

"Where?"

"How? What started him down the path? It's usually money. We're all craven in our own way. The director's rule. Remember? He wanted a small cadre of good men with a passion for anonymity. That's what he called it. His rule was that only men with money were worth recruiting because they didn't have to rely on a salary for living expenses, and therefore they were incorruptible. This job doesn't pay well enough to put up with the crap we take. You, by the way, fail that profile. I, on the other hand, fit the profile. For what it's worth."

"I have an advantage," Mueller said. "You have money, yes, but I don't care. About any of it."

Altman smiled. "You failed the polygraph. They care."

Mueller gave a short choking laugh. He thought of Beth, whom he saw silhouetted in the window, looking out at them. He looked at Altman. "My indifference is a life preserver against a tide of joyless disappointments."

Altman clapped twice. "Well said. You always could turn a phrase. A little cloak. A little gown." Altman leaned forward and looked directly at Mueller. "You're not indifferent about your son. That's your weakness." Altman looked over his shoulder at his sister, and then continued in a quiet voice. "The first lie is always easy. The difficulty with an untruth is to continue it and to reinforce the lie with more lies to protect the original mendacity, but then the compounding lies become this ungainly artifice that draws attention to itself. Secrecy is about what you don't say, what you say wrongly, what you say too much of, so words become a coil in the listener's mind. The man I trust, George, is the man who remembers his own lies, and it so happens, the man I *distrust* is also that man who remembers his own lies."

Mueller and Altman looked at each other. There was a moment of understanding. Two men sharing something known to them and hidden from others.

"It can get very lonely," Altman said. "People don't understand this life unless they're in it. You understand. You have to have two stories for everything to keep it all in your head. It's exhausting. You can't do it for long. It burns out the best of us."

"They"—and Altman waved at the house—"never know what it costs, the deceiving, the tricks, the isolation. You need another thing to get you out of bed in the morning—a faith, adrenaline, fear. It's hard on a marriage." Altman looked at Mueller. "Yours didn't last long."

Mueller had nothing to add.

"Sometimes the loneliness is intolerable."

The comment didn't surprise Mueller and he waited for it to be followed, but nothing more was said by Altman for a long time. Darkness had fallen completely and the evening surrounded the perimeter of light that came from the table's flickering candle.

"How does it end for Protocol?" Altman asked.

"He's caught or he defects."

A choked release of laughter came from Altman. "Live in a dacha outside of Moscow? Get trotted out as a hero of the Communist state? Parked for life? Me . . . I couldn't bear that, or the consequence of the shame heaped on family. Of course, it's only a matter of time before Protocol is caught. I suspect he has already felt the noose tightening and he's begun to pull away from them, give less. But secrets are like heroin. It's their fix."

Altman paused. "I don't know how this started pointing to you. If I were you I'd take the polygraph again. Clear your name."

The night was late. A chill settled on the two men at the table.

Altman looked at Mueller. "Dessert? I made a pie."

"I'll pass."

"Ride home?"

"I canoed. I'll take it home. It's a nice evening to paddle. Another race tomorrow?"

Altman touched his forehead. "And give you another shot at me?" He laughed. "I don't think so."

17

SHOTS IN THE DARK

WATER HAS two states. It divides effortlessly between rocks disappearing into the tiniest cracks, but its mass resists the hard pull of a paddle. Mueller stroked against the dark bay, and then let his canoe glide silently on the calm water under the tall trees that erupted from the shore. He worked out the tight muscle of his right shoulder that had cramped crossing the cove. Through the trees he could see the Soviet mansion on the bluff.

A full moon hung in the sky. Silvery light danced on the cove's black lacquered surface. Mueller dipped his paddle and pointed the bow to a cluster of pine trees on a spit of land. He pulled the boat ashore in a protected spot. He ran across the beach and quickly gained the cover of the woods, where he dropped to one knee. He listened. Soft sounds loud in his ears. A voice somewhere off in the distance, or perhaps at the mansion. He became aware of the things immediately around him—leaves on the ground, a breeze rustling through high branches, air scented with fresh resin from a nearby pine. He pushed a bush aside and looked for Vasilenko's green Buick. There had been no contact for a week, and Mueller was concerned.

Suddenly light burst from the mansion's front door. Mueller heard men's voices speaking Russian. They spoke quickly, in short grunted commands. These men walked down the mansion's wide steps, dark shapes illuminated from behind by light pouring from the open door. Mueller counted three men in single file. The glow of their flashlights bounced along the path. Mueller made out the vague shape of a fourth man, hands tied behind his back. The group moved along the driveway for twenty yards, but then turned and made its way toward shore.

The restrained man stumbled, but he was supported by his two escorts, who held his arms and marched him forward. One swore under his breath and snapped a command. They walked a little way and stopped in a small clearing. Moonlight gave Mueller a good view of the little entourage. One thinner man who moved with a limp stood apart from the husky shapes. His flashlight pointed to a spot in the clearing. This was the leader. Mueller saw the red glow of his cigarette, and his face, jaw set. He had a dog that strained on a leash. It barked once. At the same moment a gurgling cry cracked like a whip in the quiet night. Startled, Mueller looked closer. The man in the middle had slumped to his knees, hands pulling madly at his neck. Another unhuman moan and the man doubled over like a rag doll. The dog barked loudly twice.

The grave dug by the men was only a temporary place to hide the body. Mueller came to this conclusion when he scraped away the sandy top soil. He worked quickly with bare hands digging in the earth, careful to place what he removed so he could return it to hide the disturbance. The soil was wet, cold, and as he dug deeper he felt winter's bones. The first evidence was the damp cotton of a man's shirt. He pushed dirt away from the dead man's mouth, eyes, forehead, and neck. Mueller struck a match. A necklace of blood ringed the throat. Mueller had not expected to know the man, so he was startled to discover the corpse belonged to the driver who'd run him off the road.

Suddenly, a cry. Someone had found the canoe. Mueller was on his feet. He took a measure of the darkness all around and settled on the excited voices—two men at the shore. Their flashlights illuminated trees and brush in search of the owner. Their cries brought a group of men down the mansion's steps and they hustled in a chaotic pack astride the driveway.

Think! Mueller looked at the corpse. He moved earth to cover his discovery, but his hands couldn't undo in a minute what they had taken fifteen to accomplish. Men from the house were spreading out along the driveway and entered the trees at intervals. The two men at the shore moved their search to the slope. Mueller quietly filled the hole with scattered leaves, working quickly, but in haste he snapped a twig.

Mueller saw one man's beam shift, seeking the source of the sound. In that instant, Mueller looked toward the bay's shimmering surface. He knew that a run to the water risked alerting them to his presence, but there was a greater risk of being found at the grave. The corpse's garroted throat filled Mueller with dread. That could be him. He looked left to the man coming up the slope with a beam pointed head-on, washing him in light. The man held a gun. Men from the house formed an arc closing around Mueller.

"Hey, you," a nearby voice said in a husky accent.

Mueller waited a moment, but then took off. His arms pumped as his legs sprinted in long strides to avoid fallen logs, darting one way, changing direction when he saw a clearer path, hunters in pursuit. The first report of a gun came quickly, followed by the dog's incessant barking. Darkness cast by the canopy of trees covered his escape, but his thrashing through the brush left a trail of sound. Excited voices all around. He kept himself fixed on the beacon of reflected moonlight on the open water. His pursuers had made a judgment about Mueller's intentions and they too changed course and headed to shore. Their flashlight beams bounced erratically as they ran.

Mueller stopped at water's edge. He undid one laced shoe and then did the same with the other. His fingers ripped off socks. He shoved his thighs into the shocking water, stepping from one stone to the next until he climbed a flat rock projecting from the surface. He made a long leaping shallow dive into waist-deep water. Cold locked in around him, knocking out his breath, and the frigid embrace of the bay numbed him. He rose to gulp air and saw tiny splashes to his left where their shots had missed their target. More reports from a gun. In his luckless adventure his fortune changed. One cloud moved in, blocking the full moon, and made it hard to be seen. He went under again, hands pulled in a breaststroke as his legs pushed with froglike thrusts. When his lungs could resist no longer he surfaced, gasping, greedy for air, and then went under again. This he did in an unthinking pattern until completely exhausted.

He had no sense of time. He had counted four shots, but there might have been more. His hand struck a piece of splintered wood floating on the surface and near it, a chunk of scoured Styrofoam.

Mueller paused, head bobbing on the surface, and looked around. The only markers were the distance he'd come and the amount left to swim to the opposite shore. The shrieking in his ears began to subside. He looked back where he'd left the shore. Dark shapes stood at some distance, looking across the dark water with flashlights. Head barely above water, Mueller gasped, and took a measure of the danger. He saw he'd come halfway. Beyond the cove the ghostly four-masted barque rose like a chimera from the water's surface.

Loud voices from homes along the cove called into the night. The gunshots and barking dog had brought out residents who wanted to know what the commotion was all about. Jazz from one brightly lit home filled the evening and guests had moved to the docks and peered across the cove to the Soviet compound. These witnesses gave pause to the Russians who stood beside their docked motorboat.

Mueller moved his arms in the water in a weak crawl and headed to the nearest spit of land. He felt the smallness of his body in the immense indifference of the water.

• • •

Mueller paused when he approached the cottage. He didn't think he'd left the porch light on. He was further surprised when he found the kitchen door open. Mueller glanced at the driveway, and then back to the county road, but he saw no cars and no sign of trespassers. Was someone inside? He peeked in the cottage's window, saw nothing, and then he cautiously entered.

"Hello?" Quiet. He listened. "Hello?"

Mueller crossed the kitchen, containing his fear so it didn't subvert his ability to think clearly. Mueller knelt at his duffel bag and fumbled with the zipper, catching the fabric, biting his tongue against an urge to curse. He jerked the tab through and felt for the old sock with his Colt service pistol. His breathing slowed when he had the gun in his hand.

"Hello!"

He saw a tan raincoat covered in nettles thrown across the back of a kitchen chair, and beside the chair, a battered leather suitcase covered in faded luggage stickers. A man's muddy shoes were on the floor near the door to the sunroom. Mueller followed the progression of clues.

A sound. Behind. Mueller pivoted, pistol raised.

"Shit," Mueller growled. He lowered the pistol.

Vasilenko laughed. "I frightened you, my friend. Didn't I? You're jumpy."

"You did," Mueller said. "Yes, you frightened me. Frightened me so much that I almost put a hole in your head."

Vasilenko wiped his hands with a towel he'd taken from the bathroom. He shrugged. "No one was home. Fall in the water?"

Mueller flicked the room's wall switch, flooding the room with light. "*No one was home?* That's not an invitation to enter. Are you alone?"

"You should change your clothes. Your lips are blue. Here." Vasilenko tossed his towel at Mueller. "Am I alone? Yes, I am alone. Very alone. But I'm not crazy. The water is freezing. You must have a good story."

"How did you get in?"

"A child could get in."

"It's late. Why are you here?"

"Why am I here?" He paused. "I need a place to stay." He looked at Mueller, evaluating his bare feet, wet hair matted to his skull. "I need help. You need to change."

"Help for what? What's up?"

Vasilenko shook his head disparagingly. He offered his judgment without raising his voice. "You are a fool. A bloody fool. A wet bloody fool. There is so much you don't know."

Mueller put down the towel. "What's going on?"

"I have not been working for you."

There was a beat of silence. "What does that mean?"

Vasilenko went to the unopened bottle of scotch on the counter. "May I?" Vasilenko gulped one glass and poured a second. He slumped in a chair at the kitchen table, legs stretched in front of him, and stared at Mueller. His fingers caressed the glass. "What does that mean? Yes, a good question. What does it mean," he repeated almost to himself. He looked up. "Sit, George. Join me. Change your clothes and join me. I have something you will want to hear. It is better if you aren't shivering."

Mueller returned in dry clothes and took the chair opposite the Russian.

"You made contact in Washington," Vasilenko said. "Do you

remember? There was the offer you made of the shotgun. An obvious lure. I reported the contact to the *rezident*. He said proceed. Let yourself be recruited, but don't make it look too easy. So I went along with your game and I let myself be surprised when the cleaning girl approached me."

Vasilenko paused. He glanced at the door, an instinct. "You were sloppy, like your door here. Amateurish. I saw the man's ring on the night table, and I knew you were behind the mirror. But it was my job to let you think you were landing a fish." His hands gestured wide and theatrically. "A big fish." He laughed his mocking gruffness. "So we let the CIA have its little victory."

Vasilenko was quiet. His head turned to the window at the sound of a car traveling along the shore road, and when the car was gone he looked again at Mueller. "It's not safe for me. How much am I worth to you?"

"What's happened?"

Vasilenko waved off the question and threw back another drink. The smoky scent of scotch made Mueller want to pour himself a shot, but he rose and took milk from the refrigerator and drank from the bottle. "What was in the bag you left in Union Station?" he asked.

"I don't know. I was the delivery boy. I never saw what I turned over. They said take it, so I took it. Chernov is the handler. He's the one you want."

Vasilenko leaned forward. "I want to defect."

Mueller was quiet, thinking, hand on his chin.

Vasilenko spoke. "There are changes. Arrests. Old grudges are being settled. Chernov." He spat the word. "*Mudak*."

Mueller looked at the Russian. "Why?"

"Why?" he snapped. He had risen excitedly in his chair, but he slumped back down. "You were getting close to Protocol. Asking too many questions. Chernov couldn't risk having his prize asset compromised. It would be a big loss. Now is not a good time for a big loss. What I gave you . . ." He searched for the word. "I was a plant."

"Who is Protocol?"

"You think I know!" He paused. "It's not you."

"How do you know?"

He scoffed. "You? If you are Protocol, it's my death sentence." Vasilenko looked at Mueller. He lifted a finger to make a point. "The date in Vienna. That evening in May 'forty-eight. You were in the Soviet zone. They picked that date because you *were* there, and Chernov knew Coffin would know. A magician's trick. The eye watches one hand while the real action is elsewhere." Vasilenko paused. "It's not you because Chernov wants them to *think* it's you."

Mueller pondered that. "How was he recruited?"

"I want to defect."

"My question first."

Vasilenko raised his voice, then calmed himself. "Do you know what is happening in Moscow Center now? The long knives are out. Beria was taken from a meeting of the presidium in handcuffs. The head of state security publicly arrested. Have you any idea what that means? Stalin is dead. *Stalin is dead.*"

Vasilenko lowered his voice, but he arched his eyebrows, and he spoke almost in a whisper. "No one is safe." He drew a cutting finger across his throat.

"My question first."

"Are you authorized? Is this an official conversation?"

"No."

Vasilenko shifted his bulk in the chair. "I have been recalled. My flight is in two days. When I arrive in Moscow I know what to expect. I will be taken directly from the airport to Lubyanka Prison. They will present evidence against me—all made up— for a crime they've made up. I will be declared an enemy of the state. I will be taken to a small cell, hands bound behind my back, asked to kneel. If I refuse they will force me to my knees. A guard will come up behind and put a bullet in the back of my head. This is how it is done." His face had lost color. "I want to defect. What do you need from me?"

"How was he recruited?"

"Do you have a plan for me?"

"You have to trust me."

Vasilenko shook his head skeptically. "Our jobs require that we lie to each other."

Mueller's fingers toyed with the bottle of milk. "I could be lying. That's true. Let's stipulate that I am lying. What choice do you have?"

Vasilenko reached for his whiskey, but stopped when he found the glass empty. He lit a cigarette and inhaled deeply, relaxing with the tobacco. "I am taking you on your word." He inhaled again. "Here is what I was told. He was compromised by the Nazis in Vienna in nineteen-thirty-nine. He helped the Nazis fence art taken from wealthy Jewish families using his connections to the business world in London. German intelligence caught him with an underage boy. Protocol's acquaintance with Goering kept him from arrest and saved him from scandal. He had every reason to believe the incident was covered up. When the Red Army took Berlin they found Goering's private files, which included a record of the incident. Chernov was head of GRU in Berlin at the time and he took possession of all the files. When Protocol came to Vienna after the war Chernov prepared a trap. Chernov had a German boy brought to the Soviet zone and something was done to make the boy available to Protocol. He was caught a second time. Chernov told him, 'Now you work for us.'" Vasilenko looked at Mueller. "Is that enough?"

Mueller considered the Russian. "How do I know it's true?"

Vasilenko looked at Mueller with a cold, hard gaze. "You don't." He stood and poured himself another whiskey. "Some of it is true. Some of it has to be true so that parts that aren't true *could* be true." Vasilenko took a shallow breath. "You have one day, maybe two, before Chernov gets to Protocol."

"How will that happen?"

"I don't know. They will know something is wrong when they discover I'm gone. The plane is the outside date. They know I don't have his name. If they can't protect him they will eliminate him." Vasilenko's cheeks had the rosy blush of alcohol. He added carelessly, "They have the girl too."

"Girl?"

"From the apartment. The one who called herself Jane. She was compromised from the start. They say they caught her stealing from the apartments she cleaned. She is being held because she is useful to them. They'll ask her questions. When they're done they'll dispose of her, or exchange her."

"Where is she?" Mueller demanded.

"Embassy. Top floor. There's a small room."

Mueller closed his eyes, pressed fingers into his forehead. "You can sleep on the sofa. I'll get you a blanket. What happens to your wife and son?"

"They are on a train to the border. I have always thought of you as a friend."

Mueller looked at him. "We have been friendly. But we are not friends. Friendship is a dangerous luxury in this business."

Mueller couldn't sleep that night. He lay in bed wide awake and listened to Vasilenko's loud whiskey snores in the other room. Not since his nighttime parachute drop behind Nazi lines in '43 was he frightened like this.

18

DISAPPEARANCE

W HO KNOWS?" The director looked at the two men sitting opposite him at the conference table under snarling African lion heads mounted on the wall. His question hung in the air like a bad smell. The director regarded Coffin, who looked out the window to avoid meeting the director's eyes, and then the director settled on Mueller. It was just over twelve hours since Mueller had delivered the news that Altman had defected—*disappeared* was his exact word.

"It's a simple question, George. I'm looking at you because you're the one who seems to know the most." The sturdy rotary telephone with its direct line to the Oval Office mocked the look of helplessness on the old man's face. It was the lunch hour and the director's routine was not to be interrupted, so his conference table was set with linen cloth, a carnation centerpiece, crystal glasses, and plates with the distinctive maroon design of the CIA shield.

Mueller's tight necktie made his slightly oval face look puffy; his hair was parted to the side and combed straight back.

The director lifted his fork to his bibbed neck. "Who else knows about Altman?"

"Just the three of us." Beth didn't count. She didn't know the full story.

"Keep it that way. No one else can know until we understand the full scope of what is at risk. And what they want with him. I don't want a goddamned call from the White House. I don't want them thinking we're a rabbit warren of spies and perverts. Do you understand? Look at me, each of you. Do you understand?"

Coffin and Mueller nodded.

Mueller had seen the director angry on other occasions and he'd seen how the old man's volcanic temper erupted to intimidate. The tweedy professor wielded a cane against classroom misbehavior that he would not tolerate.

"Just the three of us," the director said. "Let's keep it that way. We are in a pretty pickle, gentlemen. He was our colleague." The director paused. "Defected. You're sure?"

The question was put to Mueller. Altman was gone from the home in Chesapeake Bay, gone from his townhouse in Georgetown, gone from the office, and gone from the places Mueller expected to find him. No one had seen Altman enter the Soviet embassy, but Vasilenko had heard that a room on the fourth floor had been prepared for a special guest. "They have him. I don't know if he was taken or if he walked in."

"How can you walk in and not be seen? *Christ.* Do you want to explain this to the senator?" The question was put to Coffin.

Coffin cleared his throat, but the director cut him off. "I'm not going to blame you, James. You had your suspicions. But on this we hang together, or surely we'll all hang separately. And we will hang, make no mistake about that."

No one answered. The director's eyes drifted back from the view of the gray Potomac. His crimson house robe was open at the neck and he abandoned lunch to light his pipe, puffing until the tobacco glowed red. "I should have suspected something. He took over in Bern when I was transferred to Berlin. I got little clues, but there was nothing to act on and nothing specific or concrete. I knew his father. I didn't want to believe what I might have suspected. His suggestion that we use George to reach out to the Russians should have been a red flag. George, go ahead. What is it you want to say?"

"We've jumped to a conclusion," Mueller said.

The director puffed. "I can do that. It's a prerogative that comes with this office."

"Do we have facts?" Mueller snapped. His anger showed.

There was a beat of silence and the flow of conversation stopped. The rebuke startled the director, whose fingers began a restless drumming.

Mueller softened his tone. "It may be him. It looks bad, yes. But I don't think he ran to them. He has disappeared. He deserves the benefit of the doubt until we have facts. I'm not defending him. I'm defending how we go about this."

The director nodded at Coffin. "Share with us your facts. What have you got?"

Coffin pulled a thick file from his bulky attaché case. His

shoulders slumped, his pale skin was shiny from exhaustion, and he had the shadowed eyes of a man who had been up all night. His pleasant tenor voice had acquired a raspy huskiness, and he cleared his throat with a smoker's cough.

"We have an idea," he said. "Some facts, yes. A theory. We have gone through what we have to understand about when he started, our losses, and what's still at risk. Shall I start at the beginning?"

Mueller listened. Coffin spoke with the authority and condescension that Mueller found distasteful. A tiresome pompous ass, he thought. But the game had shifted.

"Knowing it is Altman helped us solve the problem from within," Coffin said. "Knowing it is him we could work backwards. We think he was turned in Vienna. January nineteen forty-eight."

Coffin looked at Mueller. "You were there too, which is why suspicion could fall on you. We don't know where the first contact was made. Vasilenko said you were in the Soviet sector, which raised a suspicion, but Altman had no clearance to travel there. They probably got him to one of those bars near the Russian zone that allied troops visited. Smoke, cheap beer, prostitutes with a good line. Chernov had his file and a photo. Chernov has terrible English so he probably had someone to interpret. A short conversation. All he had to do was show the photos. The meeting would have led to another that dealt with logistics, what signals to use when alerting there was a dead drop. He was fully turned by February, I suspect."

Coffin looked up. "We know from Altman's service record that he had no access to missions run outside of Austria. So he gave them what he had. It wasn't much to start. A little bit of intelligence he got on currency support for the schilling. The cryptonym of an agent in Berlin, but no name. Our contact in the Italian Social Democrats who came through Vienna on his way to Moscow. A date here, the address of a hotel in the Soviet sector used by MI6, the names of Red Army deserters who we interrogated, minutes of meetings among Czech partisans who we were training to parachute behind Soviet lines.

"Altman knew the Soviets already had some of this information so he could believe that he was satisfying his obligation to Chernov without doing damage. And he could let himself believe the information was random, inconsequential, of little value. This would be the most forgiving explanation for what he did. He passed along information that Chernov already had, or was of little operational value. We were protected for a time because each link in our network was sequestered from the others. And maybe Altman convinced himself that he wasn't hurting anyone." Coffin paused. "This is stage one."

Coffin opened a second file. "Stage two started when Moscow Center assembled these fragments into a map of intelligence possibilities, pointers to places, dates, names, actions that became situations of interest. We do the same thing. Slowly, their men in Moscow assembled a puzzle and saw the shape of the missing pieces, and once they had the shape of those pieces they could look for them. The picture came into focus. They could create a run on the schilling. They could see our success running a Soviet asset, and then identify a suspect inside GRU or NKVD. They targeted these suspects until they were able to catch them in an act of espionage. This happened with Orlav in East Berlin. They trapped him with a prostitute in a safe house in Karlshorst. The dates align with Altman's trip to Berlin. Orlav is the first loss we can link to Altman."

Coffin leaned forward, palms on the table, eyes red from his long night of forensic research. "Altman had to see our losses mounting and he had to know that the information he passed along resulted in executions."

Coffin turned over a page on which several names were typed. "Altman is responsible for these deaths. He killed these men as surely as the man who put a gun to their heads."

Mueller scanned the list. He was struck by the sheer hypocrisy of it all. How could they not see that the Agency did the same thing, eliminating men who were no longer useful. Where was the outrage for the death of people like Mrs. Leisz, and the answer that came back to Mueller was, of course, they were not moral at all.

Mueller went down the list, stopping on each name, each life. He had known two personally, double agents who turned up dead in Berlin, one shot in an alley, the other found floating in the river. Poor dead souls, he thought. He read the captions.

Adolf Motorin missing in Berlin in August 1948. He remembered Motorin's jaunty style and his obviously false hairpiece. Prescott Goodyear gone missing in Istanbul near the Blue Mosque in 1948, and assumed dead. His death had been a surprise. Gunther Hesse, twenty-eight, ex-Nazi turned double agent, or triple agent, depending on what you believed, found executed in West Berlin. Leonid Varenik executed in Munich.

Found slumped over the steering wheel of his sedan, young wife in the passenger seat, also shot. Collateral damage. The people on the list were not just names to Mueller. He'd met them, or known them, and their names triggered memories and incidents from the past. The last was Alfred Leisz, the gaunt, chain-smoking Hungarian he'd found in a displaced persons camp and brought to Washington with infant son and pregnant wife. Damn fool. Leisz ignored the rules and was sloppy. Mueller looked up at Coffin, who had not stopped talking.

"We have another list of assets who are still in place. We don't know if they've been compromised. We know Altman is familiar with them. We don't have a way to contact them. They come to us when they have something they want to pass along, but we don't have a way to reach them. They are now at risk."

Coffin sipped his coffee. Lunch plates had been cleared. "They knew we were getting close to Protocol. They took Altman before we got to him. They will begin to debrief him, if they haven't already begun. They'll squeeze him and then silence him. Or park him in a dacha. We need to find him, to get him back . . . silence him."

Coffin closed his folder and looked at the two men across the table. The mood had darkened. Coffin added, by way of a confirmatory remark, putting a period at the end of his indictment, "The shopping bag Vasilenko left in Union Station points to you, George, if you know what you're looking at, and Walker didn't, which is why they couldn't make sense of the papers. But I could. You were set up." Coffin spoke with cold affection for his certainty.

The director stared at Coffin and then at Mueller. "It makes us look like a bunch of incompetent amateurs. The man was in this room talking about the traitor, knowing all the time that it was him. We were played." The director stood and stretched fingers to toes of his slippers, and then moved to the window. He gazed out at the Washington Monument piercing the low gray clouds. In a moment he turned back to his colleagues and spoke calmly. "We have let down brave men who entrusted us with their lives." He slumped in his chair. "We will all be looking for new jobs if they get him to Moscow and trot him out to the press."

The director looked at Mueller. "What's next?"

Mueller contemplated what else he could say in Altman's defense. "They will try to get him out of the country. How? That's the question. They won't risk taking him out under his own name. We have three days, maybe four, before they get a false passport via diplomatic pouch. They have to assume the FBI has been alerted and that the airports are being watched."

"I don't want the FBI involved, understand?" The director shifted his foot thick with gout, and massaged the swollen ankle. "*Sonofabitch*, this is a mess. I will not sacrifice this Agency, and our hard work, to the hyenas in Washington. Gentlemen, what do you suggest?"

Mueller saw a bead of perspiration on the director's upper lip. Worry pleated his large forehead, but for the first time in their acquaintance Mueller couldn't tell how much of the man's worry was for the work, how much for himself. Perhaps there was no difference. The thin line of judgment was porous with error, rank with self-interest. Washington was a terrible place for honorable men to work.

The director slapped the morning's *Post* on the table. "We're in one of those silly seasons." He pointed to the front-page banner headline, "Oust More Sex Perverts in State Department." He intoned solemnly, "There are those in this town who dress their conscience in the latest fashion." He paused. "We need to make sure the overzealous vice squad hasn't rounded up a man with those tendencies who points a finger at Altman, and that starts a witch hunt here." The director looked directly at his two subordinates. "Gentlemen, what do you suggest? James, you're always good at brainy suggestions."

Coffin raised his eyes from his coffee. "They don't know we have Vasilenko. We should use him to our advantage."

The director pondered the comment. He looked at Mueller. "You have him?"

"He's safe for now."

"Does he trust you?"

Mueller considered the question. "Up to a point. He wants asylum. He has few options."

"Will he cooperate?"

"Bait?"

"Yes."

Mueller was incredulous.

"What options does he have?"

Mueller gazed at the director. "It could be a death sentence."

"There are no good options here, George." The director lifted his chin in the way he did when he was about to give a little speech. "He got into this business knowing the risks. Just like each of us. I'm sure your clever imagination can come up with a way to make this suitable for him. He must have a family. There are things that we can do."

Lunch was over. The director removed his bib and limped back to his desk. He lifted the small statue of Nathan Hale. "There is a difference between losing one's life and giving one's life. We do the latter willingly for some higher purpose, you know, because we believe in something larger than ourselves, and a man of courage, a man of the world will rise to the occasion. Vasilenko might be such a man. You will have to find out."

Mueller couldn't tell if the director believed his little speech, but Mueller did not. There was nothing romantic about a spy's death. Dead. Gone. Forgotten. It was a shitty job.

• • •

A few people in the Agency were told that Roger Altman was out of the office on special assignment. His secretary was spoken to so she wouldn't contribute to loose talk. No one was to know. The assignment was code for a classified job. It happened all the time in Operations that one of the officers went dark for weeks at a time, dispatched secretly overseas. There was no more than the usual amount of chitchat about Altman's absence. Someone speculated that he had flown to Berlin to support the severely understaffed team working on the uprising of East German construction workers. Altman, everyone knew, was fluent in German.

19

BETH GETS A VISIT

BETH DIDN'T recognize the two men who visited her at the house. She'd been in the kitchen when she heard the loud knocking. Beth found them just outside standing side by side, cordial, polite, each holding his hat in two hands. They had short hair, both wore cinched trench coats, both had ties knotted tightly on starched collars, and she found them hard to tell apart except that one was short with wire-frame glasses and the other taller with a pencil-thin moustache. Not much alike at all, she thought, after the first impression wore off, but she thought they were peas in a pod. Two men with polite smiles who were more polite than friendly. They could have been members of a cult religion recruiting converts until she saw the holstered pistols.

"Yes," she said, holding the door open but not letting them in. "Can I help you?" She wiped her hand vigorously on her flower apron.

From behind her father called, "Who is it, Beth?"

"It's for me," she said in a definitive voice, calling back inside. Beth stepped outside, closing the door behind.

"Yes?" She looked at the shorter man and then at the taller man. The same trench coats, the same polished black shoes, the same expressionless faces that made her believe that she, or someone, was in trouble.

"Can I help you?" she repeated.

"Are you Elizabeth Altman?"

"Yes."

"We have a few questions for you," the taller one said.

A few questions? "What questions?" The words produced a spiral of speculation in her imagination. She had been worried all morning that her father would ask about Roger and she'd have to make a decision about speaking up, or staying silent. She felt the terrible burden of keeping his disappearance to herself. The events of the past week had been a series of disconnected episodes in that way that life itself was only random events that had no order, no beginning, and no end, but were merely things you had to react to. She found it hard to assemble a coherent picture of things. And there was no one she could ask.

She tried to smile at the two men, but it was uncomfortable to pretend politeness. She released her apron and met the taller man's eyes with a concerned look. "What questions?"

The taller man flipped open his wallet to reveal a badge, and said, "Special Agent Walker. FBI." He spoke quickly and she didn't catch the name. "Walker," he repeated. The shorter man didn't smile and he didn't introduce himself.

"Are you here to ask about the dog?" Beth said.

"The dog?"

"There was a terrible barking two nights ago. It went on for an hour. It started at midnight. We heard gunshots and then the barking. We called the sheriff."

"No," he said. "Barking dogs don't usually interest us. We understand you know George Mueller."

She hesitated. "Yes, I do."

"How do you know him?"

"He had an accident on the road not far from here. I found him and brought him here. Is he in trouble?"

"Did you speak with him?"

"With George?"

"Yes, we're talking about George Mueller. He was here for a few days and I wondered if you talked much to him?"

She stared coldly. She didn't like the way he was getting her to say things that he already seemed to know. "What is your interest in George?"

"We're talking to people who know him. People like you. Background check."

"I haven't known him long. Is he in trouble?"

"No. We're just asking a few questions. I have a list of things we'd like to ask. Can we go over the list?"

Beth nodded. She preferred not to, but knew she had no good reason to refuse. She wrapped her chest with her arms and glanced at the typed page Agent Walker held.

"You're chilly," the shorter agent said. "Do you want to go inside?"

"No." She almost snapped her response.

"He worked for the National Labor Relations Board. Did you discuss that?"

"We've never talked about his work."

"Did he mention he volunteered for the American Civil Liberties Union?"

"No, as I said. We didn't talk about his work."

"So you don't know what he does for a living?"

It was the way the Agent Walker framed his question that made her think that it was wrong for her to know. "He works in the government. That's all I know. That's what he said."

"That's all he said?"

"Yes."

"Did he say that he works for the CIA?"

CIA? She felt like she'd been punched in the stomach. She wasn't breathing. Her mind went blank. She knew there was a right answer and there was a wrong answer. The wrong answer would put him in trouble if he wasn't already in trouble, and the right answer would keep him out of trouble, or not make his trouble worse. She looked down at her shoes because she didn't want them to see her confusion.

"That's the Central Intelligence Agency," Agent Walker said.

"Yes, I know what it is. What was the question?"

"Did he tell you he worked for them?"

"He didn't say that. He said he worked in the government." She didn't like the men. It was their presumptuous manner—the false friendliness of men asking questions using blandishments because they were not in a position to demand answers.

"Beth?"

She turned her head to her father's voice. "Yes, be right there."

"Just a couple more questions," agent Walker said.

She turned her back on them. Anger at their prying insolence made the words leap from her lips. "I think we're finished. Next time call ahead."

• • •

Mueller was at his sink splashing water on his face when he heard pounding at his door. He looked up, alert. More banging from the front of the apartment. He toweled moisture from his face and slipped into a bathrobe. On his way across the living room he closed a file and considered where to hide it, looking at the box of packed books, then a drawer, and when the pounding continued he stuffed it under a sofa pillow.

Mueller put his eye to the door's peephole and saw Beth, absurdly distorted in the fisheye lens. He undid the police lock, setting aside the steel bar, and undid both dead bolts.

"I need to speak to you," Beth said urgently. "Can I come in?"

There were hints of greasepaint on her neck, left when she'd rushed to leave the dressing room after her evening performance. She still wore mascara, and she'd been crying, which had made her eyeliner run. He stepped aside. She wore gloves and an overcoat that she made no effort to remove. She stopped by the round table in the center of the room and turned abruptly to face him.

"I need to talk," she said.

Talk? *About what?* It was a dreadful moment. He was close

to her, at her side, holding her coat and helping her remove one arm from the sleeve. Her forehead was creased with preoccupation, lips tight and unsmiling, eyes alive with concern. He could see her measure the distance between them, and deciding it was too close, she took a step back.

"You're CIA, aren't you?"

Mueller felt the sting in her voice, the intensity of her scrutiny. Quietly. "Yes."

"And Roger too?"

"Yes, we both work there."

"I've always hated the CIA. You're all self-righteous men thinking the world needs to be saved. God, how did I not know?" She stared at him. "How did it start?"

Mueller was now standing away from her, and he dropped her coat over a chair. Mueller used the moment of silence to organize his mind to shape a scenario for her that was believable without being entirely true.

"When did he join?" she asked.

"He was OSS during the war and when the war ended he joined. He'd won that medal and he had a good story. He recruited me out of a New York law firm, so he was already part of it. He said to me, 'The free world is at risk.'"

A pause. "He said, 'We need smart men like you down here. It's something new. I can't tell you about it. The pay isn't great, but this is about democracy.' You know him. All that bravado, all that enthusiasm. It meant something then."

Mueller met her eyes. "I didn't buy the pitch, but I was at a point in my life when anything was better than what I was doing.

Hours were long. I worked twelve-hour days. The cases were dull. I drank too much. . . ." Mueller paused. *Leave it at that.*

All he got back was a sullen grunt. She glared. "What else should I know about you?"

A baby's cry came through the airshaft window, cracked open for the breeze, and there followed a woman's heckling shriek and an argument between the couple who lived across the way. Mueller closed the kitchen window. He answered her question with one of his own. "Tea?"

"Tea?" She slumped in a chair. "I'd prefer a drink. Go ahead. What else?"

In a minute a kettle hummed softly on the gas stove and then he poured her a cup of tea. He drank his quickly like medicine while she sipped hers gingerly. A long silence opened between them.

The thought of a lie made Mueller sick, as sick as he'd felt in the stairwell of Mrs. Leisz's apartment building. "I'm quitting the Agency. Moving." His hand made an arc of the room. "Leaving all of this for the next tenant. Everything but the books."

Loud sounds of domestic violence came from the apartment across the airshaft.

"I didn't mind their fighting when I first moved in," Mueller said. "I wasn't looking for a charming place that would brighten my life."

"I don't think of you as someone who feels sorry for himself."

"There are things you don't know. That's one. I tolerate disappointment."

She grunted. "I know."

Her hand plunged in her pocket and she produced a handwritten note in Roger's precise cursive script. "Read this."

Dear Beth,

Don't worry about me. I will be gone for some time. I don't know how long. I won't be able to write for a little while, but when I can I will. You are in my thoughts and always will be. There isn't much I can say, but there is a favorite poem that comes to mind. "My worst sin is in my blood and now my blood pays for it." I shall think of you always. And don't think too harshly of me.

Your loving brother,
Roger

It was as close to a confession as Mueller expected to read. Mueller met Beth's eyes.

"They have subpoenaed him to testify. You have seen what they've done to the others. Demonized them. For what? For having personal lives that they don't want splashed over the headlines of the morning newspaper!"

She had looked away, but she again met his eyes. She slumped on the sofa and spoke prayerfully from a place in the past. "I remember him as a boy standing on the bed with a little broom he'd taken from the closet. He stood there and I was behind—his recruit. He enlisted me when he needed an army to lead, or an enemy to slay. He'd cry, *'Half a league, half a league, half a league onward. All in the valley of Death rode the six hundred.'*"

Her eyes reddened. "Roger has a right to his private life. We all do. We don't know how important it is until it's taken from you in this mad prurient baiting that passes for civilization. You know him, or at least you know the person he lets you see. I know him in a different way. I know the little boy who could not get his father's attention."

She braved her tears. "My father didn't want Roger. I've never told you that. He wanted a different type of son. That's a hard thing for an eight-year-old to take in. How does that boy understand the disappointment he sees in his father's eyes? Is it possible to overcome that?"

Mueller put down his cup.

"And now they want to put him in front of television cameras, interrogate him, and use him to demonize Father." She wrapped her arms on her chest. She looked up at Mueller. "Where is he?"

Mueller moved to the window. He saw in the dark chamber of his mind that constructs such pictures the pain that would flow from all that she did not know. He felt the pain she had yet to endure. Was there any way to spare her? Him? Them? Evil hatched long ago would become a flock of black crows flapping madly around their heads. He felt a terrible responsibility to protect her.

He gazed down at the empty sidewalk and didn't stir for a long time. How did he get to this place in his life, living in a grubby apartment on a grim Washington street? Nothing he'd ever imagined about his future prepared him for the moment he was in.

He was surprised when she came up beside him, and he only noticed that she had taken his hand when he felt her head on his shoulder. She stood beside him, eyes closed, strangely peaceful. She was plain, ordinary, with a face that wouldn't turn heads on the street. A careworn face, a kid sister's face. The scent of her hair and the touch of her skin had the power to alter his life. He felt the bigness of her heart. He always thought it was the way women looked that counted, and it had been that way for him twice, but his feelings for Beth had nothing to do with her looks. He never meant to fall in love with Beth.

Love. He wasn't sure what the word meant, and he had never said it seriously. It was a vague, sentimental, romantic word, an appalling word that only led to terrible disappointment. He embraced her and felt her trembling.

20

UNDERGROUND

Final arrangements to capture Roger Altman fell into place quickly. In exchange for a promise of asylum, Vasilenko agreed to cooperate. Vasilenko confirmed that a room on the fourth floor of the Soviet embassy had been set aside for a special guest, and this could only be Protocol. Chernov had boasted he could secretly transport Protocol to Moscow and become the Communist hero who'd reeled in his big prize.

"Tomorrow night he leaves," Vasilenko said. "No later than that. The *Sedov* sails in two days. Protocol will be on it."

Coffin snapped, "The embassy is watched round the clock."

"What you don't know is this." Vasilenko surprised the men in the conference room when he explained that he'd found a cellar door that led from the embassy's subbasement to an abandoned tunnel that ran under Sixteenth Street past the Carlton Hotel toward Lafayette Park. He had found the passage when he looked around for a way to leave the embassy unseen. He needed a way to come and go without being followed, surprising Mueller in the Whiskey Bar, appearing beside him in the bar as if he'd materialized out of nowhere. "Yes, George, that was my trick. I came and left clandestinely. The FBI had their binoculars on the embassy's gate, the roof, and the windows, but I moved underground. I found an old iron door in the wine cellar behind a wall of Château Latour. I had to break a few bottles, so, of course, I couldn't tell anyone what I'd found because they'd say, 'Yuri, good work, but you'll have to pay for the wine.' So, it's my little secret. Chernov will be glad to have it. I can lead him to the hotel, through the cellar, and there will be a car to take us to the *Sedov*. You'll surprise him when he steps out to the street."

Beneath Washington's streets is an unmapped web of old tunnels built in the aftermath of the British sacking of the U.S. capital. These subterranean defenses were forgotten in time and mostly abandoned to the seasonal flood waters that channeled in meandering paths to the Potomac. Sections were used in the Civil War by freed slaves arriving or departing in the underground railroad; others reclaimed to satisfy the city's hunger for secrecy, becoming archive vaults, or passageways for congressmen to move unseen for votes in the House of Representatives, or to hasten them to hotel dalliances, and later, portions were converted to bomb shelters, or annexed by the city's new trolley system.

The trap was baited. Low clouds laid a dampening gloom over splendidly dressed guests who arrived for the Republican gala in the Hotel Carlton's ballroom. Diligent doormen opened limousine doors and led celebrities past eager onlookers restrained by velvet rope, and through the spectacle of light from paparazzi camera flashes. *Perfect cover*, Vasilenko had said, to move unnoticed in the open. These had been his last words that morning before he strode purposefully into the front gate of the Soviet embassy.

"They're late," Coffin said, checking his watch. "It's past nine. Or, we've missed them." This he snapped impatiently.

Coffin stood beside Mueller in the gray mist across the street and watched the buzzing crowd gathered under the hotel's canopy. Washington was not a European capital and there were no graceful benches to sit on, no quaint sidewalk cafés from which to clandestinely spy on a subject. No one designed the city for strolling. Certainly not in the open, subject to the city's miserable climate. With the low clouds came a light soaking drizzle that fell on Mueller and Coffin. They had left without umbrellas and water fell in rivulets from their hats, chilling them to the bone, adding to their impatience.

"They'll come," Mueller said optimistically.

"I don't trust him," Coffin said. He coughed his smoker's cough, and puffed on his cigarette again.

Inside the telephone booth at their side the handset began to ring. Coffin answered it. Mueller split his attention between a Buick parked just down the block on the opposite side of the street, and the half-heard conversation from the booth.

"Yes, we're here," Coffin said. "Nothing so far. The fog makes it hard to see. Yes, yes, I know. There's no room to fail. I'll call when I know something." Coffin hung up and turned to Mueller. "He doesn't trust Vasilenko either."

The director? "He'll come. He'll bring Roger. He has no

choice. His family is at risk. It's not a game for him. *There!* Look. The Buick is moving. They're on their way."

This is what Vasilenko had said. When the Buick left its parking spot, that meant that the Russians and Altman would have entered the tunnel and be on their way. The Buick entered the queue of cars waiting to reach the hotel drive-through.

Coffin rubbed his hands against the chill and nodded at a Cadillac delivering a couple into the doorman's sheltering umbrella. The man was stout like a penguin in tuxedo and his right-wingism announced itself in a patriotically striped cravat. On his arm was a taller, younger woman, wonderfully pleasing to the eye with her doll's face, pearl skin, topaz teardrop earrings, amber-colored scarf pressed over her shoulders, and a fine head of blond curls sculpted into an updo. Eyes of the curious onlookers followed as she made her way along the velvet rope, indulging all the attention with a coy smile.

"There is a word for all this," Coffin said. "Sometimes you need the word first and only through the word do you know what you are seeing. Everything is inchoate until you have the right word. The word, George, is *diversion.* This is all a diversion. There, beyond the tall woman, is a tight group of men. You see that. Our bait and our catch." He added in a perplexed whisper, "Why are people pointing?"

Under the hotel canopy Mueller saw four men moving behind photographers and onlookers all pressing forward to ogle at the woman. Vasilenko was the first to emerge, hatless, eyes darting, and he was joined by a thinner, shorter man in wide fedora pulled down on his forehead.

Mueller recognized Chernov's angular face, faint pock-marks, and pronounced clubfoot, which swung around when he moved it forward in his hobbled walk. Mueller felt a tinge of anxiety. Was it fear or concern—or just nervousness triggered by the sound of the gimp? For danger always poked its head out whenever Chernov appeared, as he had done in Vienna and Bern, each time offering another lure in his deprecating manner—and of course one was always tempted. The Soviet colonel had a grim visage and his nose smelled for danger.

Roger Altman was half a step behind, unmistakable by his height, Hollywood good looks, and the double-breasted blue blazer he'd been wearing when he disappeared, but different. Humbled, nervous. Eyes alert. Crimson pocket square missing. Here he was, Mueller thought, on his way to the dacha he'd dismissed. He was in the open, vulnerable, and there would be a terrible reckoning. He didn't look defeated, but then Mueller never thought Roger Altman was a person who allowed himself to look defeated. He was a refined man of good taste who never conveyed the image of a grubby man living a triple life. There was only this picture of confident coolness moving quietly along the perimeter of Washington's hoi polloi.

"Why are they pointing?" Coffin repeated.

A camera's magnesium lightning flash went off. One paparazzo and then another snapped Altman's photograph, and onlookers turned their attention from the tall woman to the discreet Altman and his nondescript companions, and then suddenly the crowd surged in a rabble, pens thrust out seeking a scribbled autograph.

Mueller didn't say what was on his mind in that instant. Some idiot forgets the plan, or a chance case of mistaken identity disrupts the intelligent working of a self-conscious plan. There is no way to apply coherence to the error and all bets are off. Mueller was already moving across the street in a run, signaling to Downes and two companions, ex-football players recruited for security work when the Agency decided it needed more muscle. They pushed through the crowd to cut off the escape route along the sidewalk. There was shoving and a few indignant protests from women pushed to the side by photographers eagerly clawing their way to snap Altman's photo. Blind mob frenzy didn't notice, or care, that the tall man in the blue blazer was someone's look-alike.

What happened next was this. Chernov saw the trap. He, his two Russian companions, and Altman, hustled through the hotel's revolving doors and disappeared inside to retrace their steps to the tunnel and the embassy, where Altman would be untouchable. Coffin, Mueller, and Downes convened on the street and agreed on a plan. Downes and his men would enter the tunnel from the hotel, giving pursuit, while Coffin and Mueller would race ahead to a grated manhole and intercept underground.

Mueller's foot searched beyond the last rung of the iron ladder that descended through the narrow ventilation shaft. From above, Coffin's flashlight shone into the blackness below and showed Mueller he'd come to the end. Mueller relaxed his grip and dropped to the tunnel floor, knees flexed, but still he crumpled on impact. He pointed his flashlight into the underworld. Noise from the street was far away and he found himself in a dark, confining quiet. Telltale sounds of water gurgling over rocks came from somewhere and he smelled the dankness of old stone. Water droplets on the ceiling gleamed in the beam of his light. As he moved it around, exploring the space, darkness opened up and revealed a vaulted brick ceiling fifteen feet above his head that curved into a wall thirty feet opposite. A creek bed had formed into the grooved channels of old rail tracks laid in the stone floor. He saw rusted iron shackles that lay where they'd been thrown off in a freed slave's flight.

Mueller saw he'd come down in a spot where tunnel tributaries converged in a roundabout, and these dark passageways led outward like spokes on a wheel. Arched tunnels disappeared into darkness, except down one where dim electric lamps glowed. At intervals, ghostly light seeped into the tunnels through ventilation shafts, making dim, perfectly round spotlights on the floor. Mueller searched for the entrance to the Soviet embassy, which Vasilenko said was an iron door set inside a wall cavity.

Coffin was suddenly at Mueller's side. "Turn off your light," he said. "They'll see us."

Mueller obliged. He had always disliked the dark, its surliness, its menace. The threat of being seen and not being able to see. It was a childhood fear. Near total darkness surrounded them.

Suddenly, a high-pitched screech filled the space all around them. Far down one tunnel Mueller saw the bulging brow of a modern trolley come around a sharp curve, iron wheels grinding on the rails. Its head lamp pierced the space, sending vast illumination into the dark. Light blinded Mueller, and then as suddenly as it came, the trolley completed its curve and darkness returned.

"Listen. Voices," he whispered.

Coffin and Mueller pressed against the damp walls, ears alert to approaching voices speaking in an unconcerned register. Mueller's eyes were of little help in the surrounding obscurity, but he made out a duo of flashlights being used by the men trying to find their way in the dark. Mueller had no idea how much time elapsed before he heard the faint sounds of footsteps. Then he heard it, the slap of leather, and the pattern repeated itself, one footstep followed by the percussive tap of a clubfoot, Chernov announcing himself.

The Soviet colonel appeared in the dim light of a ventilation shaft. He entered the circle of illumination, hesitated, and then drew back into shadow, but for a moment his face was visible. He and his companions moved away from the center of the tunnel and hugged the perimeter, moving toward a wall cavity they'd found with their lights.

Mueller saw his mistake. He and Coffin had entered the tunnel at the roundabout, and the embassy door was down a tributary. They weren't between Chernov and the embassy but catty-corner. Downes and his two men trotted down the tunnel, moving with alacrity, eager to get to the action, recklessly swinging their flashlights in the haste of their pursuit, unaware they were making themselves easy targets. Mueller saw the danger all at once.

"Stop!" he yelled.

The effect of Mueller's command was immediate. Chernov's flashlight went dark and Mueller sensed the unmistakable threat of an intelligent adversary.

A gunshot in the dark. A brilliant flash created a momentary burst of light. Explosive sound broke against the solid darkness like a slap on the face. The blast's echo decayed in the tunnels and what remained was the plaintive moan of a wounded man.

"It's Downes," Coffin whispered. Louder. "David, we'll get help."

Hustling footsteps moved in the dark, stumbling on unseen rocks, scrambling on the stone floor toward some destination. More footsteps running, one with Chernov's distinctive percussive signature. All flashlights had gone dark. There was only the palpable presence of adversaries maneuvering in close proximity to each other, and as hard as Mueller tried, he couldn't tell foe from friend, or which direction to move.

"George, be careful. He's got a gun. He won't play fair."

It was Altman. Mueller turned his ear to one spot, but then Altman called again, and the sound seemed to come from a different spot. Sound had no direction in the dark. Altman's voice bounced off the vaulted ceiling and put Altman everywhere. Coffin too had left Mueller's side and he was now alone, surrounded by muffled whispers, grunts, and the angry curse of someone in pain. He took his Colt service pistol out of his coat pocket.

"George, careful. He'll shoot me. He'll shoot you. Look for his cigarette. I'm not sure what they want with me, but I'm glad you're here. We'll have a good talk when this is over."

"Is that what you call it, a good talk?" Mueller said. "There is a lot to explain."

"You know the line, old boy, 'Nothing good or bad but thinking makes it so.'"

Altman's words were drowned by a screeching trolley far down the tunnel, and its head lamp's dazzling light put everything in stark relief. The men were caught in a petrified tableau, suddenly revealed to each other. Chernov had his gun out, Altman was pressed into a wall cavity, and Vasilenko was making an escape along the center of the tunnel following the tracks. He was startled by the light and momentarily confused. He looked one way, then the other, seeking cover, the fox out of his hole.

Mueller yelled to distract Chernov from the fleeing Russian. "It's over. Finished. Don't do anything stupid."

Vasilenko sprinted from one wall cavity to the next; trying the door in each but finding it locked, he moved to the next and the next, until he had exhausted all chances and broke in a run down the tunnel toward the trolley. His thick arms pumped as he presented himself in perfect silhouette.

"No!" Mueller yelled. Chernov had raised his pistol and sighted his 7.62mm Tokarev, one hand stretched out, cigarette dangling nonchalantly from his lips. The shot resounded in the confined space. The first shot seemed to throw Vasilenko forward, the second one made him crumple, and he lay motionless where he'd fallen.

Trolley passengers, who'd disembarked to see what was happening, scattered at the first gunshot. A woman screamed.

Chernov turned to Mueller. He was a dozen feet away. Angry. Livid. "Shithead. You had him sabotage it." His eyes had a reptile's beady glint. His pistol whipped around in his hand and he raised it at Coffin, then shifted a few degrees to Mueller.

Passengers who saw what was about to happen dropped to their knees, appalled and curious, the two sentiments existing at once in the bystanders. They pressed against the tunnel for cover. A second trolley car stopped behind the first and those passengers also became witnesses to the man lying facedown on the railroad tracks.

Another report of a gun. And in quick succession a fourth and a fifth. Brilliant strobe flashes from within the dark perimeter tunnels. It was impossible to see who was firing, or being fired at, or how many guns discharged. Stray bullets ricocheted against stone walls and one clanged on the trolley's iron brow.

Mueller saw Chernov. Heard him grunt. An animal sound that took the wind out of him and he too fell to the floor. Chernov had kept his gun and still, even wounded, he rose to one knee and aimed confidently.

Mueller had never killed a man. Metamorphosis is a painful process. He felt the excruciating agony of the caterpillar turning itself out of its skin, cracking open its hard carapace. Deep within him, in a process he was only dimly conscious of, he left behind the deep-thinking deskman who commanded death with the stroke of a pen. The gun in his hand was immediate and consequential. He lifted the pistol. Aimed. Fired. One shot.

Mueller was at Chernov's side. He saw crimson stains spread across the man's tan jacket. Eyes flickered and then became glassy and fixed. Mueller lifted his pistol and fired once more into the lifeless body. *Bastard.* Mueller confirmed the kill when he put two fingers on the man's carotid artery and felt no pulse. Mueller looked at the dead man with respectful contempt.

Then quiet. There was a fragile eerie moment that waited to be shattered by another gunshot and for the violence to resume. But the moment didn't come. Mueller knew things were over, one danger removed. He came up off his knee. He looked at his watch: 9:17 p.m. For some reason that seemed to matter. It had been just a few minutes, but it felt like an eternity.

Mueller went over to Vasilenko and confirmed that the Russian was dead. He took the Russian's wallet. He wanted something for the man's son. He lay there bleeding out from a head wound and there was nothing Mueller could do, but the wallet seemed like a good gesture. Though they were adversaries, or because they were adversaries, he respected the man. Friends in a different life.

• • •

Opinions differed later as to what happened in those few minutes of chaos underground near Dupont Circle. An inconclusive investigation by the Metropolitan Police, FBI, and State Department concluded that two Russians killed each other in a spillover of the violent purges taking place in Moscow. A forensics investigation confirmed the chest wound came from an American-made pistol, but the ownership of the gun, indeed the presence of the CIA, never came to light.

It surprised no one in the Agency that Roger Altman was put

on temporary medical leave. He was connected to the incident in the rumor mill in the office that always got things precisely wrong but vaguely right. There was speculation that Altman had been working harder than he should on the Berlin crisis, and had been brought home. The process of burning out started with continuous late nights in the office and usually ended in a breakdown. Work pressure had broken other men and now it was breaking Roger Altman. Altman, people in the Agency were told, would be promoted after he returned from rest leave.

21

THE RECKONING

"WILL YOU need me more tonight?" the middle-aged black housekeeper asked.

Roger Altman smiled. "No. I'll do the dishes. You can go home."

Altman looked at Mueller. The two men sat at the dining table in Altman's town house on P Street in Georgetown. They sat in the parlor floor's formal dining room with tall windows that looked onto the tree-lined street. The curtains were drawn, giving the room an intimate feeling. Warm light from a cut-glass chandelier illuminated a vibrant cubist painting on the wall. The mantel's clock's ticking punctuated the solemn quiet of two old acquaintances sharing reminiscences at a table set with china, crystal, and silver flatware.

"She's been with me four years," Altman said. "A wonderful cook, don't you think? Her own recipes. She has two sons she raised alone. So—"

The unfinished thought floated in the air waiting for a conclusion.

Mueller had gone to the window, lifting the curtain, and watched the housekeeper go down the steps. Across the street he saw a couple alone at a tree.

"They're watching the house," Altman said. "The director had them follow me after our talk."

Mueller returned to his seat. "What did he say?"

Altman was slumped in his chair. "He gave me a little speech on how personal compulsions destroy careers. He talked about our work together in Bern and the trust we put in each other. He said it's his job to see that the Agency is not disgraced. He never confronted me—that's not his style—but he led me to believe there was no way out. He talked about honor as if it was a suit you take from the closet. It was a pleasant conversation, pleasant in tone, but he'd made up his mind. He's never really liked me. You're his favorite. I suppose if there is such a thing as a favorite spy. I think he's impressed by your indifference."

Mueller fingered the stem of his wineglass filled with milk. "Is that his word?"

"No. Intelligence. That was his word. . . . I have disappointed him. I know that."

Mueller looked up. "Disappointment is a polite way to put it. What forgiveness can there be?"

"I don't want to be forgiven, George. That implies I've wronged them. They've made up their minds about me because it conveniently fits the world they live in." He looked at Mueller and leaned forward. "You stood up for me. I should be grateful, although, given the circumstances, it's a little surreal, don't you think? You, of all people, standing up for me."

Mueller slowly put down his glass. He felt the unerring stare of the man across the table and an awkward silence descended between them. Mueller's fingers went cold. Colors in the room washed out in the intensity of the moment.

"I didn't know how to bring it up, so if this is sudden and tactless, it's because it only came to me an hour ago, and I suppose, if I had any doubt, your expression now incriminates you. There's no manual for this. No guidebook you can read. My suspicions came in the tunnel. Chernov knew you. I could see that. His anger was intimate and familiar. So there it is. I'm right, aren't I? It's always been you?"

Mueller's mind was strangely calm. Never in his wildest imagination did he believe this moment would come, but it was happening now, in the present—Altman sloughing his treachery onto him. What makes a man without hope cling to the ledge? Is desperation a good quality or a bad quality? Mueller pondered.

"Yes, I wondered a long time about you," Altman said, "but it was here earlier this evening that I thought, of course, it's you." Altman sipped his wine. "You have always been such a virtuous sonofabitch. And so hard to read. I couldn't imagine what they had on you. Then I remembered your ex-wife. You said she was Austrian, but I knew she was Czech. Her father was an ex-Nazi and she was scared the Soviets would pick him up. Then there was what you said at dinner with Beth. Your love for your son. I put that together. Of course, Chernov was smart. Ruthless. He got to you through the boy. They have him, don't they?"

Mueller held off an urge to defend himself.

"You must love him more than life itself. You, of all people—"
The word *traitor* slipped from Altman's lips.

Mueller met Altman's eyes fiercely. "You have no idea," he
snapped. He knew he was hearing a rehearsal of the doubts Altman would raise with their colleagues. The desperate man drags
down those around him. He added angrily, "You can't sit there
and judge if you haven't known, as I have known, the terrible burden of what it means for a boy to think that his father has abandoned him. Do you understand that? Can you understand that?
Don't conflate my failures with yours." Mueller stopped himself.
He felt anger hijack the self-control he needed to get through
their conversation. Mueller's exhale came at last. He leaned back
in his chair and met Altman's eyes. He stifled an impulse to express his disappointment and his revulsion. No words could ad-
equately account for all that had brought their long acquaintance
to this wretched moment. Mueller closed his eyes to calm his
swirling thoughts. When he opened them again he spoke calmly.

"We are both guilty men, but our failures are different, and
the thing I have not done, that you did, is betrayal. I stood up
for you. But you allowed your treachery to attach itself to me. I
wanted out, and you said that made me the right candidate to
approach the Russians. The envelope in Union Station implicated
me and I became a person of interest, like the magician's hand
that attracts the eye while the real action is happening elsewhere.
The Soviets didn't want to lose their prize asset and you must
have known I was being set up. You let me hang."

Mueller paused. When he continued, his voice was confessional. "You have some things right. They have my son. She took him to protect her father and she believed their false promises, their greedy needs, the dirty game they play. You're right they are ruthless. I was important to Chernov. He found me in Vienna that night we saw each other coming from the Soviet sector. I'm not surprised that we never talked about that night. I didn't want to know what you were doing there. Perhaps, if I'm generous, you had the same reluctance. Whatever friendship we had was worn thin by then. You've filled in the mystery of that evening with convenient fabrications, but the truth is sadder than that."

Mueller told a story. He said he'd seen Altman save the girl from the oncoming Soviet jeep, and then he saw Altman return to the dark alley where a handsome boy waited. He was curious about Altman's intentions, and afraid as well, and he believed he could intervene if the boy was being used to compromise Altman.

"I lost you," Mueller said. "You moved from one alley to the next in that long black coat that made you blend into the night. It had rained. Cobblestones glistened in the streetlights. It was dangerous with Soviet troop carriers moving fast down the broad avenues toward the rampaging protesters. And then suddenly you were gone. I looked around the park at smashed statues and trees cut for firewood. You were gone. I made an effort to find you—to save you. Yes, to save you. Can you imagine I'd have that impulse? Well, I did. And I suspect that was the night they trapped you. But I lost you. I had my own appointment to make."

Mueller explained that he had arranged to collect his son

from the Soviet sector, answering a plea for help. He'd arrived at a checkpoint where Soviet guards were distracted by the commotion on the far side of Schwarzenberg Square. Pushing up his collar, he walked purposely on the edge of the light cast by the arc lamp and slipped into the first alley. The call to get his son had come from the child's grandmother—who had a difficult relationship with her daughter—and the proud older woman was fond of Mueller. He'd encouraged her with cigarettes and chocolate, which became their way of communicating, since he spoke no Czech and her English was limited to a few phrases.

A Soviet command car was parked in front of the dark apartment house when Mueller arrived on foot. The grandmother followed her daughter down the front steps, fretting and pleading, but all the years of anger left no room for anything other than the obvious outcome. The grandmother was a former actress, vain, Mueller said, and she had no tolerance for her beautiful, rebellious daughter.

"Johana gave me an angry look when I joined the little group. 'You're late,' she said. The boy in her arms was too young to know what was going on. *Late for what*? I said. Chernov came out of the vestibule accompanied by two soldiers. He'd already approached me twice with offers to work for him. I knew he was there before I saw him, announced by his foot. Funny, isn't it, a top spy so obviously exposed by his clubfoot. He looked at me and said, 'You know what we want. Soon all this will be over and you'll have the boy back. No one has to know.'"

Mueller lifted his eyes and met Altman's gaze. "Yes, I love him very much. You can't possibly know my pain for the day he is grown and he asks me why I didn't protect him. I abandoned him to loveless neglect in a stateless purgatory." Mueller slumped in his chair, face gray with anger.

The two men sat across from each other for a long time without speaking. Altman gazed across the table at his companion. "I was mistaken about you from the beginning, even at Yale. Being the public school kid, the outsider, among all the self-important nonsense must have been hard on you. I saw that and that's what I liked about you. You didn't let yourself be seduced by the nonsense. In the end," Altman conceded, and his voice became a whisper, "in the end, I was not strong enough to purchase integrity at the price of scandal. This must sound a bit like a confession. We confess and feel better afterward."

"I'm not your priest."

"No, you're not."

"What's next?" Mueller asked.

Altman gazed at Mueller. He pondered the question. The room was quiet except for the tyrannical ticking of the mantel clock. He spoke at last. "What's next for you? What's next for me? I'm scheduled to testify tomorrow against my father in the Senate. They will make a public spectacle of me to impeach him." He laughed in stubborn grievance. "So there I will be, if they have their way, incriminating my father because of slanders they'll bring against me. Odd, don't you think, how our roles are similar. You abandoning a son, me punishing a father."

Mueller grunted.

Without ceremony Altman stood and moved to his jacket, hanging on the door. He returned holding a glass vial, lifting it to show Mueller the small dose of poison. Altman's eyes were steady, calm, peaceful, and they fixed on a nervous Mueller.

"The director gave this to me. He talked about honor. It's a word he used a lot in his little speech, as if somehow, I wouldn't get the idea." Altman lifted the vial so it glinted in the chandelier. "Gottlieb made it, so I know it will work." Altman said that with a trace of irony. "Strange how the director's mind works," Altman said. "I can't imagine how he thought there was a chance I would do this."

The conversation took a strange turn. Without a conscious plan the two men reminisced about their undergraduate days, both happy to steer the conversation away from the grimmer present. They were happy to share memories of their campus youth, and each story of some antic provoked another memory, and another story. The mood between them lightened and each retreated into the safer world of harmless recollections. They laughed a good bit, willing themselves into pleasantness. Someone watching these two men would never suspect what was to follow. They talked about little things, silly and stupid things; they talked about everything except the looming jeopardy.

Altman paused and drummed his fingers on the table. "George, your choices are terrible. You know that. You kept quiet about the boy and a cloud of doubt hangs over you. I can't be an accomplice to that silence. Suspicion is the end of a case officer's career. You'll be blacklisted, maybe sacked. That job in New Haven won't last long."

Altman leaned forward and made Mueller a proposal. There was a tunnel in the basement that led to an alley. They would leave together that night in time to make the *Sedov*. The ship would leave at midnight and they could make the hour drive in his car. "I don't trust you," he said. "I'm sure you can understand. I need to keep you close." Altman assured Mueller that he'd get his son, confident he could deliver on the promise. "We can sit with my contacts in Moscow. I'll explain your role, the help you've provided." Altman suggested Mueller could be turned, doubled. He would return to America with his son and continue to work for the Agency, but he would be managed by Altman on behalf of the Soviets.

"Defect?" Mueller snapped.

Altman considered the thought. "Yes. You're good at this, George, and you've got experience. If you do well it could go on for years and to the outside world it would appear as if nothing has changed in your life. You'll have your son. Continue to see Beth. We can sit with Moscow Center and explain everything. I think they'd find this a reasonable bargain."

Sitting before Altman, Mueller felt an urgency to punish the contempt within the offer that was being made. This man with whom he'd shared his deepest pain, pretending friendship, had used the intimacy of the conversation to induce a relaxed mood in which Mueller would warm to an anodyne choice. Mueller was offended by Altman's coy blandishments, so cynical, so self-serving. He looked at the doorway.

"Go ahead," Altman said. "You can leave but that won't end it."

Mueller had always been the taller of the two, but he lacked Altman's muscular bulk, and it was useless to think he could win a fight.

Mueller saw the path to Altman's salvation in the offer of his own purgatory. He felt his future slip away. In the dark corner of his mind that evaluates these things he felt a rapid fluttering of flightless wings incapable of keeping him from falling in the abyss. A quickening tremor seized his chest like a giant hand reaching across the table and squeezing his heart. The future he wanted, the future he planned for, hung in balance. The path before him forked. One path led to opprobrium, isolation, poverty. The other path took him deeper into the secret world, everything calibrated twice, every lie having a counter lie, and he'd become a shadow man cut off from human contact.

Facing across the table, Mueller asked for a moment to be alone so he could consider the offer, and he pleaded understanding for his obligation to his son and yes, Beth too, and also the director, to whom he felt a certain loyalty, and if he was going to do this he had to be certain he was ready to give up his claim on leaving the spy business. His theatrics succeeded. Altman removed the dinner plates to the kitchen, and on his way out he said he'd return with coffee and dessert to accompany the rest of their conversation, particularly the script they'd need to agree on when they told their story to the NKVD officers aboard the *Sedov* (and, though he didn't say it, how this arrangement would crown Altman's career as a double agent). While Altman was gone, Mueller augmented his indignation with courage and removed Altman's trophy Luger displayed inside the glass doors of the breakfront. He slid back the barrel to charge the firing chamber. The fact of its being loaded surprised him and sealed his decision. Mueller pointed it at Altman when he kicked open the kitchen door holding two cups of coffee. Mueller took two steps forward so he was close and pulled the trigger once at point-blank range. The bullet entered Altman's mouth, which had opened wide in astonishment. Curses readied in his mind were extinguished before they found voice. Altman's fit body flew back with the force of the blast and came to a rest on the Persian rug. One leg was painfully bent under at an awkward angle, his cheek pressed against the floor, his eyes wide in fury. Mueller confirmed he was dead.

He looked down at his old acquaintance. He felt no grief for this man he'd known, and in place of regret there was only the lingering thought that everything between them was a series of incidents that made this final catastrophe inevitable. He cursed his life that it was for him to make things right. He turned away from the terrible sight. There was nothing alive there, except his memories of the man, and he surprised himself when he offered an apology.

Mueller finished his work quickly. He swept the broken china cups and carefully removed any sign of spilt coffee from floor and rug. He cleaned the table of all remaining dishes, but left the empty wine bottle and Altman's glass. He cloth-wiped the Luger, placed the pistol in Altman's grip to transfer fingerprints, and then kicked it away a few inches so it looked like it lay where it had fallen. When he was satisfied with the room, Mueller dialed a number on the black rotary telephone on a side table. He heard the director's voice when the call went through. Mueller spoke in hushed disbelief. "I came at your suggestion. He was morose and despondent at dinner. I was already outside on my way home when I heard a gunshot. I found him on the floor. He killed himself . . . as you suggested he might."

Mueller let himself out of the town house being careful not to be seen. Arriving at the bottom of the stone steps he turned quickly and walked away. The sidewalk was empty, the warm night alive with the alien buzz of cicadas. But passing the end of the block he happened to turn. The instinct he'd acquired in Vienna. There at the corner the young couple against a tree had turned and watched him. Mueller crossed the street and was gone.

22

HERO

ROGER ALTMAN was buried in Arlington National Cemetery early on a spring morning a few days after his housekeeper discovered his body in the dining room of his Georgetown home. She called the police, who investigated, but a call from the director to the Metropolitan Police officer who liaised with the Agency on security matters assured that the death was handled quietly, and the death was leaked to the reporters on that beat as an unfortunate accidental discharge by a war hero cleaning his souvenir Luger. At the director's request the police kept confidential evidence that he died of a self-inflicted gunshot to the head. Roger Altman was identified as an employee of the Department of State, victim perhaps, again via the rumor mill, to the fact that he was one of the talented men in the department whose bachelor life drew attention. Altman's absence from the Senate witness table was decried by the senator whose peevish fit of demagoguery was caught on live television. He lashed out at unnamed agents undermining his investigation and declared he would not abandon freedom abroad by deserting freedom at home. The vile tone of the senator's huffing petulance, and his incoherence, appalled some of his colleagues and the national audience who saw his televised performance—replayed on the evening news. There followed spirited denunciations of the senator's disrespect for an American veteran whose courage had earned a Bronze Star. People who knew Altman were convinced that there was more to the story, but the senator's smear tactics brought these people to Altman's defense.

It was a small group at the grave under a gray sky. Trees were fully leafed and the sprawling green lawn was a riot of daffodils. The unhealthy sun was small and lusterless like a withered lemon. Beth was there in black veil and a shawl against the brisk morning air. It was early. She wore dark glasses and clutched her father's arm at the grave. The two of them were quiet, alone together, a few steps apart from the six men who made their own little group.

There were Roger's colleagues from the Agency. James Coffin wore a dark suit, his long, delicate fingers held his black homburg in a prayerful way. The director was there, of course, with his cane, and wearing a lumpy suit that hung sloppily on his heavy frame. Wind lifted the few long, thin strands that covered his baldness. The case's notoriety had drawn several news reporters who were collected in a gaggle a respectful distance from the grave site.

George Mueller stood between two other men who had worked with Altman and had known him from years together in the OSS. Mueller lifted his eyes from the mahogany coffin and glanced at Beth. She stood straight, face calm and proud.

A priest stood across the open hole between two army sergeants resplendent in full dress blue. They stood at attention on either side of an easel mounted with a wreath of lilies and roses. The priest made brief remarks about duty, honor, service, sacrifice. He read Psalm 23 in a strong voice, but his words were carried away in the breeze, lost on the group of mourners unless you stood in the very front. Mueller thought the priest could have spoken louder, but it was the mood he was in, the mood he'd been in for the last few days. Nothing felt right to him.

FBI agent William Walker was there too. Mueller noticed a man hanging back in the shade of an oak tree, watching, a man on surveillance. He was alone. He wore standard black and disguising sunglasses, but Mueller recognized his swept-back hair and the thin moustache. When Mueller looked again, Walker was gone.

Mueller looked at Beth in her defiant grief. She stared at the casket suspended above the hole in the ground. She supported her father, who supported her back, and they found strength in each other. There was nothing so isolating as having the burden of unanswered questions.

The director gave a little eulogy. Short and brief, and interesting only in what he left out. "He gave his life for his country," the director said. "Few of us can say as much."

The whole ceremony was over in thirty minutes. These things have a way of being momentous in their buildup and then are over in a flash. Once the coffin came to rest at the bottom of the hole, there was no reason to hang around. Mueller felt an eagerness among his colleagues to leave.

The director pulled Mueller away from the grave, but Mueller hung back a moment and lingered at the casket, contemplating all that had happened to this man and all the events that had brought him to this moment on this day. He wanted to pray, but he had no God to address.

Mueller made his way beside the director along the winding path. He calibrated his steps to the director's slower pace, and he looked around the vast lawn of dead soldiers whose lives were lost in the service of their country, honored with tiny flags.

"And this too will pass," the director said. "With what we know, what forgiveness can there be?" They continued in silence. "You looked distracted, George. What's on your mind?"

"He was a troubled man."

"He made mistakes. Unforgivable mistakes."

Mueller waited for the director to finish his thought and then understood that the long silence meant the director had no more to say. They walked at the pace of the director's gimp leg and the cane he planted ahead of each step. Mueller put his sunglasses on against the glare of the gauzy sun.

"It's a grubby business we're in, you and I," the director said. He nodded at the FBI sedan parked in the lot, distinguished by its being undistinguished among the roadsters. The director spoke in a tone of cool observation. "We got lucky on this. The newspapers are content to believe that an accident killed a decorated veteran. They're looking for heroes." He nodded at Beth and her father, who walked ahead on the path. "What does she know?"

"Nothing. The old man has taken it hard. He was surprised. Ignorance or wishfulness. Who knows? She gave him the story that Roger was being hounded for being queer. That's all she knows."

"Let's leave it that way." The director cleared his throat, inflected with tentativeness. "You'll be going to New Haven soon, I expect." He looked at Mueller. "You'll be back. You'll get bored."

Just then they were passing the assembled news crews, and one reporter, recognizing the director, separated from the pack of cameramen and klieg lights. He stopped in front of the director, blocking his path, and thrust his microphone forward. "Sir, can you tell the American people how you feel about Roger Altman?"

Mueller stepped aside so he wasn't caught on film. The director hesitated before he answered, but when he spoke his voice was stentorian. "Were the senator from Wisconsin in the pay of communists he would not be doing a better job of sowing mistrust in our Great Land. He owes this young man's family an apology."

Mueller joined the director in the parking lot to hitch a ride across the Potomac. Mueller had to walk past Beth's red convertible to get to the director's limousine, and he had to walk past her. She came around the back of her car to open the passenger door for her father, and the two of them, Mueller and Beth, found themselves face-to-face. She observed Mueller, eyes meeting. They were stopped and they stayed looking at each other, she at him and he at her, each waiting for a sign, or for the other to speak. They looked at each other across the few feet of parking lot. Mueller didn't have the courage to say the one thing he wanted to say. The thing he'd ruined. He accepted that all he saw on her face was anger and recrimination and, yes, pity. In the long silence of the moment he knew everything she'd felt for him was clouded by grief. When nothing was said she walked away.

Mueller was in the backseat of the limousine when she came over to the open window. There was no emotion at all on her pale face, but as soon as she spoke, Mueller stiffened.

She said angrily, "You're just like all the others." She walked off.

Mueller went for the door to follow her. The director forcefully put his hand on Mueller's arm. "Let it rest for a while."

ACKNOWLEDGMENTS

O N THE morning of April 1, 1953, James Speyer Kronthal was found dead in the upstairs bedroom of his brick town house in Georgetown by Metropolitan Police, who had been summoned by his longtime housekeeper when she arrived at 8:30 and found the home suspiciously quiet. He was fully clothed, sprawled on the floor, an apparent suicide. He wasn't shot, as Roger Altman is in the novel, but in many other respects my character is based on the sad, troubled life of James Speyer Kronthal.

Kronthal was a brilliant young deputy of Allen Dulles's who had worked in the OSS with Dulles in the Bern Station during World War II. He was one of the original sixty or so people whom Dulles brought to the CIA. Those initial recruits were not required to take a polygraph test, as would later be the case with all new agency employees. Kronthal came from a wealthy banking family, attended Yale and then Harvard, where he earned a graduate degree in Art History. CIA investigators would later discover that Kronthal led a questionable life in the art world, working with the Nazi regime, brokering art stolen from Jews. It was during this period that German intelligence caught him in a homosexual act with an underage German boy. Kronthal, through his banking relationships, and his art interests, was acquainted with Hermann Goering, head of the Luftwaffe, which kept him from arrest and scandal.

When the NKVD followed Soviet troops into Berlin in 1945, they found Goering's private files, including the file on Kronthal. Kronthal had replaced Dulles as the Bern Station Chief in 1945, a key intelligence position, and the NKVD prepared another trap for him, filming him with a young boy. The Soviets blackmailed Kronthal, and he became the first Soviet mole in the CIA. He worked for Dulles and during this time reported his meetings at the highest level of the CIA to Moscow.

Kronthal's homosexuality came to light in Washington within the inner circles of the Agency at the time that Senator Joseph McCarthy was conducting witch hunts for homosexuals in the State Department. Dulles treated what amounted to an intelligence catastrophe as a political problem, not as a counter-intelligence problem. Dulles was a sharp student of history, and in his memoir he referenced the case of Alfred Redl, counter-espionage chief in the Austro-Hungarian Empire's military uncovered as a Russian spy, who was "invited" to commit suicide as an honorable way out of an intelligence mess—and to prevent the political embarrassment that would follow if the incident came to light.

Dulles invited Kronthal to dinner when the betrayal was discovered. He gave Kronthal a speech about honor and duty, and how compulsions destroyed careers. Kronthal walked home to his town house in Georgetown, where the next morning the police discovered him on the floor of his bedroom, an empty vial on the floor. The note he left for his sister spoke about the difficulty his homosexuality posed for his career. The entire episode was hushed up and didn't come to light for many years.

The hostile political environment in Washington, D.C., required that the episode be kept secret to prevent a McCarthy witch hunt of the CIA, which Dulles, and even Eisenhower, knew would jeopardize the effectiveness of the Agency at a time when the Cold War was at its height. I happened upon the incident while reading Joseph J. Trento's *The Secret History of the CIA*. I was intrigued by the idea of an Ivy League–educated young man who lived a secret life within a secret career. If you worked for the CIA, you couldn't tell anyone, even your wife, what you did for a living, or even where you worked, and being a closeted homosexual compounded the layers of secrecy. I wondered how Kronthal managed all this in his mind.

Several characters in the novel quote lines of poetry or prose. The sources are: John Webster: "Oh, my worse sin was in my blood; Now my blood pays for it"; T. S. Eliot: "Tenants of the house. Thoughts of a dry brain in a dry season"; William Shakespeare: "In offering commend it" and "Why then 'tis none to you; for there is nothing either good or bad, but thinking makes it so. To me it is a prison"; Rudyard Kipling: "We're poor little lambs who've lost our way. Baa! Baa! Baa! We're little black sheep who've gone astray. Baa! Baa! Baa!"; Ezra Pound: "In her is the end of breeding. Her boredom is exquisite and excessive. She would like someone to speak to her, And is almost afraid that I will commit that indiscretion."; Lillian Hellman: "I cannot and will not cut my conscience to fit this year's fashion."

Several books and websites were indispensable sources of information about Soviet and American espionage in the 1950s. They are: *Confessions of a Spy* by Pete Earley (G. P. Putnam's Sons, 1997); *The Secret History of the CIA* by Joseph J. Trento (Basic Books, 2001); *Spy Handler* by Victor Cherkashin with Gregory Feifer (Basic Books, 2005); *Legacy of Ashes* by Tim Weiner (Random House 2007); *Cloak and Gown* by Robin Winks (Yale

University Press, 1987); *The Lavender Scare* by David Johnson (The University of Chicago Press, 2004); *Farewell* by Sergei Kostin and Eric Raynaud, translated by Catherine Cauvin-Higgins (AmazonCrossing, 2009); *Widows* by William R. Corson, Susan B. Trento, and Joseph J. Trento (Crown Publishers, 1989); Frank Olson Legacy Project at http://www.frankolsonproject.org/.

I owe particular thanks to my agent, Will Roberts at The Gernert Company, whose probing questions led to important revisions to an early draft; and to my editor, Emily Bestler, whose fine editorial eye found gaps in the narrative. Special thanks go to my fellow writers at the Neumann Leathers Writers Group—Mauro Altamura, Amy Kiger-Williams, Aimee Rinehart, Dawn Ryan, Brett Duquette, and Rachel Friedman—who were the novel's first readers; and to my sons, Joe and Arturo, with whom I had long discussions that helped me see things I hadn't considered. Eric Olson shared the torment of a family from whom the CIA withheld the terrible circumstances of a father's death. To my readers: Robert Boswell, David Gernert, Alex Miller, Kelly Luce, Carin Clevidence, Nahid Rachlin, Rivka Galchen, Andy Feinstein, Polly Flonder, Rae Edelson, and Sujata Shekar. To my advocates: Brendan Cahill, Lauren Cerand, Alex Miller, and Milena Deleva. I also wish to thank Jayne Anne Phillips, Alice Elliot Dark, Rachel Hadas, and Tayari Jones at the Rutgers Newark MFA—teachers, writers, and mentors. And to my wife, the remarkable Linda Stein, partner, teacher, reader, critic, muse.